Juggernaut

Book 2 in *The Ixan Prophecies* Trilogy

Scott Bartlett

Mirth Publishing
St. John's

JUGGERNAUT

© Scott Bartlett 2017

Cover art by: Tom Edwards (tomedwardsdesign.com)

This novel is a work of fiction. All of the characters, places, and events are fictitious. Any resemblance to actual persons living or dead, locales, businesses, or events is entirely coincidental.

Library and Archives Canada Cataloguing in Publication

Bartlett, Scott

Juggernaut / Scott Bartlett ; illustrations by Tom Edwards.

ISBN 978-1-988380-05-6

To those who refuse to be stopped by something so paltry as failure.

CHAPTER 1

Full Compliance

"We can't let that support ship rejoin its capital ship. If we do, the system's lost."

Fesky spun her Condor along its short axis and blasted apart yet another Slag that thought it could sneak up on her. That was the name they'd settled on for Gok fighters—Slags. "I can see that, Spank," she squawked. "Do you intend to continue interrupting my concentration with the bleeding obvious?"

The Ixa's gambit for taking this star system had involved hiding their support ship behind a nondescript asteroid, guarded by three squadrons of Slags. Luckily, Husher's message to a friendly element on a human colony otherwise covered with radicals had given them access to several well-placed orbital sensor arrays, and they'd been able to spot the hiding ships.

"Can you calculate how long the support ship will take to join up with the destroyer next to that gas giant?" he said. "I'm kind of busy here." Three Slags had broken from the swarm protecting the fleeing support ship to try separating Husher from his squadron.

They must have identified him as its leader, Fesky reflected. *The Gok are getting better at this.* "I'm kind of busy, too," Fesky grumbled as she watched another pair of Slags line up to make a run at her. Nevertheless, she set her computer to calculating the timeframe Husher wanted as she swung her guns around to face the nearest Gok. Within seconds, she had an answer: "Twenty minutes. Less, if the two Roostships tying up the destroyer fall."

"We need to act now, Madcap."

"Easier said than done. The Gok aren't afraid to kamikaze us the moment we get close to that support ship."

"Then we need to get rid of our own fear."

"Okay," Fesky said, trying to keep sarcasm out of her voice. She just loved it when humans got cryptic. "What do you have in mind?"

"Let my Haymakers form a protective cone around your Divebombers. As the Slags try to kamikaze us, my pilots will peel away from formation, one-by-one, to take them on in dogfights to the death. If the Haymakers win those, they'll live to fight the next one, but if the Gok manage to crash into them, at least we'll be taking down one of theirs, too."

Fesky wished the UHF would upgrade its terminology. "Dogfight" wasn't right, since it referred to planet-based fighter combat, in which there was a down. *There is no down in space.* She brushed the thought away. "So *we'll* be your payload. My Divebombers."

"Exactly."

"Could work, Spank. I'll pass on the plan to my fliers."

It took their pilots under a minute to regroup as Husher had described. "I want everyone accelerating at six Gs toward that ship," he said over a wide channel. "Use your Ocharium boosts to reach that rate as fast as our birds can handle. *Now!*"

Together, both squadrons screamed toward the enemy, and Fesky started performing the exercises every fighter pilot was taught to combat that much pressure on the body. Two squadrons of Slags sprang forward. *Not enough.* Though she wouldn't stroke Husher's ego by saying so, his plan was decent. The Gok wouldn't expect them to act as suicidally as their own pilots did.

Unfortunately, at the moment, this was also sort of boring for Fesky. If she fired at the Gok, she'd risk hitting one of the Haymakers protecting her fighters. So she watched the tactical display instead.

Husher was the first to break formation, to take on two Slags. He feinted a chicken-run at the first, twitching his attitude upward at the last second and rotating around his short axis to blow up the dimwitted Gok from behind.

Undeterred, the second enemy fighter charged at Husher, which was exactly the wrong thing to do. The human made short work of the poor dope and moved on to engage another.

Other Haymakers fared less well. Fesky's battle calm was shaken as three Condors fell to Gok firepower in quick succession.

Under normal circumstances, the kamikaze technique would be next to useless in the vastness of space. But Gok did seem to excel at limiting the room their enemies had to meaningfully operate in.

The Condor formation had nearly reached the support ship when the last Haymaker left to engage another pair of Slags. The final Gok squadron defending the Ixan support ship sped forward, then.

Too late, dimwits. "Ignore the enemy fighters," she told her squadron. "Execute an alpha strike on the support ship and prepare to turn around for another pass." She'd plotted the course she wanted them to follow while waiting for her turn to fight, and now she sent it over to their computers.

Another pass proved unnecessary. The support ship exploded under their coordinated salvo of Sidewinders.

Habit made her raise her talons to her helmet, ready to activate the transponder and tell her squadron to save their celebrating till they returned to their carrier.

But no cheering came, of course, and she lowered her talons again. *A nice change.*

Neon-green letters flashed across her heads-up display: "MISSION SUCCESS!"

Fesky lifted off her helmet and placed it on the side of the simulator, which resembled the bottom half of a Talon fighter. Beside her, Husher did the same.

"Solid run," he said.

"Sure. But it'll have no actual application unless you're willing to spend your pilots' lives like that in real life."

"To save an entire system from the Ixa? Yeah, I would be willing."

"Hmm."

"Anyway, you're the CAG. You'd be the one giving me authorization to do it. So I guess the real question is, would you have the balls?"

Fesky stood, stretching her wings, which felt amazing after spending an hour cooped up in the simulator. "Considering not even Winger *males* have balls...I guess you'll have to wait for the next engagement to find out."

Husher chuckled. "I'm glad we were finally able to program Condor specs into these things," he said, slapping his simulator as he climbed out. "I was tired of flying your species' shitty Talons. How close to accurate do you think we got with the Slags?"

"They seemed close enough."

"Yeah." Checking his com, Husher said, "Uh oh. The war council's in fifteen minutes. We'll be late if we don't get moving."

"I'm not going."

"Seriously?"

"I hate those drawn-out circle jerks. We're going to war, and I have a lot of Gok and Ixa to kill. There's no need to complicate things any more than that."

"There may be a bit more to it, Fesky."

"Whatever. I'm going flying." She stalked toward the simulator room's exit. They both knew why she wasn't attending the war council, so she resented Husher pressuring her about it.

Of course, he lacked the exact details, but he *knew* how strained her relationship was with her species. Her fellow Wingers remembered the reasons behind her exile well, and they remembered her shooting down their pilots as the *Providence*'s CAG even better.

Still, at the room's exit, she turned to face the human. Despite how annoying he was, she had to admit she'd come to respect the cocky young officer. Maybe even like him. *Not that I'll ever tell him that.*

"Don't let the Directorate push you around, Husher. Flockhead Bytan has their ear, and she doesn't consider you on equal footing with our Interplanetary Defense Force. She sees the *Providence* as a single rogue ship whose rebellion against the UHF could very well prove short-lived. So she expects full compliance from Captain Keyes."

Husher chuckled. "Watching her try to get that should make for a good laugh."

CHAPTER 2

Supernova

The day the world ended started like any other.

Yan Arnarsson stumbled into the lab to continue his grad work, clutching a coffee with one hand and a badly aching head with the other. The previous night, he'd heavily sampled the Christmas brandy his folks had given him, and now he paid the price.

Settling down to compile the data collected by the Pasnoori space telescope overnight, Yan groaned. This promised to take hours. Pasnoori was nearing its apoapsis—the farthest it got from the sun in its solar orbit—meaning they'd entered the optimal window for stellar observation.

In turn, that meant an increased workload for Yan, hangover or no hangover.

Forty minutes into his work, his hands stopped moving on the console. He checked over the data he'd just processed. Then he rechecked it.

When Professor Leifsdóttir arrived, Yan was looking at the image that corresponded with the anomalous data. He'd downloaded it a half hour before, and he'd done nothing except stare at it since.

"What's that?" she said.

"It...it has to be a glitch. Maybe something wrong with Pasnoori's software."

"What would it be if it weren't a glitch?"

"It would be Epsilon Leonis going supernova. Which would be..."

"Impossible. It's not due to go supernova for millions of years." The professor sat at the console next to Yan's and filled its screen with code. "I'm not seeing any bugs," she muttered to herself, as she often did. "Well, Pasnoori isn't the only orbital telescope in the Campion System." Leifsdóttir glanced at him. "Check this against Cos-V. I'll compare with data from ROSAT 8."

A few minutes later, Professor Leifsdóttir's hands also stopped moving on her console. Wearing a helpless expression, she turned to him. It was the first time Yan had ever seen her act with anything but confidence bordering on arrogance.

"Could this be a new Winger weapon?" he said. "It would be the perfect attack. No colonies orbit Epsilon Leonis, and it'll take years for the shockwave to reach us, long enough for us to leave the system." He realized he was babbling, but he couldn't seem to stop. "A bloodless victory. We'll have to abandon everything we have here, everything we've built. They could do this to every human—"

"The supernova happened before the war began. Its light is only reaching us now. I don't know what caused it," Leifsdóttir said. "But we have to alert the governor. Campion must be evacuated, and its darkgate deactivated as soon as possible. Otherwise its destruction will cause a catastrophic explosion in the connecting system."

"Do you...do you have access to the governor?"

"Of course not. But I'm about to get it. The supernova will be visible to the naked eye in a matter of weeks, even in daylight. The danger is undeniable."

CHAPTER 3

War Council

The Atrium looked nothing like human government buildings. It made sense that the Wingers would want their decision makers to meet under the open sky, or at least, as open a sky as you could get while remaining indoors. A transparent dome formed the ceiling, and the seating radiated upward from a small, circular floor, where individuals would take turn speaking.

Husher stumbled a little as he entered, still not quite accustomed to Spire's low gravity, and pain shot through his recently-broken leg. The break had come when he'd slammed into Spire's ocean after falling from orbit in a Darkstream reentry suit, and shortly after that, a Winger doctor had injected him with iatric nanites. The microscopic robots had realigned, reinforced, and rebuilt the bone with incredible speed, but his leg still wasn't back to one hundred percent.

The Winger Directorate was filing into the Atrium, and taking their sweet time about it, too. *Maybe they've forgotten there's a war on,* Husher thought to himself.

After spotting the officers from the *Providence* sitting near the central area, he moved toward them, trying to catch Sergeant Caine's eye as he did. She looked away the moment he succeeded, a chill washing over her face.

What in Sol is her problem? Ever since they'd last spoken aboard the Winger orbital defense platform, moments before he'd plummeted to the surface with a nuke clipped to his suit, Caine had been giving him the silent treatment.

Blackwing also sat among the *Providence* officers, though he yet held no rank, and the sun's rays shone through the dome to play across his dark-gray feathers. The respect Blackwing commanded among Wingers had earned him a seat at the war council, respect that had only grown after his near-miraculous escape from a stealth ship plummeting to the planet. The former pirate had already declared his intention to leave when the *Providence* did, to continue serving in her Air Group. Apparently almost dying had reawakened his thirst for constantly being in danger. *Crazy Winger.*

Husher took the seat on Captain Keyes's left. XO Laudano was on his right.

"Morning, Lieutenant," the captain said. "Where's Fesky?"

"She said she can't stand these 'drawn-out circle jerks.' Her words, not mine."

Keyes chuckled. "Leave it to Fesky to be a step ahead of the rest of us."

Suppressing the urge to grimace, Husher gave a curt nod. *How can Keyes be so cavalier about Fesky's situation?* They both knew how precarious her position had become since their arrival on Spire. In truth, Keyes had seemed unusually relaxed ever since his arrival on the planet's surface.

Flockhead Bytan stood and marched slowly toward the central speaking area. Except for the Tumbra and the Kaithe, the Wingers stood shorter than other sentient species, though their muscled upper bodies and enormous wingspans made them no less imposing. Paired with Spire's low gravity, their unique anatomy had allowed evolution to grant them flight.

Unlike other members of her species, who usually had trouble concealing their emotions, Bytan kept hers tightly controlled at all times. That made her even more imposing than other Wingers.

"Wait," Husher whispered, leaning toward his captain. Don't tell me Bytan's a Director. Whatever happened to the separation of state and military?"

"The Wingers do things differently."

When Bytan reached the small circle in the middle of the Atrium, she spread her wings to their full span. "The Directorate is now in session. Our purpose today is to review the information we have about the conflict currently spreading throughout the galaxy and, if we can, to decide on a course of action. We will begin by listening to the testimony of the first human to arrive on our planet recently. He has been our prisoner for almost a week."

Near the top of the Atrium, a pair of Wingers stood up from one of the back rows, dragging a man up with them. Husher hadn't noticed the prisoner before, but now he felt himself stiffen in his seat. It was his father.

"Warren Husher arrived on Spire in a shuttle of Ixan make. He's considered a traitor by his own species, but claims he is innocent. Keep those facts in mind as you hear him. However suspect, his words may hold some value for us."

Bytan sat, and Senator Sandy Bernard stood to question the prisoner. Beside her, Corporal Simpson rose as though to follow, but then sat again with a barely noticeable shake of her head.

Since Warren had been a UHF captain, and Bernard was technically still a senator of the Commonwealth, the Wingers acknowledged her right to interview their captive. She crossed the floor as confidently as Bytan had.

Husher barely recognized the man the Wingers brought before Bernard, just a few meters from the front row where Husher and Keyes sat. His beard and hair had turned iron gray, and deep lines creased his face. Whatever his years with the Ixa had truly contained, they hadn't been kind to him. *I call it the side effects of guilt.*

"Hello, Captain," Keyes said, his words low but audible.

Warren glanced, then his eyes flitted away just as quickly. "I'm no captain," he said. "Not anymore."

"You will speak only to answer my questions," Bernard said. "Your presence here is a privilege. Do not squander it."

"Says you," the traitor said.

"The Wingers say you claim not to remember your time among the Ixa. Is that true?"

"Mostly. I do remember how the Ixa made it look like I betrayed my own species."

"And how did they do that?"

"They fabricated footage of me from whole cloth," Warren said. "They made it look like I said things I didn't say."

Bernard shook her head. "You're lying. That's beyond what we know the Ixa's technological capabilities to be."

"Then you obviously don't know enough. Do you?"

"What do you remember about your supposed imprisonment? Or about how you escaped?"

"I didn't escape. I was let go."

"Why would the Ixa let you go?"

"I don't know. I don't remember. They did something to my memory."

"What *do* you remember?"

"I remember..."

Husher's lips tightened as his father's gaze left Bernard and found him.

Warren continued. "I remember them telling me I would be reunited with my son on Spire. So I came here. Vincent..."

"I am not your son," Husher said. Keyes placed a hand on his arm, but he shrugged it off.

Warren looked stricken. "Please..."

"I am *not* your son," he said again.

"No further questions," Bernard said, her face unreadable. The Winger guards took Husher's father away.

Keyes cleared his throat and stood. "I have a prisoner to present, as well. His testimony is also questionable, but he claims to have a revelation that he's only willing to discuss at this war council. He says that we will be able to verify the truth of his words soon."

"Bring him forward," Flockhead Bytan said.

Keyes nodded to two *Providence* marines, who sat several seats down with Ochrim between them, his scaly hands shackled in his lap. The Ixan stood voluntarily and stepped forward. The first time Husher had met Ochrim, in the secret Darkstream research station where they found him, the Ixan had worn a slightly bewildered look. That look was gone, now, and what struck Husher most was how rapidly the alien appeared to be aging, his scaly skin turned almost completely white where it stretched over his face's bone protrusions. *He deserves that and worse.*

"Speak, Ixan," Keyes said.

The scientist did not hesitate, and though his words sounded solemn, the snakelike grin Ixa always wore lent them menace. "Epsilon Leonis has gone supernova, and the humans in the Campion System, which the supernova will obliterate, have just detected it. News of this will reach you soon, but upon review of the Ixan Prophecies, specifically the verses that speak of a phoenix risen from ash, you will find that all of this has been foretold. Including my telling you this today."

Ochrim scanned his audience, and so did Husher. He found shocked expressions to mirror his own.

"Humanity's use of dark tech is the cause," the scientist went on.

"You gave us dark tech," Caine said. "And anyway, we don't use it anymore."

"Incorrect. Wormhole generation has ceased, but humans still use dark tech in your weaponry, your gravity simulation, your communications, and more. You harness the lifeblood of the universe, and your actions are not without consequences. Dark matter is the network that holds the universe together. Dark *tech* sends gravitational ripples throughout that network, and the ripples are combining into waves, soon to become tsunamis. More star deaths will follow as these disturbances speed up their gravitational collapse. It will begin with aging, massive stars like Epsilon Leonis, but with enough time, no star will remain. Unless you are stopped. And the Ixa will stop you."

A silence fell over the Atrium. Into it, Sergeant Caine spoke. "I'll say it again—you *gave* us dark tech."

"You would have discovered it on your own shortly after the First Galactic War. But my involvement set us on *this* course. It is why I betrayed humanity. It is why I took your future from you. Because to let you live would have meant no future at all, for anyone."

CHAPTER 4

Wisdom

"I am surprised to find you entertaining superstition, Starfarer. Your time in space has clouded your vision."

Ek gazed up at the Speakers for the Enclave, who floated above her in the perfectly spherical meeting chamber. The room was located under the ocean floor, devoid of technology, so that there stood no chance of outsider eavesdropping. The chamber's small size and spherical shape allowed them to hear each other well through the water.

"The Prophecies have mirrored reality too often to be mere coincidence," Ek said, enunciating each word carefully. Many speculated that the meticulous way Fins spoke was due to the difficulty of communicating underwater. They understood each other by speaking clearly, in close proximity to one another, and by reading each other's lips. Her own theory was that their difficulty conversing also explained their passion for intellectual pursuits, since they spent so much time in silence.

Zed, who had been a Speaker longer than any of the others, swam forward a few inches. "The Fins have progressed as far as

they have because of our dedication to reason. The Ixan Prophecies, while interesting from an anthropological perspective, have
no grounding in logic. You have asked for a team of analysts to
help you search the Prophecies for how this war between aliens
might unfold. Tell me, what led you to think other Fins would
be interested in that, or that they would even take it seriously?"

"It was a Winger who first drew my attention to the Prophecies' relevance."

Zed's gaze drifted to the ceiling, and Speaker Po folded her
arms across her chest. The other three Speakers displayed similar signs of agitation.

"Wingers take counsel from Fins," Po said. "Not the other
way around. It has always been that way."

"And yet Wingers possess wisdom, too," Ek said. For a moment, she wished she did not have metal legs, so that she could
swim up and speak to them at their level. "I have come to believe
our obsession with logic blinds us to unexpected factors...curve
balls, as the humans would say, that reality throws us. Just because we are highly perceptive does not mean we are omniscient.
We have things we can learn from the Wingers."

"The Wingers are beloved to us," Zed said. "And yet their
thoughts are clouded by militarism. Our species' unusual erudi-
tion has let us find balance. You would have us cast that aside
and involve ourselves in war."

"Not to fight," Ek said, trying to keep her exasperation from
showing in her voice. "But we have a duty, to the universe, to life
itself, and also to our own people. Right now, there are only
three species in the galaxy who acknowledge what is coming. It

is our duty to help save life itself from the Ixa. With our abilities, the Fins are uniquely positioned to see the way forward. If only we will look."

Zed swam forward once more. "I say no. Po?"

"I say no, as well. Fins all have their own projects, and I cannot think of a single one less important than this one the Starfarer has proposed today. I will not make the recommendation."

One after another, the remaining three Speakers also answered in the negative.

For a moment, Ek stood and beheld the floating Speakers, racking her brain. But there was nothing else to say. *It is over.*

"Very well," she said, and turned to leave.

"One more thing," Zed said, and Ek turned back.

"It is dangerous for you to continue your travel among the stars. Your medical examinations show alarming bone loss, along with several other negative effects brought about by prolonged periods in zero-G. Given that Fin cells reject Ocharium nanites, and given that the suit you designed does not adequately guard you against the stresses of zero-G, we forbid you to leave Spire again."

"You can forbid me nothing," Ek said.

"We can advise the Wingers not to let you board their vessels, and we can persuade the humans that the risks of your continued star travel are too great. Indeed, we have done so. You will not leave Spire again."

CHAPTER 5

Specimens

The first Winger jail Husher saw barely fit the word. It took the form of a sprawling, open-air compound dotted with buildings here and there. When he requested to see his father, a guard escorted him down row after row of what the alien called "cells," though they too looked nothing like any cell Husher had ever seen.

"Do I just go in and talk to him, then?" he said when they stopped in front of the one where they kept his father.

"No," the guard said. "We don't let visitors enter the cells, or make any physical contact with the prisoners. If he wants to talk to you, he can come to the edge. I'll tell him you've arrived."

With that, the guard strode into the cell and disappeared inside a tiny structure that sat in its center. Four tall, thin towers bracketed the grassy square that held Warren.

The cell was built for Winger criminals. On Spire, it was considered unusually cruel to deny even prisoners the ability to stretch their wings and fly. Combined with ankle bracelets, the towers created a giant, invisible cage that prevented criminals from flying away. If they crossed the boundaries of their cage, the bracelets delivered a paralyzing electric shock while simultaneously alerting the guards.

Warren could not avail of the allotted flying space, but Husher surprised himself by feeling glad his father at least had ample space to walk around.

Ochrim's words inside the Atrium had sent Husher into a sort of trance, with thoughts that went around in circles, looping back on each other until he felt moved to do something drastic. Hence, his presence outside his father's cell.

When the Wingers received word that Epsilon Leonis had indeed gone supernova, and that another star had followed shortly after—thankfully, no doomed colonies, this time—it hadn't helped Husher feel any better. What would it mean for Ochrim to truly know the future? What would it mean for the Prophecies to be true?

Did that mean Ardent was a true god, and the Ixa his chosen people? It felt absurd to think it, and yet Husher couldn't see where else the evidence pointed.

Whatever the case, it seemed clear that humanity knew far less about the Ixa than they thought. Which made him consider the possibility that his father was telling the truth about being framed. Even the chance of that made Husher burn with shame whenever he remembered how he'd denounced his father twice in front of the Winger Directorate and several UHF officers.

That said, he was still nowhere close to trusting his father.

Warren emerged from the concrete hut in the center of his cell, blinking into the sunlight. When he saw his son, he stopped. They stood too far apart for Husher to make out the expression on his father's face, but he did see the way his arms drooped and his shoulders slumped.

"I wanted to talk to you," Husher called, not sure what else to say. The guard stood near the entrance to the hut, muscular arms crossed, gigantic wings spread across the building. *I wish he would leave.*

Warren took a step closer. "I'm thankful to see the man you've become. That's all I wanted. Honestly. I never expected you to forgive me."

Husher drew in a long breath and said, "Did you expect me to renounce you in front of the entire Winger government?"

"No. I suppose I didn't."

"Come closer." He almost winced at how much like a command that sounded. But he didn't feel comfortable with the guard overhearing their conversation. Not to mention his father's fellow inmates.

"How is your mother, Vincent?" Warren said once he stood a few feet away, the deep creases across his face now clearly visible. It still came as a shock, how much his father had aged.

"I go by Vin, now."

"Vin. What's your rank?"

"First Lieutenant. Used to be Captain."

"What happened?"

"A lot has happened since my father was branded a traitor."

Warren started to nod, but it turned into hanging his head and staring at the grass. "I'm sorry. I can't imagine the hardship I must have caused you."

"Mom is okay. She's never been the same, since you...but I send her money every month. She gets by."

His father glanced behind him, at the guard, and then back at Husher. "Where's she living now?" He smiled. "Is it as nice as this place?"

"She's still on Venus, in a not-so-bad apartment." Husher looked at the guard too, and then around at some of the surrounding cells. "It's hard to believe how little I knew about aliens before I started meeting them, which didn't really happen till after I got consigned to the *Providence*."

"I hear the UHF's gotten pretty xenophobic since my day."

"Yeah. We're basically forbidden to fraternize with aliens at all. And they're banned from boarding our ships. Didn't stop Captain Keyes making a Winger his CAG, of course..."

"Keyes always was an exceptional man. I knew he'd make a fine captain, provided he managed to get a handle on his demons. You're lucky to serve under him."

Husher paused, and then nodded. "I know it."

"How are the Tumbra doing these days?"

Eyes locking on his father's, Husher squinted. "The Tumbra? Fine, I guess. As crusty as always."

"Don't speak that way about them."

"Why not?"

"I don't remember enough from my past. The last twenty years are mostly a blur. But one thing I do remember is how much respect Tumbra had for humanity's virtues. They recognized that when we aren't blinded by greed or lust, humans are truly incredible specimens."

"*Specimens,*" Husher repeated with a terse chuckle. "That's exactly the word for how Tumbra view us. You know, we have reason to believe they conspired with UHF Command to force the *Providence* down Pirate's Path."

"I doubt that, honestly. The Tumbra helped humanity during the First Galactic War. Perhaps they would again."

"How did they help us?"

Warren sniffed, gazing into the distance for a moment. Then he looked at Husher. "It was a closely kept secret, and I don't trust my judgment anymore. Ask your captain. He knows. And if it's right for you to know, he'll tell you."

CHAPTER 6

Phoenix

Planetside, Keyes did not have access to real-time communication with UHF Command, and he would have hesitated to use it even if he did. After all, it was within Command's power to deprive him of access to the micronet at any point, and if failing to do so was an oversight, he wasn't about to draw their attention to that.

The upshot was that he, Senator Bernard, and Flockhead Bytan had to wait almost two hours for Admiral Carrow's reply to his message. When it came, it took exactly the form Keyes had expected it to.

"How novel to hear from a treasonist in a time of war," Carrow spat, his gaunt face twisted into a sneer. "Spouting Ixan propaganda at me, no less, and expecting that I'll pass it on to the Commonwealth in an effort to shape public policy. Epsilon Leonis was an anomaly, and we're looking into the cause. If you think we'll suspend our use of dark tech just because you've fallen for Ixan lies, that's fine, but don't waste your time contacting me again. I found your first message entertaining, but now I'm bored with your antics. Carrow out."

The console went black, and Keyes glanced at Bytan and Bernard, who, like Keyes, sat in lush armchairs designed to accommodate Wingers.

"We received word of Mu Cephei going supernova since he recorded that," Bernard said. "Maybe he heard about it since then, too. Should we send another message to see whether he's changed his tune?"

"No. We're wasting our time," Keyes said.

"But dark matter maps show the supernovas corresponding with the galaxy's high-density areas. If we can demonstrate to the UHF that they're happening where there's a lot of dark matter..."

"They'll never stop using dark tech, no matter how many messages we send. They'd have to stop making war in order to retrofit all their ships with old technology. They'd also have to go against their corporate master, Darkstream."

Flockhead Bytan clacked her beak again. "Keyes is right. The UHF must be *made* to stop."

"Excuse me, but how in Sol do we do that?" As expressive as ever, Bernard raised her hands as she spoke. "With all due respect, Flockhead, you can't even stop them from attacking your colonies."

Keyes cleared his throat. "I'm hoping it can be done without bloodshed."

The Winger and the senator turned to face him. "We're all ears," Bernard said.

"Human militaries haven't clashed for centuries, and I'm re-luctant to change that. Sure, we've fought radicals, but an actual intra-species war..."

"Careful, human," Bytan said. "Our alliance was conditional on your help with stopping the UHF onslaught. We could have destroyed you."

"You almost did," Keyes snapped, and then took a deep breath. *Keep it together,* he told himself. "We promised to help you, and we will keep that promise. But if I can checkmate Command without fighting them, I will. The first step is to seize as many derelict UHF ships as we can. Some of the ships whose crews Ochrim killed have been destroyed in collisions, but most of them are still out there, empty."

"I do like the sound of that," Bytan said.

"I thought you might. In the meantime, we leak the footage recorded by the *Providence*'s sensors while we fought the Ixan warship down Pirate's Path. That will show the people of the Commonwealth that their military is fighting the wrong enemy. We can distribute the footage via the micronet, while we still have access. And in the same video, we can tell the public what we believe to be the true cause of the supernovas."

Bytan furled her gray wings. "What if Ochrim's words at the war council were lies?"

That drew a sharp glance from Bernard. "Do you really think that's a possibility anymore? He had no access to outside infor-mation, and yet he knew about Epsilon Leonis before we did. And he pointed us to the verse from the Ixan Prophecies that predicted all this. As crazy as it seems, I think it's time we start taking the Prophecies seriously."

It certainly seemed crazy to Keyes. He'd resisted for a long time, but after what he'd seen, it seemed undeniable. There was something to the verses the Ixa had been broadcasting throughout the galaxy for years.

They'd seemed to predict the destruction of the *Providence* above Spire, and when they'd pulled through despite the odds, he'd thought that was the end of it. But the verses Ochrim had pointed them to referenced a phoenix, a mythical bird known for coming back from the dead.

Was the *Providence* the phoenix?

By now, he'd memorized the verses:

Behold, a phoenix springs from ash atop the tower of birds.

Fly, phoenix. Fly! Remain, and the tower crumbles.

Your people need you, phoenix, even as they fall to the scythe.

Fly, phoenix. Fly! Else, they'll all die.

The disruptor speaks of starbursts in the sky.

Fly, phoenix. Fly! Let us hear you rage and cry.

If his ship truly was the phoenix, and the "tower of birds" was Spire, the Winger homeworld, then he took those verses to foretell Spire's doom if the *Providence* remained here. *All the more reason to go capture those ships. Now.*

"I've been on this planet long enough," Keyes said, rising from his seat. "My crew and I leave today."

"What about the damage your ship took from the collision with the Gok carrier?" Bytan said. "We have the means to restore your damaged flight deck."

"That would take months. I doubt we have days. Are your Wingers prepared to leave?" The flockhead had agreed to draw heavily from her reserves, as well as from surviving crews of neutralized Roostships, in order to bolster the *Providence*'s crew as well as to fly the derelict ships they would commandeer.

Bytan nodded. "They're standing by."

"I'd like to come with you, Captain," Bernard said, sweeping her light-gray hair from her eyes as she joined him in standing.

Keyes raised his eyebrows. "You'd be safer here."

"I'd also be useless."

"What do you expect to accomplish aboard the *Providence*?"

"We'll figure that out. Together, I hope." She paused. "I expect Corporal Simpson will want to come, too."

He gave a brief nod. "All right, then. Let's go get those ships."

CHAPTER 7

Cowards

Sonya Hurst's fingers curled into tight balls atop the marble windowsill of her office as she glared at the protesters amassed before the gates of the presidential residence, blocking her from attending an important meeting with the CEO of Darkstream. Her security detail said leaving was too dangerous, but why should she fear a bunch of troublemaking lowlifes? She was president of the Commonwealth!

She couldn't hear their chants through the bulletproof glass, but if she squinted she could make out some of their signs. "STOP FIGHTING OUR ALLY!" one said. "WE'RE GOING TO NEED A UNIVERSE TO LIVE IN," said another. And a third: "DOWN WITH DARKSTREAM!"

From next to the gates, armed guards monitored the protest closely, accompanied by a sizable contingent from the capital's police force. The police bore riot shields and batons, and they'd already proved they weren't shy about using them to force the protesters back. Nearby, an armored personnel carrier loomed over the whole scene, with another officer perched atop it, manning a twenty-millimeter rotary autocannon.

"How are we going to spin this, Fink?" she said, turning to Horace Finkel, her pet reporter since before the election.

"I don't know," he said, turning nervously toward the cluster of her advisors sitting in the corner of the office, which was where she liked to keep them—as far away from her as possible.

"Well, I'm going to need an angle." She'd had no idea becoming president would turn out so...messy. They'd elected her president, and so now the public needed to step aside and allow her to rule the Commonwealth, no questions asked. That's how *she* thought it should be, anyway.

Hurst returned her gaze to the outside, where some of the protesters were gathering in a hokey prayer-circle type thing. A speck of dirt on the glass distracted her, tearing her focus away from the human obstructions outside her new home. "I hate living here," she muttered.

"I've been working on finding an angle," Finkel said. "But it's tough. The public doesn't like the look of that Ixan warship. It's caused a bit of a firestorm on the micronet. Understandably, I guess...I mean, the Ixa aren't supposed to have any military, right?"

"Our monitors watch them so closely they could probably figure out how regular their bowel movements are," Hurst said. "And those same monitors say everything's fine."

"Even so, the footage from the *Providence*..."

"What about the dark tech? Have we gotten any reports back from the scientists? We're paying them good money, so they'd better have something for me soon."

One of her advisors cleared her throat from the corner of the spacious office.

Hurst hated how they listened in on every conversation. "What?" she spat.

"Madam President, the first reports from our dark matter experts are already in."

"And?"

"They confirm Ochrim's explanation for the supernovas. The consensus so far is that if we continue using dark tech for ten more years, the universe's destruction will become irreversible. That said, the collapse isn't likely to affect many human colonies until thirty years' time. We were unlucky with the Campion System. Sol won't be in danger for another forty years."

I'll be dead by then anyway. Or near enough.

"Darkstream is too big to just shut down," Hurst said. "The economy rides on that company. And anyway, the Wingers would run over us if we gave up dark tech." She sniffed. "Does the traitor Keyes still have micronet access?"

The advisor who'd spoken before nodded. "An oversight. But one that—"

"Cut it off. I have the power to order that, right?"

"Yes, Madam President. You can mandate that the UHF—"

"Just do it." Looking out the window again made Hurst grimace. "The Commonwealth can't afford for important meetings like today's to be delayed. Why do the guards and police have guns if they aren't going to use them?"

"Mm," Finkel said. He'd moved to the next window over and was peering out.

"Don't breathe on the glass," Hurst snapped at him. She turned back to her advisors, pointing out the window at the demonstration. "Give the order. I want them dealt with."

The advisor swallowed audibly. "Madam President, dragging away the protesters may prove dangerous."

"I didn't say drag them. I'm designating those protesters economic terrorists. They're endangering galactic security. I want them gunned down."

"Madam—"

"Give the order. Now!"

"Yes, Madam President."

Sonya Hurst turned back to watch. It only took a few minutes for her order to be acted upon. Apparently, the officers and the guards were just as eager as her to teach a lesson to anyone who thought they could obstruct the governance of the Commonwealth and get away with it.

The first spray of bullets caught the protesters totally off-guard, and the targets went down in a heap. The others reacted immediately, turning to flee toward the streets of the capital, tripping over each other. *Cowards.*

Another volley took the next row in their backs, making them pitch forward in comical fashion.

"Prepare my convoy," she told her advisors without taking her eyes off of the carnage.

CHAPTER 8

Derelict Ships

As expected, the *Providence*'s micronet access was cut off shortly after they leaked the footage of the Ixan warship to the public, but not before Keyes saw civilian footage of police and armed guards killing protesters in front of the presidential residence.

They'd almost reached the derelict UHF warships floating in stellar orbit. But before they proceeded with anything, his crew needed to see that video.

He marched from his office toward the CIC, barely registering his crew snapping to attention and saluting as he progressed through the ship.

When he entered the CIC, he barked, "Coms, check your inbox and prepare to play the footage you find there on every screen aboard this ship." He settled into the Captain's chair, which was as hard and unyielding as ever. "Patch me through to shipwide."

"You're on now, Captain."

Leaning forward slightly, he spoke into the air. "Women and men of the UHS *Providence*, this is your captain. Go to the

nearest viewscreen. I am about to play you a video that will inform our approach to this conflict. It's likely you haven't seen it,
since as far as I'm aware it hasn't been mentioned by the news
shows available to you in the crew mess. Civilians have been
sharing it around the micronet. Know that it will likely shock
you." With a glance at his Coms officer, he said, "Play the clip."

No one spoke as the scene played out on the CIC's main
viewscreen—as the police and security personnel opened fire on
civilians exercising their constitutional rights. As those civilians
fell and died, and as the survivors panicked, fleeing into the capital's streets.

When the video ended, no one spoke, or even moved. Except
for Keyes. He leaned forward once more.

"Clearly, the Commonwealth cannot be reasoned with. Clearly, they cannot be persuaded. I'd hoped I could pressure them by
alerting the public to the dangers faced by our species, but they
refuse to heed them. The reason for their suicidal indifference
doesn't matter, because we know what we must do. Our government has used up every ounce of legitimacy, and therefore it
isn't our government anymore. It is the enemy. To stop them
from destroying humanity, it will be necessary to fight them
with everything we have. It will be necessary to overthrow them.
I am hereby committing the *Providence* to doing that."

After pausing a moment to let his words sink in, Keyes continued. "To the Winger pilots, soldiers, and other personnel
newly aboard our ship, I would like to extend to you an official
welcome. You bring us closer to a full complement of personnel—closer to our full potential. You are crewmembers of the

Providence, now. Crewmembers of the *Providence* learn from each other, and they support each other to reach their highest level of effectiveness. Any crew, human or Winger, found violating those principles will be disciplined appropriately. That is all."

He settled against his chair's stonelike back. "How soon will we reach the derelict ships, Werner?"

"Minutes, sir," his sensor operator said. "And our three traveling companions are close behind us." He meant the trio of Roostships, which were packed full of the Wingers who would crew what ships they commandeered.

Wingleader Korbyn captained the lead ship, and he'd assembled a team of Winger navigation adjutants who'd been given a crash course back on Spire in a feature that the UHF had started including in its warships after the advent of dark tech. Barring a critical malfunction in another system, every modern human ship could be steered by a single knowledgeable navigator using a simple override command, provided they had access to that ship's CIC.

Korbyn had only a handful of navigation adjutants qualified to take advantage of the feature, but it would be enough to relocate a reserve battle group to Pinnacle, a nearby Winger colony—their most populous world, after Spire. Following the mission to recover as many derelict ships as they could, Korbyn and the other Winger captains planned to join the fight to defend their colonies under attack by the UHF, backed up by as many derelict ships as they had the crew to fully operate.

"Very good, Werner," Keyes said. "Coms, tell Lieutenant Fesky to prepare to launch Condors at a moment's notice. And instruct Sergeant Caine to ready the ship's full contingent of marines for deployment. I don't want to take any chances."

"Sir..."

"Yes? What?"

"One of the UHF ships is moving. It's the *Tucker*, a missile cruiser."

"Moving where?"

"Toward us."

CHAPTER 9

Everyone Has a Hobby

"I want two squadrons of Condors in the air, one led by Lieutenant Fesky and the other by Airman Gaston. Tell them to move it." Launching Condors was mostly for extra missile defense, since the chances of encountering enemy fighters here were quite low. Other than the *Providence*, no UHF ship had carrier-strike capabilities.

Of course, I should probably know better than to assume that. He remembered a certain battle during the First Galactic War, when Captain Warren Husher had taken down five Ixan warships by hitting them with fighters launched from ships that had no business carrying them.

And that reminded Keyes of his most recent encounter with the Ixa. *I let Teth get too close. Just like this missile cruiser's attempting to do. And I paid for it.*

"Helm, reverse thrust at once. We're going to keep our distance until we have a better handle on exactly what's happening, here."

"Yes, sir."

"Send the *Tucker* a transmission request, Coms."

"I'm on it, sir." After a handful of moments passed, his Coms officer spoke again: "They aren't accepting."

"They're accelerating, Captain," Werner said.

"Increase reverse thrust to seventy percent. Coms, try again."

As the supercarrier accelerated backward, her momentum caused Keyes's body to press forward against the straps for the brief moment it took the Ocharium nanites distributed throughout his uniform and body to compensate, tweaking their interactions with the Majorana matrix in the ship's deck.

"Still nothing," Coms said.

"Sir, the missile cruiser is now coming at us under full power."

"Increase to eighty-five percent, Helm." Keyes's body tilted forward once more as his order was carried out. "Coms, tell them they have ten seconds to respond before we blast them to Hell."

"Done. They've accepted our request, sir."

"Put it on the screen."

The viewscreen came on, showing a Gok stuffed into the Captain's chair of the *Tucker*, making it look like a child's toy. "Sorry for rudeness," it said. "Was busy preparing this."

Before Keyes could reply, the alien winked out of view again, and Werner went rigid at his console. "They've launched missiles, sir—thirty of them!"

Keyes winced. The *Providence*'s main capacitor was fully charged, meaning if a single missile hit them they'd all die, likely taking out several more UHF ships in the process, not to mention the accompanying Roostships. "Full reverse thrust, Helm, and hard to starboard! Are those Condors ready yet?"

His coms officer pressed a hand against her headset. "Fesky says they're still preparing to scramble, sir."

"Tell her I needed them in the air five minutes ago! Send a message to Wingleader Korbyn asking him and the other Winger captains to target as many of the missiles as they can. Alert Fesky that we've done that, so her pilots know to watch out for friendly fire." He turned to his Tactical officer, hands curled into tight fists atop his chair's armrests. "Arsenyev, I need you to whip up a firing solution on that cruiser, pronto, and keep it updated in real-time."

Arsenyev nodded, bending over her console, not wasting any time on words. *I can't make her my XO soon enough.*

"How long till the first missiles reach us, Werner?"

"Two minutes, sir. And the cruiser just launched twenty more."

Panic crept up Keyes's body, constricting his throat, threatening to muddle his thoughts and shut down his brain. *No.* "Arsenyev, where's my firing solution?" He knew it was far too soon to ask, but—

"I have it, sir."

"Excellent work. Now, start firing Banshees to pick off some of the incoming missiles. The minute you've done that, ready point defense turrets."

"Captain, Condors just launched," Werner said.

Be careful, Fesky. "Put a tactical display on the main screen."

Keyes watched as the pilots chose their targets, engaging them in several perilous games of chicken. There was no time to come at the missiles from the side: his Condors were forced to run at each one head-on, and hope that if they missed, they would have the instincts to pull away at the right time.

His eyes stayed glued to Fesky's fighter as she took out one missile, then another, then rotated around her short axis to hit a third and a fourth. That didn't surprise him. Airman Gaston was the next-most successful pilot, and he only accounted for two. Several of the others didn't get any.

Not good enough.

"Sixty-five seconds to impact, sir."

Keyes's lips tightened, and a tremor went through his jaw. He clamped his teeth together. "Tactical, prepare to discharge our primary laser."

Arsenyev glanced at him. "Sir, the Condors are in the way. We risk hitting them if we fire on the enemy."

"I know that. We may need to discharge it in another direction, just to release the energy." *This is a disaster.* Larkspur was a heavily populated system, with lots of traffic, and he hesitated to fire the laser in a random direction. But letting a missile hit them with their main capacitor charged would be an outright catastrophe.

The Roostship missiles arrived, then. Winger warships weren't known for their artillery, but their missiles packed enough punch to explode the Banshees before they arrived. The cloud of Winger missiles collided with those targeting the *Providence*, taking out ten...fifteen...

Still not enough.

"Sir, the second group of missiles has been neutralized," Werner said. "But nine still remain of the first group."

Arsenyev turned her full body to face Keyes. "Captain, if we don't fire the primary now, our window will close. Our point defense turrets are only likely to destroy seven of the incoming missiles."

"You're right. Fire..." He trailed off as something on the tactical display caught his eye. It was Fesky, breaking away from the other Condors and hurtling toward the *Providence* under full Ocharium boost.

"Holy shit," Werner said, and Keyes looked at him. "Sorry, sir. But she's doing ten Gs."

"Hold, Arsenyev." Keyes gripped his chair's armrests so hard it hurt, but he couldn't force himself to let go.

The missiles had reached the range of the ship's turrets, which proceeded to spray kinetic impactors at them. The front missile went down. Then the next. And the next.

Fesky fired two Sidewinders while the point defense turrets took down three more missiles. *Three left.*

Arsenyev leapt to her feet, and Keyes resisted the urge to do the same. "Sir, they're going to—"

The turrets took down one more missile, and Fesky's Sidewinders slammed into the remaining two. Keyes knew their shrapnel would rain down on the *Providence*'s hull, but it wouldn't be enough to make her main capacitor blow.

"Coms, patch me through to Fesky's Condor."

"You're patched through, sir."

"Lieutenant Fesky, what is it with you and coming to the rescue at the last minute?"

"Everyone has a hobby, sir," she said. "Some people do crochet."

He chuckled, and told his Coms officer to cut the transmission. Turning to Arsenyev, he felt the corners of his lips curl upward. "Turn our primary on that cruiser and wipe it out."

His XO, Commander Laudano, cut in. "Captain, the *Tucker* is among the most advanced missile cruisers the UHF has ever developed."

"And it won't be the last UHF ship we destroy today. I plan to obliterate every ship we don't have enough personnel to commandeer. This is war, Commander."

CHAPTER 10

Caesar

Among the ships whose crews Ochrim had killed with his subversion of dark tech, the UHS *Caesar* was the most formidable. It was a destroyer, and had been the flagship. So it was the one Captain Keyes sent Husher to investigate, with a platoon of marines at his back. If the Gok had infiltrated the *Tucker*, they almost certainly had some sort of presence aboard the *Caesar*.

"You all have access to the ship's layout via your HUDs," he said to the marines gathered in front of him in the destroyer's shuttle bay. He'd posted two marines at the entrance, to give them ample warning if any Gok tried to take them unawares. "I'm splitting us into four squads to secure four important areas, with each squad taking a separate route that I'll designate on your display. Wahlburg, I'm sending your squad to check out the cargo holds. Markov, you get the weapons lockers. Caine, Engineering. Proceed with caution, all of you. Don't let the enemy take any tactical advantage, if you can help it. Meanwhile, my squad will double-time to the CIC, where we can access the cameras and see exactly where the Gok might be hiding. Questions?"

There were none. A longstanding tradition of UHF marines involved ribbing squad members endlessly if they missed anything from a briefing, so they'd all learned to listen and understand the first time.

There were Winger soldiers dotted throughout the platoon, too, but they also remained silent. *Probably don't want to give their new crewmates an excuse to taunt them.*

Caine's squad was the last to roll out, and before she left, he touched her shoulder, switching to a two-way channel. "Hey. You okay for this?"

"I'm fine." She shrugged off his hand and took her squad into the corridor.

Keyes had deemed her fit to lead a squad again—she'd proven that on the Winger orbital defense platform, although she'd gone on that mission without the captain's permission, something he'd overlooked given the mission's success.

It wasn't as though they had their pick of squad leaders, anyway. Markov had no experience with leadership, though he'd also proven himself in the fight over Spire. Husher had seen Markov get shot during the final battle on the orbital platform, and he'd assumed the corporal dead, but his UHF-issue pressure suit, reinforced with a para-aramid fiber, had spared him anything more than some nasty bruising.

Husher preferred not to dwell on how risky he considered putting Wahlburg in charge of anything. But with Davies dead, who else was there?

Still, Caine hadn't been cleared to resume her post as marine commander, and that had to bother her. *Maybe that's why she's being so distant.*

Husher took point, his squad following behind, swift and silent. Two of the ten were Wingers, who the humans towered over, but the aliens' upper body strength meant they could carry around medium to heavy machine guns without straining too much.

As far as he knew, the *Providence* was the first military vessel in galactic history to deploy mixed-species squads. Figuring out the battle applications afforded by a more diversified marine contingent was at the top of Husher's to-do list. If he was being honest with himself, he was looking forward to it.

A hatch burst open as he passed by, and a towering Gok barged into the hallway. Husher had time to register its lighter armor, signifying it belonged to a raiding party. *Not military.* Then the alien reached for him, and Husher aimed his assault rifle at what he knew to be the armor's weak points. He pulled the trigger.

The bullets found their way into the giant's forest-green flesh, and it listed to the left, but its charge didn't slow. Husher fired again, his bullets lodging in the Gok's left forearm, which didn't stop it from lifting him off the ground, its hands like small boulders against Husher's sides. Before he could react, he was airborne, followed by his head slamming into the bulkhead.

His vision twinned, but he forced himself to regain his feet and run down the corridor, away from his assailant, to get a chance to clear his head. *I'm useless like this.*

A glance backward showed him two corridors, two marine squads, and two Gok attacks, with more of the aliens pouring in from adjoining compartments. He shook his head. Slowly, his mirrored sight merged into one reality. A tense reality. The Gok nearly matched his squad in number, which didn't bode well for the squad, given the aliens' incredible might.

Worse, several of the newly arrived Gok wore the titanium-reinforced pressure suits of their military. Those Gok bore energy weapons similar to those Husher had faced on the orbital defense platform above Spire, and they'd make short work of the marines if Husher couldn't find a way to end the engagement quickly.

He raised his assault rifle to his shoulder, picked the nearest target, and fired. The Gok he'd shot fell forward, but it brought a marine down with it. *Nothing I can do about that now.* He drew a bead on another berserker and fired, simultaneously screaming over a wide channel: "Caine, Wahlburg—I need backup, now!"

His marines held their own, taking down three more Gok. Husher's mad dash down the corridor had afforded him some distance, and he was able to neutralize two more as he walked slowly back toward the fight.

But that was all. Gok strength soon prevailed. One of them picked up a marine and charged at the wall, holding her like she was a battering ram. A sickening *snap* reached Husher's ears, and a red smear remained on the bulkhead where the Gok had pounded her head against it. Then it threw her body at another marine.

A private managed to sink his combat knife into a Gok, but it simply picked up its attacker by the neck with both hands. The marine's back was to Husher, so he could do nothing to help. The Gok crushed the marine's throat cartilage like it was paper mâché.

The entire marine squad lay dead and dying, and now the four remaining Gok turned toward Husher. He doubted they wanted to talk, and so he opened fire on the one closest to him as all four enemies rushed toward him. His target came crashing down a few feet away, and he drew his combat knife, but the next Gok backhanded it out of his grasp and punched him in the chest, knocking him to the deck. His assault rifle skittered away.

Instantly, he pushed against the metal flooring with his hands, scrabbling against it to try to gain enough distance and regain his footing. With one stride, the Gok who'd batted his knife away planted its foot on his chest and pointed an enormous energy weapon at his head.

A bolt of energy lanced through the air, but not from his assailant's gun. That Gok slumped forward, and Husher rolled out of the way just in time to avoid getting crushed.

He turned onto his back again to see one of the surviving Gok wrestling with the other. Heaving himself to his feet, Husher spotted his assault rifle lying on the deck, and he crept toward it while the two berserkers warred with each other.

As his hands closed around the gun, he heard a crash, and he looked around to see one Gok dragging the other to the floor. *One of them saved my life. But which one? Who am I rooting for, here?*

The one who was pulled down regained the advantage, and gripping its opponent's head in both hands, it slammed it against the deck over and over.

Scarlet droplets sprayed both the deck and the Gok's arms. The supine Gok had ceased moving, but still the other continued, rendering its victim's head a bloody mess.

"I think it's dead," Husher said, his assault rifle pointed at the beast, who'd dropped its own weapon at some point.

The Gok stopped, its tiny black eyes settling on Husher. Then it rose to its full height, military-grade armor gleaming darkly under the corridor's halogens.

"Easy," Husher said.

Raising its dark-green arms toward him, the Gok took a step forward.

Husher gestured with the assault rifle. "One more step and you're done."

The Gok turned toward the bulkhead and pressed its forehead ridge to it. Then it reared back and smashed its face against the metal. Again. Again.

Caine appeared around the corner where Husher's squad had come from, her eyes darting from Husher to the Gok and back again. Her squad formed up behind her as she took in the bodies that littered the deck.

"Come on," Husher shouted, dropping his assault rifle and running to subdue the Gok. "Help me get this thing under control!"

CHAPTER 11

Tort

Trying to keep his shock and revulsion from showing on his face, Keyes studied the Gok as it strained savagely against its chains. It had already broken one of the sick bay beds, and so they'd been forced to chain it to a steel pallet to prevent it from harming itself further. As for the energy weapon Husher had brought aboard for study, Keyes had ordered it stored well away from here, inside a secure weapons locker.

Husher and Caine stood on the opposite side of the Gok, clearly struggling with their emotions as well. *Especially Caine.* She'd gone through a terrible ordeal, here. In fact, the Gok occupied the same space she had during her psychosis. It had broken the bed she'd been restrained in. *She's handling it well, all things considered.* Keyes knew that she still experienced delusional thoughts, but she'd broken through the full-fledged fantasies her mind had concocted, and she was able to distinguish reality from delusion well enough. *As well as we need her to, anyway. Hopefully.*

"Why did you try to kill yourself?" Keyes asked the alien.

The Gok fell still for a moment, then it heaved upward against the chains once more. "Wasn't trying that." Its clipped words came out as a tortured yell.

"What were you trying, then?"

"Was trying not to kill your man."

Private Ryerson, who was still recovering from his bullet wound in a bed across the way, gave a humorless laugh through the maroon curtain. "That was a threat, Captain. The thing threatened you. We shouldn't have it alive on our ship. You need to kill it."

"Not an it," the Gok yelled, though Keyes detected no increase in its agitation. "Am a he."

"You're done participating in this conversation," Keyes told Ryerson. "Speak again, and I'll have you moved to the corridor." He returned his gaze to the Gok. "So you're male, then."

"Yes."

"Explain to me what you meant. How did harming yourself stop you from killing my lieutenant?"

"Only way. Needed to point rage somewhere. Was the only option."

"Why are you so angry?"

"Was not always this way. Before Ixa, was calm. Slow to anger."

"Before the Ixa? They did something to you?"

"To entire species. Play with brains. Using virophage. Make Gok more aggressive. Much more."

"When did they do that?"

"Started in Great Fight. What human calls First Galactic War. Been getting worse ever since. Many Gok love what Ixa did."

"But not you."

"*Hate* it."

Husher ran a hand over his mouth. "What's your name?"

"Am Tort."

"You saved my life, Tort." The young lieutenant's voice wavered, reminding Keyes that Husher had just witnessed an entire squad slaughtered, and one under his command no less. *I'll need to monitor him for signs of psychological distress. Some talk therapy with Doctor Brusse is likely in order, too.*

"Hoped human could find a way to change back," Tort shouted.

Keyes cleared his throat. "Our ship's doctor is the closest we have to the type of scientist who might be able to manage that, and she's studied only human anatomy. In fact, our knowledge of Gok biology is extremely limited, given the general lack of contact between our two races." *Except to kill each other,* he didn't add. "I'm grateful you saved Lieutenant Husher's life, but even if curing you were possible, I can't afford the time or resources it would take to do it. We're in the middle of a war."

Tort's muscles bulged once more as he pushed against the chains. "Maybe you *get* motivated to help." He fell back again, panting.

"What do you mean by that?"

"Maybe you learn more about virophage by fighting human version."

Caine squinted down at the Gok. "Human version? What are you talking about?"

"Ardent-worshiper humans on planet Thessaly. Work for Ixa. Develop virophage for release into human population. Make humans even more aggressive than Gok. Never stop killing Wingers. Start killing one another, too. "

Keyes knelt at Tort's side, so quickly that he caused the great alien to start, rattling the chains once more. He laid a hand on the giant's green shoulder. The skin felt like rock to the touch. "How close are they to finishing their work?"

"Almost done."

"Do you know exactly where on Thessaly they are?"

Tort raised his head off the pallet in a nod. "Found out. Give you coordinates."

Keyes rose to his feet, locking eyes with Caine, then with Husher. "We're going there. Now."

CHAPTER 12

Command and Control

Tennyson Steele studied Hurst across the unnecessarily mammoth table in a meeting room deep inside the presidential residence. She was older than him, but he had to admit that life had been friendlier to her, at least where appearance was concerned. No one would call Hurst beautiful, but she didn't have the smooth fleshy protrusion that he had connecting his chin and neck.

I suppose I could have looked after myself a little better. Barbara regularly urged him that it wasn't too late to start, and that may have been true for a man one-quarter as busy as Steele.

"Two meetings in as many days, Madam President," he said, smiling over his folded hands. "I'm beginning to think you like me."

"I need your advice."

I imagine you do. "Would this happen to have anything to do with our nosediving economy?" He parted his hands momentarily, to adjust his horn-rimmed glasses. Then he folded them again.

"The markets are freaking out, Tennyson. My donors won't stop harassing me."

Steele widened his smile in sympathy while reflecting that Hurst was the only politician he'd ever met who talked openly about serving her donors instead of the public. "After the incident with the protesters, people are worried." *To put it mildly.* "More importantly, investors fear that business might not proceed as usual if democracy is replaced by a command-and-control society."

"Oh, is that all?"

Her sarcasm almost made him laugh in her face. *If she thinks she can disrespect the CEO of Darkstream and remain unscathed, a stern lesson will follow.* "Well, there's also the concern that you'll favor the colonies where you have business interests, though I'm sure the wool can be pulled over the public's eyes about that. But when the galactic economy starts to fail altogether...well, that's a little harder to manage."

The president's bravado wilted as quickly as it had sprung up, along with her leathery face. "What do I do, Tennyson? You've always had a grand vision for where we're headed as a species. Anyone who knows you can see that."

Ah, flattery. A better tack for you, no doubt. He had to admit, he did love being flattered. "Here's what you do. You declare that the reason you've been out of touch with the public is that you've been working around the clock to bring to justice whoever gave the order to kill those civilians."

"But...*I* gave the order." Her voice had dropped almost to a whisper, which Steele found comical. Actually, he found basically everything about Hurst comical.

"I know. Even so, you'll hold a press conference and tell them you *didn't* give the order. You'll say that the cops were acting on their own and will be disciplined proportionately. I'd recommend choosing a scapegoat from within their command structure, preferably someone disliked by their subordinates, to pin it on."

"That will amount to giving in to the protesters. I don't give in to economic terrorists, Steele."

Steele shook his head, and he could feel his neck flesh wobble. "I'm not suggesting you give in to them. This is about repairing the economy, and there are ways to quash protests without suffering the political fallout that comes from killing them."

"What about the whole dark tech thing? People will never stop protesting if they think I'm catering to a company set to destroy the universe."

Removing his glasses, he squinted at her, though he kept his smile in place. "I'm sure you're not suggesting *failing* to cater to that company."

Hurst threw up both hands, palms facing him. "No, of course not. That would be absurd."

"Indeed. Where dark tech is concerned, my advice is to launch a...public awareness campaign, let's say. Spin the real danger as a conspiracy between Keyes, the Ixa, and scientists who say dark tech is destructive—even government scientists.

Dark tech isn't destroying the universe. Of course it's not. That's nothing but a hoax designed to take away people's freedoms and creature comforts. And people do love their creature comforts, don't they?"

"Yes. That's brilliant, Tennyson."

"Oh, it's nothing, really. But it should scale the unrest way down, and whoever remains in the streets...well, we can quietly deal with them. I'm sure the media will cooperate."

"Of course they will. If they know what's good for them."

"And they do. They know who signs their advertising checks." He stood, and Hurst followed suit, her hands clasping before her. "A fine meeting, Madam President," he said. "Now, if you'll excuse me, I have an economy to carry."

CHAPTER 13

Forgotten Instincts

A ghost shark swam toward Ek, and she almost wished it would attack her. The thought shamed her instantly, and only served to highlight how different she was from other Fins, who valued harmony with all ocean life.

Every Fin carried a stunner to repel predators without causing them harm, but today, Ek's did not become necessary. The ghost shark swam by her, its gray, soulless eyes making it impossible to tell whether it had even noticed her.

She kicked at a rubbery sea fern with her metal foot, and it bounced back to its original position. Curling her hands into fists, she marched on.

The Speakers sentencing her to remain on Spire had clouded her thoughts with anger. *How dare they?* She was useless here, as useless as they were.

Except, she still had access to the Prophecies. Even if they would not allocate any resources to helping her decipher them.

Ek took out a tablet from her rubber satchel, and it turned on at her touch, illuminating the murk for only a few meters. Her ancestors had not had access to such a device for their scholarly work. They had written on treated rubber paper with the durable ink of the cuttleslug. Ek took a moment to give thanks for the modern tools at her disposal.

After watching footage of the war council between the humans and the Wingers, she had become fascinated with the verses Ochrim had identified, about a phoenix.

According to Flockhead Bytan, Captain Keyes considered the phoenix a reference to his ship, the *Providence*. But Ek did not feel as sure about that. She could not quite place her doubt, but she considered it well worth exploring, especially considering the verse that warned: *Remain, and the tower crumbles.* The "tower" had to mean Spire, and if the true phoenix was still here...

Your people need you, phoenix, even as they fall to the scythe.

She expected that referred to civilians getting massacred in front of the Commonwealth's seat of power, news of which had reached Spire just hours ago. *Starbursts in the sky* meant the supernovas, clearly, and Fesky had already figured out that Ochrim was *the disruptor*.

The verses held nothing else for her. Scarlet anger flashed again at the edges of her thoughts, but she pushed it away. *There has to be something I am missing.*

She began flicking aimlessly through page after page of the Prophecies. Four flicks later, and a passage caught her eye.

Ardent's chosen let a bird fly free, didn't they?
Didn't they.
The bird chased instincts it forgot it had. Didn't it?

Didn't it.

Vermin stuffed it in a cage, didn't they?

Didn't they.

Birdsong brought down Ardent's rage. Didn't it?

Didn't it.

It struck her, then. The bird from this passage was the phoenix, which did not represent Keyes's supercarrier at all. It represented Warren Husher, who the Wingers had imprisoned. She did not have to stretch her imagination very far to accept that the Wingers might be called "vermin" by the Ixan Prophecies.

She instructed her tablet to calculate the most efficient route to Flockhead Bytan's office, and then she ran along it as fast as she could, using her fins and tail to speed her along the ocean floor.

CHAPTER 14

Suffer His Wrath

C aine checked her action for the umpteenth time before peering around the next corner. Her determination not to let her recovery interfere with her performance had made her overly cautious about everything, which wasn't necessarily a bad thing. *Unless it makes me too slow, and I die while I'm triple-checking that I loaded my gun.*

Pairs of marines crept down the branching alleyways to scout for enemies, or for anyone who might alert radicals to their presence. Caine's squad was creeping through Larissa, the capital of Thessaly, and Husher's squad followed behind, keeping their distance in case Caine ran into trouble and they needed to execute a flank.

A local warlord named Thresh had conquered Larissa, taking advantage of the instability brought by the war, which had diverted the UHF's attention elsewhere. In normal times, it would have been the *Providence*'s job to root the warlord out. *In normal times. Not now.*

The first two marines returned, and Private Simmons reported. "Looks like some of Thresh's goons are harassing some followers of that new branch of Ardentism."

Caine nodded. "I'm gonna go check it out."

She saw the skeptical looks that passed between her marines. Ignoring them, she pushed down the alleyway, which let out onto a square. Kneeling in the shadows and holding her rifle at the ready, she took in the scene, sweat rolling down her forehead.

Just as Simmons had relayed, five radicals were shoving around a group of Ardent worshipers. This new branch of the religion promoted peace, even in the face of persecution. The radicals were forcing them to their knees and jabbing them with gun muzzles.

"Ardent frowns on your heresy," one of the radicals yelled, loud enough for everyone in the square to hear. "I spit on your perversion of his teachings." The radical spat on the closest pacifist, in case anyone thought he was speaking figuratively, Caine supposed.

Someone knelt on the other side of the alley, and Caine glanced over. It was Husher.

"We're wasting time," he said over a two-way channel. He'd been fairly quiet since the incident aboard the *Caesar*, where Gok had killed his entire squad. When he'd radioed for Caine's help, she'd been so worried for him that she could barely think. She didn't like experiencing the anxiety Husher caused her on a daily basis. It angered her, in fact. *No one should have the power to make me feel like that.* And no one had, not for almost a decade. *I have to keep fighting this. I can't afford to be so preoccupied with anything other than winning the war.*

In the square, another radical was yelling. "Denounce your sick interpretation of Ardent's teachings or suffer his wrath." She leveled a pistol at one of the pacifist's heads.

"We gotta help them," Caine said.

"It would blow our cover." Husher's head cocked sideways, and she could see him squinting at her from inside his helmet. "I seem to recall, on our last mission to this planet, you were ready to shoot civilians if they endangered your marines. Which is fair enough, but now you're ready to risk our mission to help people we don't know?"

He was right. She'd changed, and it wasn't just her psychosis that had done it. It was this entire war, and the role they'd been playing in it.

"Isn't this what serving on the *Providence* is about?" she said. "I mean, maybe we can't beat the UHF. Maybe we'll never stop the Ixa. But we can always do the right thing. Can't we? Nobody has the power to take that away from us."

No answer from Husher.

"I'm tired of everyone questioning my judgment just because of what happened to me," she said. "I'm the same Caine, Husher. I've just been through some stuff."

"You're right. Pick your target."

"What?"

"Come on. Who are you going to shoot? These people are out of time, so if we're rolling the dice, let's do it now."

"I'll take the one on the farthest right. You start at the left. Work our way in."

"Okay." Husher switched his assault rifle to fire short busts and raised it to sight along the barrel. "Ready."

Caine took aim. "Fire."

The gun shuddered in her hands, and her target went down, jerking backward as her bullet took him in the throat. Smoothly, she lined up the muzzle with the next target to the left and squeezed the trigger. He went down. Caine's and Husher's rounds took down the fifth radical simultaneously.

Husher leapt to his feet and rushed into the square as he started giving orders over a wide channel. "I want my squad roaming the area surrounding this square in pairs. Caine's squad, take up positions on the perimeter. Hopefully we won't be here long, but until we leave I want to hear about everything that moves."

She followed him to the group of pacifists, who were rising to their feet, looking shaky.

"We thank you," said a woman who Caine took to be their leader. No one contested her right to speak, anyway. "Ardent thanks you."

"Tell him he's welcome," Caine said. "What intel can you give us about the way into the inner city? How many of Thresh's people should we expect to encounter? What defenses have they set up?"

The pacifist leader bowed her head. "I'm sorry. We don't involve ourselves in conflict."

"I'm not asking you to involve yourself. I'm asking you to give me information to keep my men and women from dying."

"It is against our beliefs. We do not provide intelligence to soldiers. We are leaving this city."

Caine exchanged disbelieving looks with Husher. "Useless," she said over a two-way channel.

"I guess we're done here," he said. "I'll call back the others."

As the pacifists trickled out of the square in the direction of Larissa's outskirts, one of them lingered behind, a young boy. Once the others were gone, he approached Caine.

"Soldier," he said.

"Yes? You're not about to try to convert me, are you?"

He shook his head, eyes on the ground. "Thresh has set up a blockade, six blocks from here. They've pieced it together from whatever's around. Cars. Rubble. They have snipers every-where, and every alleyway is monitored. You won't make it through."

I can't believe that other one kept this from us. "Is there any way to get through underground? A sewer system, maybe? Subway?"

"There is a sewer, but Thresh has filled in several passages with dirt. It will take you days to get anywhere."

"Okay. Thank you. You've done the right thing."

He nodded and ran in the direction of his fellows. Hopefully they wouldn't pick up on what he'd done. Judging by their be-havior, they wouldn't hesitate to throw him to the wolves in the name of their beliefs.

Caine switched to a two-way and turned to Husher. "You heard that?"

"Yeah."

"So...you thinking what I'm thinking?"

"Pretty sure I am." He switched to a wide channel. "All right, marines, proceed with extreme caution. There's a heavily fortified blockade six blocks ahead, according to a local. I want the first one who sees it to use their heads-up to paint it for an airstrike. We're gonna blow our way through. You hear that, Condor pilots?"

A squadron of Condors outfitted for aerial bombing runs were standing by in Thessaly's mesosphere. "Copy that, Spank," one of them said.

"Let's move, marines."

Caine switched back to a two-way channel between her and Husher. "Hey...lieutenant?"

He turned back, eyebrows raised behind his faceplate.

"Thank you," she said.

"Sure thing." Turning, he started toward the enemy fortifications, where Thresh's radicals were waiting to rip the marines apart at their first miscalculation.

Caine followed.

CHAPTER 15

The Shape the End Takes

Bytan spread her metal-gray wings in a rare display of irritation. "With all due respect Honored One, I'm not sure what you want me to do. You say Spire is in danger, but we've bolstered our orbital defense platforms' nuclear arsenal since the human warship broke through and crashed to the surface. Our sensors will spot any threat that approaches across the Larkspur system. This is as safe as we can be."

"It is not," Ek said. "You can recall the fleet. Including the UHF ships you gained."

The flockhead's beak clacked. "Out of the question. They are fighting to keep our colonies from being completely overrun."

"The colonies can hold their own while you stop your entire species from getting decapitated. Without Spire, the Wingers will be lost. And so will my people."

"Spire is just as valuable to me as it is to you, Honored One. And the Fins are even more valued, as you know. But I can't just abandon the strategy we settled on at the war council, with the full Directorate present, no less. At least, if I am to abandon it, I need a better reason than Ixan poetry."

"You know that it is more than that. It has reliably predicted events."

"It didn't predict Lieutenant Husher breaking through to the surface of Spire, or the *Providence* surviving that battle. I'm sorry, Honored One, but you aren't even able to tell me exactly what form this threat will take. I can't formulate battle plans based on flights of fancy. You're asking something I can't do."

Ek bowed her head deeply. "Your words do not anger me, Flockhead Bytan. They sadden me. I have deep respect for you, and it brings me no joy to see you destroyed by the bonds you place on yourself."

"Honored One..." The Winger's dark eyes shone, and Ek could tell she felt helpless. "I don't know what to say."

"Say nothing, and know that it has been a pleasure to know you. I hope you survive what is to come."

Ek left Bytan's office, feeling numb for the first time since she took to space aboard a battered asteroid miner. *I have failed. And now all is lost.*

There was one thing she could do. According to the Prophecies.

Your people need you, phoenix, even as they fall to the scythe.

She ran through the Winger army base, alarms blaring even before she left.

"All personnel to battle stations," a panicked voice said from every loudspeaker. "Talon pilots, take wing. Reserve forces,

prepare for transport to your designated orbital defense platforms. A Gok fleet has appeared in-system and is headed
straight toward Spire."

So this is the shape the end takes.

Wingers could reach almost anywhere on land simply by flying, but for more urgent purposes they took a speeder. When
Ek reached the vehicle bay, she was relieved to find several of
them ready to deploy, their sleek contours glimmering in the
dim lighting.

Dashing to the one nearest the exit, she hopped inside and
got its systems running as quickly as she could. Then she burst
out of the vehicle bay and onto the network of roads.

Traffic was heavier than normal, though that was still fairly
light. Wingers preferred to use their wings, and they took the
barest excuse to do so. When Ek did encounter other speeders,
she simply drifted around them. Back when her legs had been
new, before she found a ship willing to take her off-planet, she
had spent a lot of time cruising in speeders, and the skills she
acquired then proved useful now.

At last, she arrived at her destination—the prison where the
Wingers were keeping Warren Husher. The guards stopped her
at the gate.

"What business do you have here, Honored One?"

"I must speak with Warren Husher."

The guard bowed low. "By all means. Please carry on
through. The human is being kept in row omicron, cell five. Another guard will meet you—"

Ek accelerated through the gate before he could finish, braking and turning so that the speeder ended up perpendicular to the rows of cells. The first half of the alphabet flashed past, and she turned hard into the row the guard had named, preserving most of her speed with the maneuver.

When she reached cell five, the guard meant to meet her had not arrived yet. *Good.* She drove straight onto the grassy expanse.

Warren Husher was sitting outside the small structure that provided him shelter, his legs spread on the ground before him. "Get in," she shouted.

He stood. "A Fin outside the ocean. Now I guess I have seen it all."

"The planet is about to be attacked by the Gok. If you would like to survive, I suggest you heed what I say."

Warren raised his foot, drawing his pants up to reveal a gray ankle bracelet. "I'm not going anywhere."

Ek turned off the speeder, popped the hood, and leapt out to walk around to the front, cybernetic legs whining softly. In the center of the motor, a large magnet was slowing to a stop. She pointed at it with a black-clad hand. "Place your foot next to that."

"What? Why?"

"It will wipe the data on the bracelet's memory, so that it forgets when it is supposed to shock you. Hurry."

"All right." Warren heaved his right leg onto the engine and nestled his foot next to the magnet. "Will that do it?"

"It should."

"I hope you're right. If you're not, this thing won't stop shocking me until I go back in my cage."

"Let us try." Ek closed the hood and got in the driver's seat once more. The human climbed in beside her.

Without hesitating, Ek accelerated across the cell, passing between the towers that formed the box that had been her passenger's prison. In her haste, she almost hit a Winger guard, who had finally arrived to make sure she could communicate with the prisoner safely. Warren waved to the Winger as they zoomed past.

"I take it you were not shocked," she said.

"By getting sprung from jail by a Fin with metal legs? Shocked doesn't begin to cover it, actually."

"I meant by your ankle bracelet."

"I know what you meant, sweetheart. What's your name, by the way?"

"It is not sweetheart. And you will find calling me that will not prove viable for you, long-term."

As they sped past cell after cell, Winger prisoners emerged from their shelters, or settled to the ground from flight to watch them pass.

I hope they are not doomed.

CHAPTER 16

A Little Experiment

Private Simmons scouted ahead, and Husher's heads-up display gave him access to what the scout was seeing in real-time. *We're so close.* They'd come within two blocks of the coordinates Tort had given them, but they'd reached an impasse. Radicals milled about in the street in front of the building Husher needed to access. *Are they defending it? Is Thresh helping develop the virophage?*

An idea struck him. "Wahlburg, check the next street over, to the west. Tell me what's adjacent to the building we need to access."

The air strike had cleared their way into the inner city, but it had also stirred it up worse than a kicked hornet's nest. Ever since, they'd been inching their way through Larissa. *If only there were tunnels we could access, this would have been so much easier.*

Remembering his last time fighting in an urban environment, Husher regularly reminded his marines to think in three dimensions. The difference was that last time, they'd been able to take advantage of that third dimension themselves. Now, Larissa held far too many radicals, making it a bad idea to dig in and fight. Meaning the vertical offered them nothing but stress.

"It's a business," Wahlburg said, patching his feed through to Husher's helmet. "Looks abandoned. Broken glass. Probably looted when the radicals took over the city."

There'd been a time when Wahlburg's report would have come with a sarcastic quip. Husher would have never guessed that he'd miss that. "Thanks, Wahlburg." Then he switched over to a wide channel. "All right everyone, Wahlburg found us a more viable avenue of ingress. An abandoned business butts up against the back of the building we need to get to, so we're going to mouse-hole through. Let's go."

The marines pushed forward as quickly as possible while creeping from shadow to doorway to alleyway. Husher encouraged them to split up whenever necessary. One-by-one, they arrived at the store, slipping inside and gathering in the front room.

"Both buildings' rear walls are flush with each other," Wahlburg said. "One blast should do it."

Husher nodded. "Good work. Markov, go set the satchel charge. My squad, be ready to rush through to locate and defend the next building's entrance—the explosion is going to draw radicals. Sergeant Caine's squad will defend this store. We should be able to dig in and defend our choke points for a while, but that's no reason to screw around."

Within minutes, the charge was set. "Blow it," Husher said.

Markov started the timer and ran out to join them in the store's front room. Seconds later, a blast rumbled through the floor and walls.

"Move! Sergeant Caine, you're with me. Everyone else, set up the best defense you can, as quickly as possible."

They followed Husher's squad into the next building, where shouting could already be heard from the street out front. Husher expected the biochemical work to be happening underground, and it didn't take long to confirm his suspicions. They found a large trapdoor in one of the back rooms.

Caine looked at him. "What if there are more radicals down there?"

"We neutralize them," Husher said, grabbing the latch and flipping the trapdoor open so that it leaned against the wall.

But they didn't find any radicals downstairs. They didn't find anything, except a light switch that made the ceiling fixtures flicker and come on with an unsteady glow.

The staccato of gunfire began upstairs, dulled by the basement's ceiling. Husher and Caine dashed through, searching room after bare room. Nothing.

"Have they cleared out?" Caine said. "Maybe they got word we were coming and relocated somewhere else in Larissa."

"If that's the case, we have to keep searching the city."

"Easier said than done, considering all the radicals we just called down on top of our heads. After this, our only option is a swift evac."

Husher was about to agree with her when his com pinged. He took it out and saw that he he'd received a video message. When he played it, an Ixan face came on the screen—the captain they'd fought just before retrieving Ochrim from a Darkstream research facility hidden beneath a remote moon's surface.

Teth. The Ixan didn't speak. He only smiled the creepy smile Ixa always seemed to wear. Husher showed the com's screen to Caine.

"Is that Ochrim?" she said.

"No, it's Teth. The one who fired on the *Providence.*"

"Well, is he going to say anything?"

"Why yes, Sergeant Caine, I do intend to speak. I was waiting for Lieutenant Husher to show you my face, so that I would have your undivided attention."

"Wait," Caine said, her eyes locked on Husher's. "That can't be real-time...is it?"

Slowly, he shook his head. "It's a video message. A recording."

"Correct," Teth said. "But let's conduct a little experiment, shall we? I know you humans are still at least somewhat skeptical that the Prophecies are real, that the Ixa can truly predict the future. So please treat this like a real-time conversation. Answer me as though I were standing right next to you."

Husher looked from the com's screen to Caine. "Not a chance. I'm not playing his game. Let's just let the entire video play out."

"But, wait. Wouldn't it be sort of useful to know if the Prophecies are real or not?"

Teth remained silent, still smiling at them like a predator sizing up its next meal.

"Sure. And we can test that by not answering him. Clearly, he's predicted that we'll play along. By refusing to do that, we prove he doesn't know the future."

"All right."

They both stared at the screen, and Teth stared back at them. "I'm waiting for you to treat this like a conversation," he said.

Husher and Caine exchanged glances, but stayed quiet.

Teth's smile widened. "I fed that Gok aboard your ship false information about what you'd find inside this building. If you'd like to know *why* I would do that, I think you should probably speak to me."

"Why, then?" Caine said. "Why'd you do it?" Husher shot her a sharp look, and she ignored him.

"I thought you'd never ask, Sergeant Caine!" Teth said, chuckling. "That was a joke. Obviously I knew that you would. Ixa find humans especially predictable. Maybe it's because we're so much alike."

"We're nothing like you," Caine spat.

"You're very much like us. Have you ever noticed that humanity and the Ixa are the only two sentient species in the galaxy to have invented corporations? Immortal entities, legally bound to elevate profit over every other consideration, including the survival of the species. Of course, we've learned to control *our* corporations."

Caine spat on the basement's dirt floor. "We're in the process of that."

"You're in the process of going extinct, actually. You're very quiet, Lieutenant Husher. How predictable. I expected you would remain stubbornly silent during our conversation."

"Well, I'm speaking now," Husher shot back. "So I guess you were wrong."

"Actually, I was lying. I only said that to trick you into participating. Imagine that! Someone as smart as you assume you are, so easily tricked."

Husher clenched his teeth, hard enough that his jaw began to ache.

"Back to the silent treatment, I see. No matter. Sergeant Caine has already proven to be a pliable interlocutor. You've come here to stop Ixan sympathizers from releasing a virophage that will make humans aggressive, but you see, there's no need for such a virophage, because humans are aggressive enough already! Aggressive enough to kill each other off, along with your own allies...softening yourselves for us to swoop in and dominate you."

"Then why did you lead us here?" Caine said.

"Simple. Thessaly is on the opposite side of the Larkspur System from Spire, and it would take the *Providence* the better part of a day to return there. By then, the Gok will have cleansed Spire of all life."

CHAPTER 17

Intercept Course

A wave of nausea swept over Keyes as he listened to the final words of Teth's message. To him, the recording had sounded like a bizarre one-sided conversation, but according to Caine and Husher the video had played out just like a real-time exchange.

By then, the Gok will have cleansed Spire of all life.

"Lieutenant, I'm deploying a combat shuttle to evac you and your marines, but I can't wait around for you. I'm taking the *Providence* to Spire."

"Yes, sir. Good luck."

"Keyes out." He twisted around in his chair and fixed his Nav officer with his gaze. "As quickly as you're able, calculate the most efficient route to Spire that allows for maximum acceleration. Don't worry about fuel efficiency—only speed. Helm, when Nav sends you the course, punch it. Engage all engines, full power."

"Aye, sir."

Keyes settled in for what promised to be the worst wait of his life. He wanted a coffee, but he forbade his crew to treat his CIC like a food court, and if he wanted to follow his own rule then he'd have to down his beverage in the wardroom. No way was he leaving the CIC for that long. Not at a time like this.

An hour later, when they were already committed to their course, Werner spoke. "Sir, there are three UHF ships moving on an intercept course. Two frigates and a corvette."

Keyes felt his nails biting into his palms, even though he kept them well-trimmed. He relaxed his hands. "Send the corvette a transmission request."

Seconds later, a man he recognized as Captain Yamat appeared on the viewscreen. "Captain," Keyes said, "Can I ask your purpose in positioning yourselves along my trajectory?"

"With pleasure, Keyes."

"It's Captain Keyes."

"Not anymore. You're in open rebellion against the UHF and the Commonwealth, and so you've been stripped of your rank."

"I don't recognize the UHF's authority to do that."

"We'll have to differ on that, then."

"State your business, Captain Yamat."

"We were ordered to investigate what you were doing on Thessaly. You're to tell me, and while you're at it you can let me know where you're headed with such haste."

"I'm going to provide aid to the Wingers on Spire. They're under attack by Gok."

"I'm afraid I can't let you do that."

"Captain Yamat, an entire species resides on that planet. It would be an unforgivable atrocity to let the Fins be wiped from the universe."

"That planet is also our enemy's homeworld. It makes strategic sense to allow the Gok to complete their attack."

Keyes squinted at Yamat. "This isn't about strategic *sense*. It's about—"

"I have my orders, Keyes, and they include apprehending you. Do you plan to cooperate or not?"

"Don't make me do this, Yamat."

"Is that a threat?"

"It's a promise. Clear out of my way."

"No."

Keyes gestured to his Coms officer to cut off the transmission, and she did. A biting remark had been waiting on his tongue, but his conversation with Yamat had run its course, and his time would be much better spent formulating a battle plan. He'd witnessed too many captains offer up valuable intel to the enemy because of their need to have the last word.

"Arsenyev, calculate a firing solution that targets the nearest frigate with our primary laser." *Burn it away to nothing,* he wanted to add. For that matter, he wanted to pound his fists against his armrests until they were bloody. But detached efficiency was what the day called for. Indeed, every day would call for that, either until this war was won or his corpse had grown cold.

I need to keep my temper's throat under my boot.

"Sir, the three opposing ships are performing retro burns," Werner said. "The other frigate apparently intends to position itself directly in our path."

"That suits me," Keyes said. "Let's take advantage of our acceleration. Launch a full salvo of kinetic impactors at it, with a one-mile spread in every direction. Coms, put Lieutenant Fesky on standby."

"Yes, Captain."

"There's no going back now," Laudano said.

Keyes turned to face his XO. "Clarify."

"We're firing on crewed UHF ships, aren't we? We've become true rebels. Hopefully we won't meet the same fate most rebels do."

CHAPTER 18

A Prisoner Again

Ochrim couldn't hear the battle raging over Spire, but he kept his eyes on the sky, and occasionally he saw a flash. A Gok ship exploding, perhaps. Or an orbital defense platform.

The platforms had the advantage of having nowhere to go, which had afforded their creators the ability to devote most of their mass to artillery. On the other hand, Gok had the advantage of not caring whether they died.

Even with their increased nuclear arsenal, the defense platforms were not equipped to repel an enemy with no sense of self-preservation. *As they learned when the UHS* Buchanan *came crashing to the surface.*

An hour into the battle for Spire's life, Gok warships started breaking through. The first ones were decimated, pockmarked and smoking, robbed of their ability to do anything but crash.

But a couple of hours after that, the Gok managed to create a hole in the orbital defenses big enough to fly shuttles through unscathed. The first such headed in the direction of Ochrim's prison.

He heard them as they rampaged through the jail, accompanied by the cries of the inmates they brutalized. The first Gok Ochrim laid eyes on seemed to take no notice of him. Instead, it forced its way inside the central shelter of the cell opposite the scientist's.

Seconds later, the Gok emerged clutching the Winger inmate, who beat its wings helplessly against the giant's forest-green bulk.

Ochrim had gotten to know that Winger, a little. His name was Pyron, and his mother had been killed in the First Galactic War. Since then, Pyron had become a pirate who'd ventured too far outside Pirate's Path.

It was widely suspected that the Winger government turned a blind eye to the pirates, since they mostly targeted human vessels. But when they strayed into civilized space, the Wingers had no choice but to take action, to avoid angering the human Commonwealth.

Pyron had a young daughter who'd visited him twice since Ochrim had been imprisoned here.

The Gok caught one of the talons beating against its rock-like skin and snapped it off, causing Pyron to emit a piercing shriek. Then the hulking alien grabbed the Winger's crown feathers and used them to smash his face against the side of the building. After several repetitions, the Gok cast the Winger to the ground and ran to the next cell.

Pyron did not move again. His eyes stared sightlessly at the sky, and his beak was a shattered, bloody ruin.

More Gok appeared, murdering the prisoners in the surrounding cells in brutal fashion. Amidst the chaos, Ochrim spotted another Ixan walking calmly toward his cell, a long, midnight cape billowing behind him.

"Brother," Teth said once he stood just outside the invisible wall created by the towers. A wall for Ochrim—not for Teth. Or for Gok. "You've done well."

Ochrim didn't answer.

"Your part is done, now. You can rest. Father says you can rest."

"I have no father," Ochrim said, surprised to hear himself echoing Vin Husher from the war council mere days ago.

"He would be sad to hear you say that."

"My father is dead."

"He's very much alive. And he will look after you. You can even rule with us, if you ever get around to feeling like it. But this war is won. With Spire's destruction, it's won. The Prophecies are undeniable. Without the Fins, the humans will never see clearly enough to subvert their destiny."

"Am I to be a prisoner again?"

"You were always a prisoner, but never a prisoner of the Ixa. You are your own personal jailor." Teth stepped through the invisible wall, producing a gun and pointing it at Ochrim's foot. When Teth pulled the trigger, the ankle bracelet popped off, making Ochrim's pants stick out from his leg. He shook it, and the bracelet tumbled out onto the grass.

Teth turned and walked away, in the direction he'd arrived from. "Come," he said.

Ochrim followed.

As they left the planet, his brother used his ship's main screen to show Ochrim a view of Spire, and of the Gok warships holding position in orbit. Teth raised his wrist to his mouth and, in an audible whisper, said, "Now."

The Gok carpeted the planet's surface with nukes, in a barrage that did not end for as long as Ochrim stared. *Meditation. Your meditation practice.* He tried to focus on the emotions the vision produced in him. The physical sensation the emotions caused.

But there were no emotions any longer. He felt nothing.

"The humans will intercept us before we leave this system," he said, as he was meant to say, his voice utterly flat.

"Incorrect," Teth said. "We are leaving the Gok to their own devices. They will spread through this sector, killing everything in their path. That should cover our exodus."

CHAPTER 19

No Less Remarkable

The volley of kinetic impactors ruptured the second frigate's hull and caused it to explode seconds later, but the first frigate didn't behave as expected. Instead of slowing like the first, it shot past the *Providence*. Though Arsenyev's calculations were good, the primary laser only had a few seconds to play across the frigate's hull as it zoomed by, inflicting minimal damage.

"Launch Condors," Keyes barked. "Tell Lieutenant Fesky to chase down that frigate and kill it."

His Coms officer relayed the order to Fesky, and within a minute Keyes saw the tactical display blossom with green dots: the *Providence*'s Air Group, bolstered by the new addition of seventy-five Winger pilots from Spire.

That left Captain Yamat's corvette for Keyes to deal with. The UHF warship was squaring off with the *Providence*.

David and Goliath. But I don't think this is David's lucky day.

For slowing his progress toward Spire, Keyes wanted to burn the opposing ship to cinders. But he'd learned to separate his desires from his actions a long time ago. "Coms, send Yamat another transmission request."

"Done, sir. He's accepted."

"Put him on-screen." Yamat appeared moments later. "Yield," Keyes said.

"I won't."

"This is insanity. You can't win this engagement."

"I believe you're right. But I also believe your victory will martyr my crew and I, hardening the other captains against you."

Keyes blinked. *Incredible.* "You have my respect, Captain Yamat. Your sacrifice serves the wrong cause, but that makes it no less remarkable."

"You have none of mine, Keyes."

"Very well." He gestured at his Coms officer, and she terminated the transmission. For his part, Keyes turned his attention to how he could end this engagement as quickly as possible. In addition to being a much more powerful ship, the *Providence* had the advantage of never having relied on wormholes generated using dark tech. Her engines were more powerful than modern ships, which had relied heavily on the wormholes for mobility, and so corners had been cut with their engines. Now that dark tech had failed...

"Captain?"

Werner's voice sounded small, which gave Keyes a sinking feeling in the pit of his stomach. He turned toward his sensor operator. "Yes?"

"Sensor data tells me...it..."

"What is it, Ensign?" Keyes asked gently.

"It's Spire, sir. The Gok have covered it with nukes."

Keyes felt his shoulders rock forward, and he caught himself by jerking his hands to his kneecaps. The deck seemed to sway as he stared at it. Acid crept up his throat, and a single tear fell to splash on the metal below.

"Captain?"

He managed to raise his gaze enough to see that Arsenyev had gotten to her feet. Werner stood, too, his concerned expression mirroring the Tactical officer's.

"I'm sorry," Keyes said, and he truly was. Nothing should break a captain's resolve, and certainly not in the middle of an engagement. Except...

He placed a hand over his eyes, breathing deeply. "Werner," he said, concentrating on not vomiting.

"Sir?"

"How is Lieutenant Fesky faring against the frigate?"

"She has two squadrons picking off its point defense turrets. A third squadron is performing the first alpha strike now."

Keyes straightened in his seat. "Tell her to devote a squadron to running missile defense near the *Providence*, and then every EW fighter she has to scrambling Yamat's systems. Ready our point defense turrets. Once Fesky's neutralized the frigate, order her to engage the corvette's missile turrets, to allow our Banshees to get through. Helm, perform a retro burn at fifty percent."

There was no longer any need for haste, and so he aimed to end this engagement without any damage to his ship.

They had the time.

CHAPTER 20

Drunk

An hour after the Condors returned to base—an hour after they played a central role in the destruction of their first UHF targets—most of the pilots sat around the crew's mess, trying to distract themselves after Fesky's half-hearted debriefing.

Husher had barely slept since leaving Spire, but he didn't want to sleep, and neither did anyone else, it seemed. Maybe they expected sleep to bring nightmares, like he did. His would certainly have lots of material to work with, not the least of which were the fresh memories of his entire squad being brutally murdered by Gok.

He'd tried to catch Fesky on the way out of Flight Deck B's primary ready room, but she'd brushed past him to disappear into her quarters. *She needs time.* Probably a lot more time than she was likely to get.

He was playing Poker with some of the other pilots, mostly from his Haymakers squadron. His hand sucked. Glancing across the mess, he spotted Wahlburg sitting on his own, clutching a mug of something and peering into it.

Dark days. For everyone. Remembering how the Wingers had reacted when the *Buchanan* had crashed into their planet made Husher wonder how they'd behave now. Back then, after a handful of Fin deaths, they'd attacked the UHF with no real hope of winning. What would they try to do to the Gok, who'd wiped out the Fins completely? And would it actually help to win the war?

He tried to envision a future for the Winger species where they didn't completely self-destruct, but he couldn't do it.

Voodoo revealed a royal flush, scooping up the pot, and Husher stood, tossing down his cards. "Congrats, Voodoo. I'm out."

"Don't blame you. See ya, Spank."

"Bye, Spank," a couple of the others chimed in. No one sounded very engaged in the game. They didn't even seem to mind Voodoo taking all of their money.

Husher walked over to stand at Wahlburg's table. After a couple of seconds, the sniper looked up. "Lieutenant."

"Private. What's that you're drinking?"

"Disgusting swill. Something they distilled down in Engineering."

"You know that's against Fleet regs, right?"

He expected some crack about what did Fleet regs have to do with them, now that they'd left the UHF. Instead, Wahlburg just nodded. "Yeah."

Frowning, Husher decided to prod him further. *See if I can't stir up the old Wahlburg.* "Technically, it's my job to discipline you now. Think I should?"

Wahlburg shrugged. "Probably."

Husher took a seat next to the sniper instead.

"You want some?" the private asked, pushing the mug toward him an inch.

"No."

"All right." Wahlburg took a long pull from the mug and set it back on the table with a *clunk*. "You probably think I'm pathetic. Depressed over a dead girl who never loved me back."

"Davies was a fine marine and a good person." Husher sniffed, never sure whether he was saying the right things in situations like these. "Anyway. If the human heart made sense, there would never have been so much ink spilled about it. I doubt there's anything that's been written about more than that."

"I always knew I never had a chance with her. Still, getting rejected never stopped stinging. But you know what the crazy thing is? Right now, I'd give anything just to get shot down by her one more time."

"Yeah." For some reason, Wahlburg's words made him think of Caine. Pushing her out of his mind, he thought of his father, and how Warren Husher hadn't seen his wife in over twenty years. And that reminded him of their conversation on Spire. *I wonder if Warren's still alive.*

"I'd better go," Husher said, pushing back from the table. "Let me know if you want to talk some more."

"Right. Thanks."

He didn't know what Keyes planned to do now, in the wake of Spire's destruction. Possibly they'd already embarked on their next mission. If so, Husher hadn't heard anything about it.

It was one of the darkest days in galactic history, but the *Providence*'s objectives hadn't changed. They still needed to get the UHF to stop attacking Winger colonies and start preparing to fight the Ixa. And at some point, they needed to stop humanity's use of dark tech.

As he strode through the ship towards the captain's office, he thought about what a galaxy without dark tech would look like. They'd have to go back to the old method of simulating gravity, which had had a lot of negative health effects. And they'd lose instantaneous communications. *Not that we have that on this ship anymore.* The galaxy would become a very different place.

Thinking of his father had reminded him of one of the last things Warren had said to him, about how the Tumbra had helped humans once. And how they might again.

"Come in," Keyes yelled when Husher knocked, and he opened the hatch to find the captain gripping a whiskey bottle, with not a glass in sight.

"God," Husher said, saluting. "Is everyone getting drunk today?"

"At ease. Have a seat." The captain waved at the wooden chair in front of his desk, his movements a little unsteady. "Who else is drinking?"

"Never mind," Husher said as he sat. "What are we doing right now, sir? Where is the *Providence* going?"

"Nowhere. We're floating in space."

"In the middle of a war zone?"

"You want a drink?"

"No. I want to talk."

Keyes sighed. Slowly, he picked up the bottle's cap and screwed it into place. Then he stowed the whiskey in its customary drawer. "I'm beginning to doubt my fitness for command." Bloodshot eyes locked onto Husher's.

Wow. He's hammered. "With all due respect, Captain, you don't get to doubt that. You led us into this rebellion, and you're all we have. So I think you'd better sober up and lead."

With the measured pace of a drunk, Keyes said, "*Behold, a phoenix springs from ash atop the tower of birds. Fly, phoenix. Fly! Remain, and the tower crumbles.*"

"What's that supposed to be?"

"Ixan Prophecies. It predicts the destruction of Spire, and I spotted that, long before it happened. Problem is, I thought *we* were the phoenix. And if we left, the planet would be fine."

"Permission to get a glass of water?"

"Go ahead. Glass near the sink."

Having a private washroom was an incredible luxury aboard a warship, afforded only to the captain. Husher opened the tiny room's door and found the glass, filling it. He returned to Keyes's desk and set the water front of him.

"I think you should drink that, sir."

Keyes did.

"Who do you think the phoenix really is, then?"

The captain set down the glass after swallowing half of its contents. Then he raised it to his lips and downed the other half.

"I don't know," he said at last. "It doesn't seem to matter much, anymore."

"Fair enough. Sir, there's something I've been meaning to ask you, and this is the first chance I've gotten. My father said you know something most people don't about our relationship with the Tumbra."

Keyes spun the empty glass between his fingers, studying it. "He told you that, did he?"

"He said that if it was right for me to know, you'd fill me in."

"Your father. I didn't speak to him, on Spire. I wanted to. And I never believed he was a traitor. But something didn't feel right about his presence there. Something inside me made me stay away."

"The past can't be changed," Husher said. "And we sell the future short by dwelling on it." *I'm just full of wise words, to-day.* "The Tumbra..."

"I've never repeated what your father told me. To anyone. I've kept that UHF secret, even after going against the UHF. They were worried about it getting out, Command as much as the Tumbra. Afraid the aliens' reputation for neutrality would shatter. And it would."

"Why?"

"During the First Galactic War, they gave us information on enemy ship movements. They admired us, then, and I suppose they were right to. I suppose we were admirable, once. Anyway, that's the secret. The Tumbra helped us win that war."

Husher felt his heart rate increase. "Sir, if we had access to Tumbran intel today, that would be a huge boon to the war effort. Right now we have no idea what the Gok will do. Where will they strike next? And what about the Ixa, when it comes to that? If we had advance warning of their approach—"

"I don't know whether the Tumbra can be trusted anymore. I've often suspected they resent us as much as the Wingers do. On the other hand, some people believe that most Tumbra have sold out to the UHF."

"But we need to try *something*. We can't hang around here like a sitting duck."

"There is one Tumbran who may help us. *May.* It's a long shot, but we've known each other a long time. He's the only one of them who ever came close to showing signs of affection for humans. Not that it came anywhere near that."

"Then let's go find him."

"Yes." Keyes rose unsteadily to his feet, frowning. He stabilized himself with both hands on his desk.

"Respectfully, sir, you can't give orders like you are now. The crew can't see you like this. I can tell the XO you're not feeling well. I'll relay the mission to him myself, as long as you can give me this Tumbran's location."

Keyes nodded. "I can. That's not the problem."

Husher hesitated. "What is the problem?"

"We'll need to travel through Commonwealth space to reach him."

CHAPTER 21

Soon

Performing pull-ups using the vertical bars of his cell made them more difficult than normal, but the horizontal crossbars weren't high enough, and in the end, his unusual approach only strengthened him faster.

Bob Bronson spent most of his time exercising, even when his muscles ached. The pain went well with his anger, which he'd also grown accustomed to.

That anger came nowhere near rage. It remained a low-level background burn, and he actually considered it a useful reminder of what had been done to him. What had been taken from him.

I am the rightful captain of this vessel.

One of Laudano's people had snuck him a safety razor, and Bronson used it in front of his cell's minuscule mirror to keep his beard as tidy as possible. He took good care of himself. Along with the regular exercise, he constantly pestered the guards for books, to keep his mind sharp. They didn't ask him how he managed to maintain his facial hair.

They're lax, but not for long. I will captain this shipwreck, and I'll whip everyone on her into shape. Then I'll destroy her. And them with it.

Some of the guards had good sense. Like the one who approached his cell now. He was one of Laudano's. *One of mine, before long.*

"What's the latest?" Bronson asked.

"Keyes ordered the destruction of most of the derelict UHF warships. And then he went on to destroy three crewed ones."

"He has to be stopped." The UHF had ordered Keyes to hand the command over to Bronson. The bastard couldn't have that, of course. Oh, no. He had to hog all the power for himself. *Not for much longer.*

The guard tossed a piece of crumpled paper through the bars, and Bronson caught it. "A message," the man said. "From the XO."

"Thanks."

Once he was alone, Bronson smoothed out the paper on his knee. It had one word written on it: *Soon.*

He considered flushing Laudano's note down the toilet, but he decided that wouldn't be secure enough. Instead, he popped the paper into his mouth and chewed, saliva gushing at the pulpy taste.

Soon.

CHAPTER 22

Rounds Away

"Transmitting now, sir."

"Very good, Ensign." Keyes settled his hands on the armrests of the Captain's chair and watched the tactical display as the *Providence* progressed toward the Larkspur-Caprice darkgate. He'd just finished recording a message to all of the UHF captains in the system, entreating them to recognize Command's current course for the madness it was. He'd invited them to join him in rebuilding the UHF as it was intended—a space military dedicated to serving humanity, to be deployed only in its defense. Not to enrich a corporation blinded by greed.

Within fourteen hours, every UHF warship in the Larkspur system would receive it. Of course, many captains had been assigned to attack Winger colonies in other Bastion Sector systems. But word would spread. *It has to.*

His head still pounded from his brief descent into depression and drink, but he valued the aching. It reminded him never to let that happen again.

The crew needed him. The *Providence* needed him. And humanity needed them all. Husher had helped Keyes remember that.

"Werner, what's the posture of the Gok fleet?"

"I don't know that I'd call it a posture, Captain. They're spreading across the Larkspur system in a wave. We'll likely make it out of here before that wave hits us, though."

Keyes nodded, thinking of Ek, Warren Husher, Flockhead Bytan. Had any of them made it off Spire alive? There was no time to search for them, but he devoted a moment to silent prayer in their names. *Come back to us.*

He turned to his Tactical officer. "Ensign Arsenyev, what do you have for them if they do reach us?"

If he hadn't known better, he would have said Arsenyev's mouth curled upward slightly at the sound of her new rank. "I've set my console to continually compile the locations of nearby Gok ships, sir. If one draws too close, they'll receive a healthy helping of Banshees."

"Very good."

After waking from his drunken stupor, Keyes's first order of business had been to conduct a brief promotion ceremony for Arsenyev on Hangar Deck G, in acknowledgment of her exemplary performance, most recently during the engagements with the Gok missile cruiser and the UHF ships. Senator Bernard had presented Arsenyev with her new insignia. Laudano had attended as well, though he'd seemed less pleased with Arsenyev's accomplishment.

"Captain Keyes," the Tumbran in charge of the Larkspur-Caprice darkgate said once they reached it. "I'm afraid you'll find official procedure even more difficult to navigate than during our last encounter. I have been forbidden to grant the *Providence* access to this darkgate."

"Not to worry," Keyes said. "I don't plan to engage with official procedure."

"I'm not sure I understand you, Captain. At any rate, I'm closing the darkgate."

"If you don't let me through, I'll blast your ship apart, and we'll see whether Tumbra can breathe in space. Do you understand that?"

"Threats do not alter, protocol, Captain—"

"Arsenyev, let's start with a round of kinetic impactors. Hold off on Ocharium boosts, for now. Fire when ready." Keyes turned back to the Tumbran. "Sorry, you were saying?"

"Captain Keyes, this is rash. Fleet response will be severe."

"Honestly, I doubt it can get much more severe."

"Rounds away," Arsenyev said.

"Let's have a zoomed-in view of the Tumbran's monitor ship on a splitscreen, Werner. Keep our friend on the other half."

But the Tumbran had ended the transmission, and the visual of its ship expanded to full-screen. Arsenyev's warning shot hit home, scoring the monitor ship's hull. The Tumbran engaged its engine, then, attempting to flee.

"Hit its engine with the secondary laser till it's melted to slag," Keyes said.

Arsenyev did so, and Keyes ordered Werner to send another transmission request. The Tumbran reappeared, looking like a scalded cat, its chin sack vibrating vigorously.

"Do you think I'm serious yet?" Keyes said.

"I'm opening the gate. I doubt you'll get very far."

"Thanks for your analysis. Oh, by the way: the *Caesar* is under Winger command, and it's currently watching us closely. If you try to close the darkgate while we're transitioning, it will come and blow you to pieces."

That was a bluff. He'd made no such arrangement, and he doubted the Wingers would send anyone away from the defense of their colonies. But he fully expected the bluff to work. Tumbra weren't known for their tactical analysis.

Indeed it did work. The *Providence* transitioned into the Caprice System in one piece.

They found it devoid of warships, which scared Keyes almost as much as a waiting UHF fleet would have.

If the Ixa struck now, this system would be completely undefended.

CHAPTER 23

Fabrication

The Wingers had honored the Fins' request to bar Ek from leaving the planet on any of their vessels. Luckily, amidst the chaos of the Gok attack, she and Warren Husher had been able to access the Ixan shuttle he had first arrived in.

Now, they were hundreds of millions of miles away, fleeing before the wave of Gok warships and fighters that radiated outward from what had been the Winger homeworld.

Ek found that their situation did not bother her. She had requested that Warren devote a small, tertiary viewscreen to showing the stars, and he had done it. So she stared at them.

I am the last living Fin.

She had been an outsider to her species, her existence considered contrary to the status quo. Now she *was* the status quo, with her breather, her bodysuit designed to keep her alive outside the ocean, all of it. From this day forward, whatever she chose to do was what Fins normally did.

The thought terrified her.

Or at least, it terrified part of her. Another part observed her body's physiological responses to the fresh genocide, gauging the likelihood that her state of shock would lead to irrational behavior.

This is what it means to be a Fin. This is what it means to be a Fin.

Her rigid dorsal fin. Her body's increased demand for moisture, causing her suit to step up production.

This is what it means to be a Fin.

"Oh my."

Warren turned. "What?"

"Just..." She shook her head, mimicking human body language, as she did with members of whatever species she happened to be interacting with. "It is a lot to process."

"Are Fins usually given to such epic understatements?"

"I was just thinking about that, actually. The fact that now, whatever *I* do is what Fins usually do."

"It's true."

"My people studied grief extensively and produced many writings on the subject. It was widely noted that one of the few things all sentient species share is that discussing one's grief is a viable coping mechanism."

"A viable coping mechanism indeed."

"Before this, as I traveled the stars, I convinced myself that I do not miss my species, and also that I do not miss my family. Now that I can never return to them again..."

Ek began to shake soundlessly. Warren put his hand on her arm. "Are you all right?"

"This is crying," Ek said, her voice hitching. "Fins do not have tear glands, so this is how we cry."

Running a hand through his dark-gray hair, Warren furrowed his brow. "I'm sorry, Ek."

She nodded. "I am sorry, too. And...baffled. Baffled that, before, I harbored such an irrational thought without even being aware of it."

"Fins aren't used to considering themselves to be as irrational as the rest of us."

"No, but..." *But once, Fesky highlighted that for me. And she was right to do so.* Ek did not finish the thought out loud, and Warren did not ask her to. "I will never forget about my capacity to be irrational," she said instead.

"Why did you come to get me? Back on Spire?"

"Because I believe you are the one referred to as 'phoenix' by the Ixan Prophecies. '*Your people need you, phoenix, even as they fall to the scythe.*' If the Prophecies are as accurate as they appear, it seems likely humanity will have great need of this phoenix."

"And you think the phoenix is me."

"Yes."

Warren hesitated. "I—I think I'm starting to recover some memories from my captivity."

She glanced at him. "Your captivity by the Wingers?"

"No," he said, chuckling. "The Ixa."

"Oh! Of course."

"I'm beginning to get the idea that I bargained with them for my release. But I don't remember what my end of the bargain was."

That made Ek study him more closely. Could Warren Husher be trusted? His people called him traitor. She did not detect any behavioral indicators of an ulterior motive, but that could be due to a blindness brought about by her current state of distress. Even if she was right about his role as the prophesied phoenix, the fact that the information came from the Ixa unsettled her.

"Uh oh," Warren said.

"What is it?"

He pointed at the tactical display. Several dots were approaching them from the direction of Thessaly.

"What are they?"

"Falcons."

"Ah." Falcons were space fighters retired by the UHF after the First Galactic War. They had found their way into many different hands, after that. *But whose hands are these in?*

Blue light bathed the shuttle's cockpit. "We're getting a transmission request," Warren said.

When he accepted it, a large human male appeared on the shuttle's main viewscreen. Stubble darkened his wide jaw. "Surprised to find a human piloting an Ixan shuttle."

"Surprised to find a radical able to string together a coherent sentence, let alone distinguish between shuttles."

Ek looked at Warren in shock. He was smiling from ear to ear.

"You're coming with us," the man said, his face flushed. "Set a course for Thessaly, unless you'd prefer getting shot down."

"Okay." Warren terminated the transmission. "Not much we can do about that," he said, hands flying over the shuttle's controls. "At least I got a decent jab in."

"How did you know he was considered by your government to be a radical? The unrest in the Bastion Sector did not begin until years after your capture."

He glanced at her. "Oh, the Wingers filled me in on a bit of the history I missed."

For the first time, Ek detected that Warren was lying to her. But what she found truly troubling was her certainty that *he* did not realize his statement had been a fabrication.

That seemed impossible, but no less true for that.

CHAPTER 24

Setback

As they traveled through Commonwealth space, Keyes tried to spend as much time in the CIC as possible without compromising his performance through lack of rest. The UHF would know that the *Providence* was behind what had become enemy lines, and if the Fleet came for them, the seconds it took Keyes to run from his quarters to the CIC could be the ones they needed to escape.

But when Doctor Brusse sent him an urgent message via his com, telling him that Private Ryerson was trying to kill the Gok, he leapt out of the Captain's chair and dashed for the exit.

"Coms, contact Sergeant Caine and tell her to order her two marines nearest sick bay to get over there," he shouted over his shoulder. "Laudano, you have the CIC."

By the time he arrived, Brusse had already restrained Ryerson, with the help of a marine who'd been wounded during the strike on the Winger orbital defense platform.

"That thing doesn't belong on our ship, Captain," the guilty party spat. "It's not just that it's against UHF regs. I know you've abandoned those, but have you also abandoned concern for your crew?"

Keyes stared down Ryerson until the private broke eye contact. Caine's pair of marines arrived, then, and Keyes ordered them to take Ryerson into Doctor Brusse's office until he reviewed footage of the incident and decided what to do. In the meantime, Keyes helped the wounded marine back to his bed.

"Hopefully that effort didn't set back your recovery, Private. How do you feel?"

"I'm fine, sir. Needed the exercise after lying around so long, anyway."

Keyes chuckled. "That's the sort of grit I like to see from my marines. You'll be commended for your swift action today."

"Thank you, sir."

With the private settled away, Keyes rejoined the ship's doctor at the Gok's pallet. Somehow, she'd managed to get two thin mattresses underneath the hulking alien. *Must have sedated him.*

The Gok—Tort, wasn't that his name?—had a clean slice across his forest-green throat, which had produced a lot less blood than Keyes would have expected. Its arm bore another cut, which had bled more.

"I've already sent the footage to your com, Captain," Brusse said.

Keyes removed it from his pocket and watched from overhead as Ryerson rushed into view and attacked Tort with a scalpel. After the two incisions, the private who had probably saved the Gok's life rushed in and tackled Ryerson.

"Gok don't have major arteries in their necks," Brusse said. "That's what saved Tort."

Tort didn't behave nearly as violently as during Keyes's last encounter with him. His eyes looked glassy, and he didn't appear to have much to contribute to the conversation. "You've managed to calm him down."

Brusse nodded. "I finally found a sedative that works on him. What will you do with Ryerson?"

"I'm confining him to quarters. We'll lock his hatch from the outside and give him a direct line to you, in case something goes south with his recovery. If it wasn't for that, I'd give him brig time. I can assign a marine to accompany you whenever you check on Ryerson, if it would make you more comfortable."

"That won't be necessary. But thank you, Captain."

He nodded. "How are efforts to cure the virophage going?"

Brusse's mouth quirked downward, then. "Not great."

CHAPTER 25

Lash Out Across the Galaxy

The *Providence* transitioned into the Quince System without any hiccups. Since the Larkspur-Caprice darkgate, none of the Tumbra had given them any trouble.

Keyes didn't know whether that was because, after two decades of using darkgates, he was known to most Tumbra, or simply because they'd heard what he'd done to the one in charge of Larkspur-Caprice and had decided impeding him wasn't worth the trouble.

Maybe they simply haven't received orders to stop me.

Whatever the reason, his luck seemed to be holding when it came to outpacing any pursuing UHF ships. Keyes had the advantage of long experience navigating the darkgate system. He knew the best routes, as well as best practices for entering each system prepared for anything. In the meantime, other UHF captains had grown accustomed to travel by wormholes they could open to anywhere they wanted.

Keyes's method ate up more fuel, which was one of the reasons he'd had to fight so hard to prevent the *Providence* from getting decommissioned. But he'd managed it, and now he found himself well-versed in what had suddenly become the dominant mode of travel. Unlike every other UHF captain.

His sensor operator's voice cut into his thoughts. "Sir, you said our Tumbran operates the Quince-Fennel darkgate, didn't you?"

"Correct," Keyes said.

"His monitor ship appears to be under attack by Winger pirates."

Keyes's insides felt suddenly cold as his gaze snapped to his console's tactical display. The thought that they'd come all this way, at such risk, just to watch Piper die...it didn't sit well with him. "How long till we reach Quince-Fennel?"

"A little over four hours, at our current velocity."

"Nav, start work on a course to cut down on that flight time and then send it over to Helm. I want engines at full power."

What are those Wingers doing so far outside Pirate's Path? Was it only the instability brought by the war that had emboldened them? Or had Spire's destruction instilled in them a reckless abandon?

"Sir," Arsenyev said, "should I work with Nav on a course to download into a Banshee or three?"

"No. Nothing we launch will reach them in time to have a meaningful effect on the situation's outcome." Keyes drummed his fingers on his chair's armrest once. "There's not much of value to pirate aboard monitor ships. They're made that way intentionally. So Piper must have refused to let the Wingers through the darkgate. That's the only reason for them to bother him."

"We could send Piper a transmission telling him to let them through."

Keyes shook his head. "I doubt our input will change his decision. Piper already knew refusing the Wingers could mean his life. He's decided to take a stand, for better or worse. I do like the idea of sending a transmission, though. Coms, contact Blackwing and tell him to come to the CIC, double-time."

Ten minutes later, the former pirate captain stood at attention in front of Keyes. Blackwing saluted. Despite his deference, his movements had an air of cockiness. *Still puffed-up by his daring escape from the plummeting stealth ship.* Hopefully that confidence would help him accomplish what Keyes wanted him to.

"The Wingers respect you," Keyes said. "All of the Wingers, but the pirates especially."

"I suppose that's true," Blackwing said.

So modest. "I need you to talk some sense into these pirates. Tell them you know they're hurting, after the loss of Spire, but they're being selfish. They may have perceived their piracy as helpful to their species at some point, but no such argument can be made anymore. They're not helping anything by attacking a defenseless Tumbran."

"Okay, Captain. I'll try."

"We don't have time for multiple takes, so get it right." Keyes glanced at his Coms officer. "I want a closeup of Blackwing's face during the entire video message. Make sure none of us humans make it into the shot."

"Yes, sir. Recording."

Keyes nodded at Blackwing, who faced the viewscreen, above which the camera's circular black eye gleamed.

"Brothers and sisters," he said, pausing to clack his beak. "Um, hope is not lost. Hope...hope is never lost. It's only ever discarded by those unable to spot it in the dimness."

Oh, God. This is a disaster.

"I'm no great speaker," the Winger said, and now his screechy voice seemed to gain a little more confidence. "I'm not a politician to fill your head with empty words. But I have always fought for our species. Everything I've done, Wingers have been in my thoughts. I ask you: what's in your thoughts, now? Yes, Spire has been destroyed, yes the Fins are gone. But we are not."

Keyes shifted in his seat. *Okay. Getting a bit better.*

Blackwing spread his wings so that the tips moved off-screen, one of them nearly batting Ensign Werner in the face. "What would the Fins counsel us to do, if they could? Would they tell us to lash out across the galaxy, helping no one but ourselves? Or would they tell us to take up arms for what we have left? We will never forget the Fins, and yes, they will be avenged. But it does not have to mean casting ourselves into the jaws of fate. Back in the Bastion Sector, there are fledglings in danger from the Gok. Our colonies are under threat. But you can help restore order. Go back to them. Use your stealth to launch attacks the enemy will never see coming. And seek out other pirates who can help you do the same. The Wingers can live on to do good in the galaxy. We can use our strengths to restore balance and justice. Or we can use them to harm the defenseless, and bring shame to our species forever. It's your call."

Blackwing lowered his wings, and Keyes motioned for the Coms officer to stop the video.

The Winger's head whipped toward Keyes. "How did I do?"

"You...that actually wasn't bad, Blackwing. Dismissed."

Blackwing saluted again and left the CIC.

And now we wait. Traveling at the speed of light, the recording would take a few minutes to reach its recipients.

"The Wingers are attempting to board the monitor ship, sir," Werner said.

"Acknowledged."

The *Providence* sailed through space, her engines straining. Nav had managed to reduce the time it would take to reach the darkgate down to less than two hours. Nearly an hour into their journey, his helmsman informed him that they'd need to start decelerating soon in order to avoid shooting past their target.

"Give it another few minutes," Keyes said. If the Wingers continued their attack, he intended to launch a salvo of Ocharium-boosted kinetic impactors before deceleration.

His sensor operator looked up from his console, wearing a wide grin. "Sir, the Wingers are disengaging!"

Keyes released a breath he hadn't realized he'd been holding. "Excellent. Thank you, Werner."

Before long, they'd drawn near enough to send the Tumbran a real-time transmission request. Piper accepted, and he appeared on-screen, looking harried but uninjured. "Captain Leonard Keyes."

"You remember my name."

"Yes. Do you recall mine?"

"Piper."

The Tumbran lowered his head slightly, his chin sack drooping.

"I'd like to invite you to my ship," Keyes said.

"Does that have anything to do with the condescending way you feel we Tumbra speak to you during transmissions?"

Keyes felt a smile make its way across his face. *That takes me back.* Sitting in Captain Warren Husher's CIC back then, hearing him say the words Piper had just spoken...everything had seemed so complicated and fraught at the time. But Keyes had had no idea what the future held in store for him.

"No, actually," he said. "It's because after the beating your ship has taken, I'm doubting its ability to keep you alive for much longer. And because I'd like you to come with us. We need your help."

CHAPTER 26

Also a Cretin

Captain Keyes seemed lost in thought while they waited for the Tumbran to join them in the conference room. Glancing around the table, Husher realized that this was the first time they'd met in here since before he'd led a strike on one of Spire's orbital defense platforms and then plummeted to the surface in a poorly functioning Darkstream reentry suit.

It was also the first time the officers of the *Providence* had held a proper meeting with Sandy Bernard. Somehow, that didn't seem right.

Fesky also sat at the table, along with Caine, Arsenyev, and Laudano. Husher's attempts to catch Caine's eye had failed. She seemed to have returned to ignoring him, despite what they'd experienced together on Thessaly. Maybe because of it.

At last, the Tumbran arrived, escorted by two marines who closed the hatch to wait outside the conference room.

Immediately, the alien's gaze fell on Husher. "I recognize this one."

"You do?" Keyes said, apparently having finished with his reverie.

"He bears characteristics similar to your old captain, Warren Husher."

"This is Lieutenant Vin Husher. Warren Husher is his father."

Provided he's alive, Husher would have added.

"Is the son also a cretin?" the Tumbran said.

Husher exchanged looks with Arsenyev, who shrugged.

"Lieutenant Husher is an exemplary officer," Keyes said. "It's been a great boon to have him serve on my ship."

"Hmm," Piper said, waddling around the table, his sallow, gray skin shifting around its body. "I suppose I'll just take a seat, since you obviously aren't going to offer me one. Typical." He pulled himself onto the chair, and when he sat, his oblong head barely cleared the table's edge.

Seemingly undeterred, Piper studied the assembled officers, one-by-one. "What sort of help do you think you need?"

At the head of the table, Keyes leaned forward, toward the alien. "We hoped you could help us tap into the Tumbran network. If we could access the sort of intelligence you gave us during the First Galactic War, we'd at least have some advance warning when the Ixa decide to strike."

"You discuss our old arrangement openly with your crew?"

"These are trusted officers. But regardless, the time for secrecy is long past. No offense, but this is no longer about the Tumbra's theories for balancing galactic power. It's about the survival of life in the galaxy."

"I see. So, humanity is on the precipice of extinction, and you turn to a Tumbran. Should I be flattered that you sought my help over that of the children?"

"We no longer trust the Kaithe," Keyes said. "The Ixan Prophecies predicted they would betray us, and indeed they did. They gave us the coordinates to find Ochrim, who they described as an old friend, and then Ochrim went on to destroy half the human fleet."

"Interesting," Piper said. "The Prophecies."

"Yes. They have a disturbing way of coming true."

"Hmm." The Tumbran looked at Husher, at Fesky, and then back at Keyes. "Have you considered that the children may not have known Ochrim would do what he did?"

"The Kaithe's behavior seems fairly incriminating all around," Husher put in.

"Let me ask it another way. Have you considered that the Prophecies may not be intended as an accurate forecast of the future, but as a tool to deceive and intimidate you? The tool may look a lot like such a forecast, but that may not be its actual purpose. After all, if the Prophecies really do provide a reliable map to the future, why would the Ixa ever give it to their enemies?"

A silence fell over the conference room as they digested Piper's words. At last, Keyes spoke: "That's a very interesting way of looking at it."

"I should think." Piper slowly raised its thin-fingered hands to touch its cheeks, as Tumbra sometimes did. Husher wasn't sure what the gesture signified. "I will attempt to restore your access to our knowledge of Ixan movements. There's a fair chance I'll be able to do so. But I believe I have a more significant contribution to make. This should interest you, Senator Bernard."

Bernard blinked, looking shocked. "Um...yes?"

Husher felt similarly. Tumbra barely ever appeared to take an interest in human affairs, and the fact that Piper knew Bernard's name did come as a surprise.

"Yes. For years, you have fought Darkstream's growing influence on your government. And for an equal amount of time, I have spent my spare time working on a tool for doing the same."

Piper paused, and Bernard gave him what he clearly wanted: "What is it?" she asked.

"My tool consists of a set of algorithms designed to operate in tandem in order to calculate how close a population is to toppling their government and replacing it with a new one. You might call it a gauge for revolutions. If given access to your micronet, it will access historical data, social networks, and news outlets both mainstream and independent. I have tested the tool using countless simulations, and I am confident in its ability to accurately assess the progress made by a revolutionary movement, within a certain margin of error. It gives that assessment in the form of a percentage, and the margin of error is plus or minus two points."

"Okay. How do you see your tool being applied?"

"That shouldn't be hard to understand, when you consider how many revolutionary efforts have sputtered out just before they achieved victory. The task at hand seems impossible, and so the people give up, never knowing how close they came to success. My tool will give them the courage to continue fighting, with the knowledge that if they apply enough pressure, they'll win."

"Your tool sounds a lot like AI," Husher said.

"It is. Just not a strong AI."

"How do we know that?"

"Because I'm telling you. You came for my help, not vice versa. Listen, human, I'm not trying to represent my tool as safe. It's dangerous. Very dangerous, to those in power. But I assumed you didn't come to me looking for safe."

"We've asked you to be an intermediary between us and your species," Husher shot back. "We didn't ask for this. This sounds like just more alien plotting against humanity. The type that's been happening in increasing amounts since the First Galactic War."

"You're wrong," Piper said. "The Tumbra remain humanity's ally. But your species has strayed from the virtues that make it great, and a true ally cannot support that. I want to see humanity rediscover its virtues. My tool is a way to help you do it."

CHAPTER 27

Drama Queen

Police Sergeant Doucet surveyed the scene outside the Ocharium refinery through binoculars from atop an armored personnel carrier. The refinery was one of only a handful on Mars, and its output was small, so the demonstrations happening outside it had only symbolic value at best. *If you can call it "value."*

Complicating the matter was the fact that the protesters weren't actually blocking access to the facility. The surrounding area technically counted as public land, though most political analysts expected President Hurst to auction it off to the highest bidder within her first year.

Still, the protests were spreading, and Darkstream market valuation was taking a hit. Facilities where protests sprang up outside the door, like this one, even saw spikes in employee absenteeism, though the company didn't waste any time firing those employees and hiring more willing workers to replace them.

"Sir, we've driven the protesters into the stream, but they're holding firm, the bastards."

Doucet lowered his binoculars to study the man who'd spoken. Corporal Bradley's uniform looked like it had just come from the dry cleaners. *That's what I like to see.* A man who could stay looking sharp in a situation like this was a man poised to rise through the ranks.

"Turn the hose on them. See how long they last under that." Technically the hose was a water cannon, but they'd been trained not to use that term, lest it leak to the media. Official police protocol did not condone the use of water cannons.

"Yes, sir." Bradley saluted and then spun on his heel, marching off to implement his sergeant's orders.

The thought of getting soaked to the bone in this weather made Doucet shiver involuntarily. It was nearing winter in Mars' northern hemisphere. *For a crowd of lazy freeloaders, they sure have balls.*

But what else could they be? Hard-working Martians would be at jobs on a weekday, not out stirring up trouble for the galaxy's most profitable corporations.

Worse than lazy, the protesters were stupid, even though you could tell they thought they were so smart. They were what his father would have called "useful idiots," and they'd swallowed this conspiracy theory about dark tech destroying the universe whole. It was just like President Hurst said: the Ixa hated humanity's freedoms, and this was their attempt to take those freedoms away.

Although, Hurst also said Captain Keyes had partnered with the Ixa to spread the lie, and Doucet wasn't sure he bought that. He'd always admired Keyes, and while dark tech was wonderful, keeping a ship around that didn't need it made good sense. In fact, Doucet would have kept a lot more than one, but then again, it wasn't his job to make those decisions.

His job was to squash this protest.

He climbed down from the personnel carrier and made the short walk to the front lines, where his police had already turned the water cannons on the freeloaders standing in the stream. Doucet saw one get knocked underwater, but she popped right back up to stand her ground and glare up at the police.

Incredible.

The protesters had taken to calling themselves defenders, and for the first time, Doucet could see how seriously they took that name. Clearly, they didn't plan to give in anytime soon.

Not unless something changed.

"Bradley," Doucet barked.

The corporal marched over from where he'd been standing nearby, coming to attention two meters away and snapping off a smart salute. "Sir."

"I told you to have the concussion grenades on hand. Did you see to that?"

"Yes, sir."

"Deploy them."

Doucet took up a position higher on the hill so that he could observe the grenades in use. All along the ranks of police, trained officers hefted launchers onto their shoulders.

"Fire!" Corporal Bradley hollered.

The grenades arced into the crowd of protesters, and a second and a half later, they exploded, sounding like kernels popping—if kernels were as loud as gunshots. Engulfed in smoke, the protesters fell into disarray immediately, their panic hitting them nearly as hard as the grenades had. Doucet watched as one man, in an attempt to keep his head above water, pushed the woman beside him below the surface.

How quickly their solidarity crumbles. Doucet permitted himself a small smile.

He raised his com to his lips. "Again."

"Fire!" Bradley screamed, and another volley launched.

The grenades blew, and this time they were followed immediately by shrieking that started and didn't stop. Doucet raised a hand to his forehead and scanned the crowd of protesters, trying to spot the source of the noise through the smoke. *Who's the drama queen?*

Then he saw her: a woman whose arm hung limply by her side, with the soft tissue between her elbow and wrist completely blown away.

Slowly, Doucet lowered his hand to his side.

"Sir?" Bradley's voice came through Doucet's com as crisp as ever. "Do you see that?"

"I see it, Corporal."

"What do you advise?"

Doucet drew in a deep breath. He was having trouble piecing together exactly what he advised. *Think, Doucet. What's wrong with you?*

"Sir?"

"They're terrorists, Corporal. Economic terrorists, just like President Hurst says. If that lady didn't want this to happen to her, she shouldn't have taken up terrorism."

"So, then..."

"Fire another volley."

CHAPTER 28

In Good Conscience

"**A**re you sure you don't want me to come to the meeting?" Corporal Simpson said, studying Bernard's face over her mug of steaming coffee. "I know what makes senior officers tick."

Bernard smiled. "I know you do, Trish. But Captain Keyes isn't much like most senior officers. I have a feeling he and I will get along just fine." She stood, abandoning her half-drunk tea. "I'd better go. Somehow, I doubt being fashionably late gets you a lot of traction on this ship."

"Good luck, Sandy," Simpson said.

To Bernard's surprise, her and Simpson had become fast friends. Their relationship had started rocky, with a long stint living together aboard a combat shuttle, followed by sharing adjacent cells in a Roostship brig. But now that they had their personal space back, they discovered that their trials together had actually caused them to bond. Bernard ran all her ideas by the corporal, finding that Simpson actually had a pretty sharp mind for political analysis. *She would have made a good senator herself.*

She found Keyes poring over something on his desk console. Stowing it, he clasped his hands on top of his desk. "Please, have a seat." The captain wore his characteristic bluff-faced stare, but it wasn't entirely without warmth. "You were somewhat coy about the purpose of this meeting, if you don't my saying."

"My apologies. It's a bad habit, left over from meeting with Darkstream's stooges and not wanting to give them too much information in advance."

"A fine strategy. What is the purpose, then?"

Bernard let out a long breath, collecting her thoughts. She resisted the urge to sweep her bangs out of her face, which she still hadn't had the time to get cut. "I believe humanity needs your help."

"I agree. However, I'm currently doing everything I can to help humanity. I can only be in one place at once."

"That's what I'm getting at, actually. I'd like to request a loan of one of your shuttles. I think that if I was on the ground with the protesters, I could help them coordinate, and maybe even inspire more to join the movement against the Commonwealth's reckless policies. I could also take Piper's revolution gauge with me and upload it to the micronet the moment I reach a planet."

Keyes extended his right thumb to scratch the back of his left hand. His lips pressed together. "Piper's algorithms are untested, outside his simulations."

"With all due respect, Captain, I don't view that as a reason not to try them out. Attempting to rid the Commonwealth of Darkstream's considerable influence is also untested."

"Indeed. And I'm not saying we shouldn't try out Piper's gauge. I see ousting Hurst from power as priority number one, right now. If we can't break Darkstream's grip on the UHF, they'll continue self-destructing humanity, leaving us woefully unprepared to fight the Ixa. What I *am* saying is that I'm not confident Piper's gauge will be sufficient on its own."

Bernard nodded. "Okay. I'm listening."

"I think we need something new. I'm not a sociologist, but I do know the Commonwealth is no stranger to suppressing traditional protests. Their arsenal for doing so is well-developed. If we stick to a traditional playbook, we'll lose. Even if it's possible for us to win that way, we can't possibly do so quickly enough. The Ixa will overrun us long before that."

"What do you suggest, then?"

"We need a new way to object to what our government is doing. A new way to dissent. Something that will embarrass the Commonwealth and put unprecedented pressure on it. Something that will drive up Piper's progress bar as quickly as possible."

"That sounds great, but I'm not sure what this new way of doing things will look like."

"I'm not completely sure, either. I also don't know that it will work. But just like Piper's revolution gauge, it's worth trying. And I think it begins with paying a visit to a man I served with during the First Galactic War. He hasn't served since, and he carries around a lot of baggage from that war. This might be just the way for him to offload it. It could be the perfect match, in fact. His name is Calum Ralston."

"Sounds like a lot of maybes. But I suppose that's all we have right now, isn't it?"

"Yes. Obviously, I'm not able to visit him myself, but I'd be willing to take you to him."

"Wait. You're offering to take me there? In the *Providence*?"

Keyes nodded. "We can hammer out the details of our plan in transit, but we need to get underway right now. If you go alone, in just a shuttle, you could get picked off too easily. Or, the Tumbra might not let you through. In good conscience, I can't let that happen just because I failed to do my part. This is too important. So the *Providence* will take you to Ralston."

The captain rose from his seat, hand extended, and Bernard rose with him. They shook.

CHAPTER 29

UHS Firedrake

Captain Vaghn squinted at the main viewscreen, which showed the wreckage of a Winger fleet, following yet another rout. A wide channel broadcasted inside her corvette's CIC, and they could hear the raucous cheering of the other UHF captains who'd fought in the battle, along with that of their CIC crews.

Vaghn did not feel moved to join in their celebrations, and her somber mood had apparently infected her own crew, who sat at their consoles stiffly.

It's funny how a culture forms aboard a ship. Even though Command decided who got assigned where, every ship she'd ever served on had its own distinct set of attitudes, beliefs, and habits. *And the culture on the UHS* Firedrake *doesn't like what we're doing in the Bastion Sector.* Maybe that had something to do with who the *Firedrake*'s captain had been before Vaghn took over.

She'd waited a long time to receive her own command. There was no getting around the fact that it was almost two decades overdue. During the First Galactic War, there had been ample talk of making her a ship captain after they defeated the Ixa. Then she'd gone on a mission to negotiate a ceasefire with the Ixa. At the time, it had seemed like the most important mission of her career. But it had ended with Captain Warren Husher betraying humanity, and that had tainted her. His defection had left her briefly in command of the UHS *Hornet*, but the admiralty transferred her the moment she returned. Her prospects of promotion dissipated into the void.

Even the fact that they'd given her the *Firedrake* felt like a message: *If you don't toe the line, if you pull something like the Hushers did, you'll be court martialed quicker than you can blink.* The *Firedrake*'s last captain had been Vin Husher, after all.

Vaghn's sensor operator tried to say something, and she cut off the wide channel's broadcast so she could hear him. "Say again?"

"Ma'am, Gok are advancing on a small Winger farming colony. The colony's essentially defenseless."

"Thank you, Chief." She shifted in her Captain's chair, where she could never manage to get comfortable. That reminded her of how relaxed Warren Husher had always appeared while sitting in his. *Command fits some like a glove. Others, it fits like a noose.*

She sighed. "Put a view of the tactical situation surrounding the Winger colony on-screen. Coms, send Admiral Carrow a transmission request."

"Done. He's accepted, ma'am."

Vaghn glanced at her sensor operator. "Splitscreen."

Carrow appeared on one-half of her viewscreen, a rictus of laughter fading from his face. A slight grimace replaced it. "Captain Vaghn. What is it?"

"Admiral, our sensors have detected Gok about to attack a Winger farming colony."

"Yes? Our sensors have detected the same thing."

"The colony has very few defenses, sir."

"So it does."

"I'm seeking permission to take the *Firedrake* and back up the colony's few defenders."

"Denied. Our mission has not changed. We will continue defeating the Wingers' forces and taking over their colonies. This Gok attack advances those objectives."

"It won't help if the Gok obliterate the colony, leaving nothing left. The Commonwealth wants their resources, doesn't it?"

"What the Commonwealth wants is none of your concern. Command has decided not to directly engage the Gok, since they have not specifically targeted us. As long as their aggression serves our ends, they are to be left alone."

Vaghn stared back at the admiral, speechless. *Have we become no better than the Ixa?*

Carrow pursed his lips. "And Captain, please don't contact me on a whim again. We're in the middle of a war, and I lack the time to entertain your every fancy. Carrow out." A black square replaced the admiral's face, which the tactical display extended to fill.

Looking around her CIC, Vaghn saw the blank expressions of people who felt as hollow and helpless as she did.

Noticing that she'd begun to slump, she corrected her posture, taking a breath. "This is imperialism," she said, her eyes moving from crewmember to crewmember. "We've become conquerers, and we're not even trying to hide it anymore. The UHF was meant to help us live in harmony with our allies and work together to defeat clear-and-present threats. We weren't supposed to be tyrants."

Her CIC crew nodded along with her words, their expressions turned grim. Vaghn turned to her Coms officer. "Patch me through to ship-wide."

"Yes, ma'am. It's done."

"Men and women of the UHS *Firedrake*, this is your captain. The Gok are about to attack a sparsely defended Winger farming colony. I have requested permission from Admiral Carrow to leave and help them, but that permission has been denied. My conscience tells me to help the Winger colony despite that. If any crewmember objects, you have five minutes to contact the ship's primary Coms officer, who is at his console now. I will order him to keep from me the identities of any objectors. If there is even one objector, then we will obey the admiral's command."

Motioning for the Coms officer to end the transmission, she looked around at her CIC crew. "The same goes for all of you. If you object, please inform Ensign Stuckless. I'll be in the wardroom for the next five minutes." She turned to her XO. "Commander, you have the CIC."

Vaghn strode calmly to the wardroom, determined not to let her maelstrom of emotions show on her face. When she arrived in the tiny room, she tried to eat a cardboard-like biscuit from the cupboard, but she found she had no appetite.

Five minutes later, she returned to the CIC and retook her chair. Her stomach dipped as her gaze fell on the Coms officer. "Ensign?"

"There were no objectors, Captain. It's unanimous."

She nodded, though the tension she felt did not subside. If anything, it increased. *I suppose that's to be expected.*

"Nav, set a course for that colony."

CHAPTER 30

Battle Group

Private Ryerson is no longer in his quarters, the message from Doctor Brusse read. I went to refresh his pain medicine but found him missing.

Keyes replaced his com in his breast pocket and turned to his sensor operator. "Tell me what Private Ryerson's com says about his location."

"Yes, sir." Werner bent over his console and worked for a few seconds. "It says he's in his quarters."

"Well, he isn't. Doctor Brusse says she went to give him pain meds, but he was gone. Use the ship's interior cameras to try locating him. Prioritize other tasks, but I want you to spend every moment you can spare searching for Ryerson. And keep an eye on sick bay. I'd rather not have to deal with another attack on our resident Gok."

"Aye, sir."

After two days of travel, the *Providence* had transitioned into the Feverfew System just over an hour ago. The system only had one planet fit for colonization, but the colony it held, Zakros, was one of the Commonwealth's most important.

Zakros boasted abundant resources, not to mention one of the few major Ocharium deposits ever found outside the Bastion Sector. It had a population of ten billion. And most importantly, from a strategic perspective at least, the Feverfew System featured four darkgates, making it a well-trafficked hub for reaching anywhere in Commonwealth space.

It was also where Calum Ralston lived.

If Bernard thought she could spark a galaxy-wide movement against Hurst, Zakros offered a tantalizing place to start it. Widespread dissent here would hit the Commonwealth right where it hurt.

His conversation with Bernard had given him another idea, and shortly after it, he'd approached Blackwing about taking a Condor packed with as many supplies as it could hold and using it to track the pirates who'd attacked Piper's monitor ship. If the Winger could enlist his old associates in the fight for the Bastion Sector, it could make a difference.

Blackwing had assured him that he could handle tracking down the pirates, even in their stealth ships. "I know the tech," he'd said. "I know how it limits you, makes you walk one of just a few narrow paths. I'll find them."

Keyes had nodded, hoping that the Winger's words amounted to more than just his usual bluster.

The *Providence* was around halfway between Zakros and the darkgate she'd used to enter the system when Werner gave Keyes some troubling news. "Sir, a UHF battle group just entered the system through the Feverfew-Hellebore darkgate."

Keyes considered that for a moment. "What does it consist of?"

"Three corvettes and two destroyers."

"They were waiting for us. The Hellebore System's a dead end, of no strategic importance." The only business those ships could possibly have had in Hellebore was setting a trap for the *Providence.* "Maybe we can still complete our mission. How long will it take them to reach Zakros from Feverfew-Hellebore?"

"At the battle group's current speed, seven hours."

And we're four hours away from Zakros. "If they accelerate, we can outpace them. Our engines are superior. Let's see Senator Bernard to the planet safely and then make a beeline for the darkgate into Caprice. It's time we rejoined the fray in the Bastion Sector."

"Yes, sir."

But less than an hour later, Werner had more bad news. "Sir, a second battle group has emerged from the Feverfew-Caprice darkgate. A destroyer, two missile cruisers, a corvette, and a frigate."

"*Damn it,*" Keyes yelled, drawing glances from a few of his officers. He drew a long breath and exhaled slowly. "We have to turn back. It'll mean going the long way around to reach the Bastion Sector, but getting to Ralston isn't worth endangering the *Providence.*"

He briefly considered messaging Bernard and giving her the chance to make for Zakros aboard a combat shuttle, but he decided against it. If he could be sure she'd actually reach the planet, maybe. But the shuttles traveled a lot slower than the supercarrier, and he could easily envision a scenario where the UHF quietly scooped her up before she ever reached the relative safety of Zakros. Bernard would be no good to anyone rotting in a warship's brig. There were other colonies where she could complete her mission.

"Sir..." Werner said.

"*What?*" Keyes snapped. "What is it, Ensign?"

"A third battle group of four more warships has emerged from the darkgate we used to enter the system. They must have been trailing us."

"No shit," Keyes said, and instantly regretted letting his agitation slip into his speech. "I can see where this is going. Nav, plot a course for the remaining darkgate, one that keeps us equidistant between the two nearest battle groups. Update it as those groups change position."

The darkgate they headed toward now led into the Petrichor Sector, which was ultimately another dead end, but at least it had a few interconnected systems where he could attempt to evade his pursuers, maybe split them up and confront them one battle group at a time.

That said, he had no expectation of ever reaching that sector. And within a few minutes, Werner confirmed his suspicions.

"A fourth battle group has just come out of the Petrichor Sector, sir. Five more ships."

CHAPTER 31

Heavy Beam

Keyes leaned back in his chair to stare at the ceiling. *Nineteen. Nineteen enemy ships.* He gave himself ten seconds to compose himself before resuming his usual crisp posture.

"Give me the composition of the third battle group to appear, Werner."

"It has a destroyer, two missile cruisers, and a corvette."

"And the fourth, out of Petrichor?"

"A destroyer, three corvettes, and a frigate."

"That's the one we like best. Nav, scrap our present course and calculate one that gets us to the fourth battle group as quickly as possible while allowing time for us to decelerate and engage. Helm, bring engines to full power along the course Nav has already sent you, but stand by to switch to the new course the moment you have it."

"Aye, sir."

Keyes cleared his throat. "The enemy captains will think they have the upper hand. Which they do. But their dominant position will make them sloppy. They won't expect a head-on charge. They'll see it coming, obviously, but they'll be scrambling to prepare for it. Coms, brief Fesky on the situation and tell her to prepare to launch the entire Air Group."

"Yes, sir."

"Werner, put up a tactical display, full-screen."

Before telling Arsenyev to start calculating firing solutions, Keyes waited to see how the opposing battle group responded to his charge. As he'd anticipated, they started rearranging their formation, since their present one didn't come close to resembling an optimal configuration for taking on a supercarrier.

The trio of corvettes arranged themselves in front of the destroyer in staggered formation, with the frigate above them and slightly ahead. Together, the smaller ships formed a screen to protect their highest-value unit, the destroyer. Which Keyes intended to ignore completely, to start.

"Sir," Werner said, "all corvettes from the other three battle groups have broken away and are traveling at speed toward the darkgate into the Petrichor Sector."

"Acknowledged." *They're trying to head us off.* "That doesn't affect our current line of action. Arsenyev, calculate a firing solution for a full spread of Ocharium-boosted kinetic impactors and space them out along a line that cuts across the center and leftmost corvettes. Work with Nav to find a timing that coincides with our top speed, to take advantage of our momentum."

"Yes, sir."

"I also want a firing solution for our primary laser, targeting the frigate." The smallest ship was likeliest to explode under three-hundred petawatts of power, so it made good strategic sense to target her first.

Keyes decided to wait to learn the outcome of their first salvo before making any more battle decisions. The longer he managed to delay formulating a plan, the less likely the enemy was to anticipate it.

His CIC fell into silence as his officers worked at their stations. Keyes spared a moment to wonder about Ryerson's disappearance, forgotten in the rush to prepare for what would likely prove one of the biggest battles in the *Providence*'s history. *If not the biggest.*

Two hours later, Arsenyev spoke. "Kinetic rounds are away, Captain. Impact in eighteen minutes and thirty seconds."

"Very good. Ensign Werner, inform me of the result the moment you have it."

When the time came, just before Werner gave him the news, Keyes saw one of the corvettes vanish from the tactical display. *Excellent.*

"The leftmost corvette has exploded, sir," Werner said. "The other managed to evade the shot. The remaining ships are distancing themselves from each other, so that we won't be able to hit two of them with a single spread again at this range."

"Laser range in nine minutes, Captain," Arsenyev put in.

"Acknowledged. Nav, I have another course correction for you. Nudge our nose two degrees to port and adjust our deceleration so that we come to rest with the destroyer between us and the rightmost corvette." The corvette's primary weapons were rail guns, and her captain wouldn't risk firing past the destroyer at the *Providence.* "Coms, tell Fesky to prepare to launch Condors on my mark. She'll be targeting the corvette that will still have a firing solution on us."

The minutes ticked by, and it felt like no time before Arsenyev said, "We're in range to hit the frigate with our primary laser, sir."

"Fire, and Werner, give me a full-screen visual of the target."

It never failed to warm his heart, watching enemy ships melt under the heavy beam his ship's main capacitor was capable of generating, and this time was no different. After several seconds of concentrated power, the frigate exploded.

Under normal circumstances, that would have caused his CIC crew to burst into cheering. Not now. They had a drawn-out slugfest ahead of them, and this was merely the opening act.

As they sailed past what was left of the enemy formation's outer screen of ships, Keyes barked, "Launch Condors."

"Aye, sir."

The tactical display exploded with a flurry of tiny green lights, each representing a Condor. With the addition of the Wingers from Spire, his Air Group had grown significantly since the last time the UHF had had the opportunity to count them. Immediately, Fesky's well-trained pilots fell into formation and began performing alpha strikes on the corvette Keyes had designated.

At last, the *Providence* came to a stop in line with the battle group's flagship as well as the corvette on the opposite side of her. "Give me a full-screen visual of the enemy destroyer and magnify."

"Yes, sir."

"Captain, the destroyer is coming about to line up a shot from its main gun," his Tactical officer said.

"We aren't going to allow that to happen, Arsenyev. Hit them with everything we've got. Open with a full salvo of kinetic impactors all down her port side, with a firing solution that targets as many point defense turrets as possible. Immediately following that, I want you to put forty Banshees in the air."

Arsenyev gave a prim nod, and Keyes could sense her satisfaction with the order.

"Would you like me to assign Lieutenant Laudano to assist with the calculations?" he asked.

"That won't be necessary, sir. I can work from a set of firing solutions I've already generated in anticipation of a situation similar to this one. It'll just take a slight adjustment."

Keyes nodded, not trusting himself to speak in light of the unexpected emotion that had flared up in him at Arsenyev's words. *Now, what's that doing there?* He cleared his throat.

"Sir, Fesky has succeeded in taking down her target and has shifted focus to the remaining corvette," Werner said. A row of explosions blossomed along the destroyer's flank, then, and the sensor operator continued. "Seven turrets down, Captain."

"Excellent. Fire Banshees."

The missiles that made it past the destroyer's remaining turrets didn't obliterate the ship, nor had Keyes expected them to. They did, however, deal massive damage, and it brought a transmission request from her captain.

Captain Stephen Cooley appeared on the main viewscreen, his face paper-white. "I yield, Keyes. We yield."

No, I'm afraid you don't. "I'm facing down three more battle groups, Cooley. I can't afford to leave your destroyer operational."

"Wait. On behalf of my crew, I'm begging you. They have families, Keyes, and so do I. We'll run to the escape pods at once."

"I don't have time to wait around for that." Keyes sighed. "I'm taking out your engines so that you can't pursue."

"Thank you, Captain Keyes. Thank you. Thank you."

"Yeah," Keyes said, and made a cutting gesture across his throat. Werner terminated the transmission.

"Fesky's just neutralized the last corvette, sir," Werner said. "She won't have known the battle group's flagship already yielded."

"That's that, then. Tactical, target the destroyer's mains with three Banshees each. Coms, recall our Air Group. The next engagement will come soon, and we have no reason to expect it will go as smoothly as this one did. Let's regroup."

CHAPTER 32

Ek and the Warlord

As the warlord's followers escorted Ek and Warren Husher into a long, cavernous room, she took in her surroundings and began digesting their meaning. The rare paintings that adorned the walls had not been arranged by someone with a true appreciation for art, but by someone who wished to impress and intimidate viewers. A Lowery hung next to a Hashyl, which made no sense from any perspective, aesthetically, historically, or otherwise.

"Kind of medieval, isn't it?" Warren said, turning his lined face toward her before staring ahead once more.

Ek joined him in gazing toward the front of the room, where a large, bearded man sat on an enormous chair that could only be termed a throne. His officers stood arrayed on either side of him, facing each other across the large space.

"A Fin has become a very valuable thing to own," Thresh boomed, before they had even reached him. "And what a remarkable Fin, at that!"

The fighters escorting them stopped several meters before their leader, drawing back against the wall to leave the prisoners in front of Thresh's throne. *Everything is calculated to send a message.* Their standing alone said to them that they could run if they wanted—they would simply be intercepted. *Or perhaps gunned down.*

"I haven't decided whether I'll keep you or sell you," Thresh said. "At any rate, if you'd like me to treat you well, you should probably answer my questions truthfully."

"By all means," Ek said.

"Good. Tell me, how did you come to occupy an Ixan shuttle, and so near my planet?"

The bombast of calling Thessaly his planet amused Ek, but Thresh had no way of knowing that, because she gave him none. "We come from Spire, where we barely escaped the Gok attack."

Thresh's eyes drifted briefly to a man and a woman standing to Ek's right, who wore identically colored wedding scarves, indicating marriage to each other. The woman wore a vest too small for her. Ek saw that she could not button it even if she tried.

"Keyes was at Spire," Thresh said. "Keyes, who shares my hatred of the UHF."

"I wouldn't ascribe hatred to Captain Keyes," the married man said. "He's too much a pragmatist for that."

Thresh glared at him. "He hates them, Saul. How could he not? But that's irrelevant. What matters is that the Fin tell me what Keyes's next move is. What does he anticipate from the UHF, and how will he thwart them?" Thresh had returned his gaze to Ek, but soon glanced again at the woman, whose hand was on her belly.

Interesting. "I will answer your question once you grant me a private audience."

Thresh laughed, long and loud, in what was clearly another power display. "Who are you to make demands of me, fish? Why in Sol should I grant you anything?"

"You are right to consider Fins valuable. Perhaps you have heard about our powers of perception."

"Yes, indeed! I'll get a high price for you. Right now, though, I'm thinking I probably won't keep you for myself. You talk too much."

"I have perceived that your entire command structure is about to descend into chaos. I will require a private audience to inform you of why."

For a long time, Thresh studied her, his mirth gone. Then he flicked his hand toward his followers. "Leave us."

Some of the guards hesitated, and Thresh bellowed, "Leave us! I think I'll be safe on my own with one land-walking Fin."

Once alone, they stared at each other in silence for some time. Ek knew that Thresh was waiting for her to speak, in an attempt to indicate he did not feel concern over her warning. But the attempt would fail. Ek was patient.

"All right, Fin," Thresh growled at last. "Tell me what you meant."

"The man Saul is your second-in-command."

"Yes. How did you know that?"

"You require me to walk you through each of my percep-tions? Then I am happy to do so. Only your second-in-command would dare speak out of turn with a leader as ruthless as you portray yourself."

"As I *portray* myself?"

"You are planning to have Saul assassinated." Thresh's eyes widened at that, but Ek continued, taking a step closer, her metal foot meeting the marble floor with a *clack*. "You resent how he questions your orders, but more important than that, you have impregnated his wife. I see the way you look at her, even if Saul does not: a mixture of concern and adulation. A level of adulation hardened warlords are not traditionally given to displaying."

"How do you know she's pregnant?"

"She wears a vest too small to button. Clearly, she has not had a chance to purchase a new one since her pregnancy. And she touches her stomach as humans touch a loved one." She took another step forward, pinning Thresh to his throne with her gaze. "You are of Asian ancestry, and so Saul will immediately know the child is not his. Therefore, he must be assassinated. But the assassination will not turn out as you hope. Saul has more loyal supporters than you believe. Many of them stood in this room just moments ago. Your lover will not be able to handle the resulting fallout. She cannot even find the time to buy herself clothes that fit, let alone cope with the guilt she will experience once her denial over what she has done is shattered. She will flee with the newborn, leaving you to deal with an uprising you have unfavorable odds of suppressing."

Thresh's shoulders rose and fell, indicating heavier breathing and an accelerated pulse. "What would you suggest I do about all this?"

"You resent how the UHF has oppressed the people of Thessaly. The bombings and occupations have angered you, as they have angered many throughout the Bastion Sector. But your people do not view you as a savior. They view you as an opportunist. If you wish to insulate yourself against your second-in-command and his followers, you must earn their love."

"How?"

"You have a fleet of Falcons at your disposal, and your counterparts throughout the sector do as well. If you join with them, using your combined might to fight the UHF's tyranny, and to defend your species from the Ixa when they come, you will be revered. You will also increase humanity's chances of survival, which I assume you view as a positive, considering you belong to it. A new world is forming. If you would like a place in it, then I suggest you join the fight to save it."

None of Thresh's bravado remained. His posture rigid, he stared at Ek as though at a bizarre spectral phenomenon. "All right," he croaked.

"Excellent. Let us get to work."

CHAPTER 33

A Second Hull

The *Providence*'s Flight Deck A had been pulverized during the battle over Spire, taken out by a collision with a Gok carrier. And so it made sense that, in preparation for the journey to engage the next UHF battle group, most of her Condors would reenter her on the starboard side, through Flight Deck B and other, smaller flight decks on that side.

At least, that was the story Husher had wanted to sell to the enemy battle groups' sensor operators, whose sensors had only been able to see the *Providence*'s port side. But instead of landing inside her, he'd suggested to Fesky that those Condors remain outside the supercarrier, hugging her stern like a second hull to avoid detection by enemy sensors. The CAG had trained her pilots well, and the Wingers came already highly skilled, so Husher knew they had the chops to pull it off.

And they did pull it off. When the *Providence* met the battle group that had entered from the Feverfew-Caprice darkgate, guns blazing, she suddenly adjusted her attitude ten degrees up from the ecliptic plane. Five squadrons of fighters blazed past her underside to hit an enemy unprepared to deal with Condors this soon.

The frigate Husher's squadron targeted did not even have time to engage its point defense turrets, and his Haymakers got in for a clean alpha strike, followed by another from the squadron behind them.

By that time, the turrets started hitting them, and the second squadron kept them busy while the Haymakers moved in for alpha strike number three. That did it. The frigate blew apart under their concentrated fire, and both squadrons scattered to avoid any shrapnel hurtling through space.

The cockpit of Husher's Condor washed red, and a glance at his tactical display showed him a missile closing with him, from the nearby missile cruiser that Fesky and her Divebombers had been supposed to deal with.

Using his Ocharium boost to leap ahead, he engaged his fighter's gyroscopes to whip around her short axis just in time to neutralize the missile. Three other pilots, including one of his Haymakers, weren't so lucky. All three of their fighters exploded, only one of them ejecting to escape death.

On the tactical display, he saw the three squadrons Fesky had taken to destroy the missile cruiser slipping out of formation and getting forced farther and farther from their target.

Husher slapped his helmet to activate his transponder. "Madcap, I thought you had that cruiser taken care of!"

"Sorry, Spank," Fesky said, her voice drained of energy. "I don't know what happened."

"Looks to me like you got sloppy. We all need you to wake up and join the battle." If Keyes thought they could pull off defeating four UHF battle groups, then Husher was happy to help prove him right. But if they did manage it, it wouldn't involve screw-ups like the one Fesky had just made.

"I'm sorry, Spank..."

God. She sounds pathetic. "Listen, Fesky, I know how hard losing Spire must be for you. But before that ever happened, you fought alongside humans against your own kind. You have a new home, now. The *Providence* is home, and we need to fight as hard as we can to protect it."

"It's not about my own kind. I lost them a long time ago, and I lost Spire, too. It's about losing the Fins. And losing Ek."

"That's crap." Husher's words sounded harsh in his own ears, but they needed to be said. "Ek would not want you to let your mourning distract you from being the CAG we all know you are. Ek would want you to harness that mourning, let it fuel your anger, and use it to fight the UHF with everything you have."

A brief silence, and then Fesky said, "You're right."

"Of course I'm right." On the tactical display, the missile cruiser was pelting the *Providence* with Banshees, and both the destroyer and the other cruiser were doing the same. Some of the shots were getting through. "Enough talk. We need to do something about these cruisers right now."

"The captain of the missile cruiser I tried to take out has the most talent," Fesky said. "So let's take out that one first. I need your Haymakers to start targeting missiles while the other squadron under your command engages its point defense turrets. My three squadrons will work on neutralizing the cruiser itself."

"Yes, ma'am."

But the captain of the missile cruiser was indeed talented, and the moment the Condors moved to target her, she performed a full retro thrust to evade them, redirecting her missile barrage at them alone. Several more Condors went down, including two of Fesky's Divebombers. The surviving pilots had their hands full with avoiding getting killed themselves.

In the meantime, the destroyer and the other missile cruiser continued to bombard the *Providence.*

Husher's mouth went dry. They'd needed to whittle down this battle group far quicker than this.

The third battle group was almost upon them.

CHAPTER 34

The Spirit of the UHF

"Fesky's run into trouble, Captain," Werner said. "The *Lightning* has started focusing entirely on the Condors."

"Launch the reserve fighters we kept in the port side and tell them to join her. In the meantime, we need to redirect some of our fire to dealing with the missiles being launched at us by the *Porcupine*. The point defense turrets alone aren't cutting it."

The main capacitor still wasn't charged from their discharge of the primary laser hours ago, and Keyes didn't feel comfortable letting it fully recharge in the middle of an engagement. *At least we'll soon have enough for secondary lasers.*

Werner spoke again. "Captain, the third battle group is nearly here."

"The flagship *Imogen* has sent us a transmission request," the Coms officer said.

"Accept."

The face that appeared on the CIC's main viewscreen belonged to Admiral Jacobs, which felt like even more of a sucker punch than the overwhelming odds Keyes faced. Jacobs counted among the very few admirals ever to gain Keyes's respect.

"Captain Keyes," she said, her voice worn-out from decades of shouting commands. Even during the First Galactic War, Jacobs had been considered old to still serve in the field. Now, everyone lived in disbelief of her continued battle prowess.

"Admiral Jacobs. I'm sorry that the UHF has ordered you to do this. It pains me to have to fight you."

"I volunteered for this mission, Captain."

Keyes closed his eyes and breathed.

"I am an officer of the United Human Fleet," the admiral went on. "This is my job, and I will never be insubordinate, as you have been. You pose a danger to the very concept of an effective military."

Keyes opened his eyes again, still trying to grapple with the thought of battling one of his oldest heroes. "With all due respect, Admiral, the women and men of the *Providence* embody the spirit of the UHF in its truest form. Ma'am, how long will you remain so dedicated to an organization that has betrayed its own species in service of a corporation? Will you still be proud of your decision when the last Winger dies? Will you stand by it as the Ixa begin destroying our colonies, one-by-one?"

The admiral slowly shook her head. "I still remember the boy who threw himself into the Ixa's teeth to save countless Fleet lives in the Coreopsis System. Now you fight savagely to take those lives away. But enough talk, Captain Keyes. Do you surrender?"

"Ma'am, I will never surrender while humanity is in peril."

"I was afraid you'd say that. You'll be brought to justice either way. Jacobs out."

CHAPTER 35

Hurricane

B ob Bronson paced his cell, humming an old military tune—the soft part in the middle, his favorite part, just before the wind instruments returned in a hurricane of sound.

Then he started in on the loud, frenetic part, and a guard shouted past the rows of cells: "Pipe down in there."

Bronson grinned. *I suppose there are worse last words you could have spoken.*

The thunder of gunfire rolled through the brig, bringing all of the prisoners to their feet and then to the edges of their cages. Not Bronson. He ceased his pacing, reclining on his bunk instead to await the visitor.

Private Ryerson strode past the cells, holding a keycard in one hand and a semiautomatic in the other.

"Too bad the on-shift guards weren't some of ours," Bronson said as the private drew near. "Luck of the draw, I guess."

The marine didn't respond, clutching his side instead and wincing.

"Don't give out on me now," Bronson said with a chuckle. "We're almost there. Did Laudano send the signal?"

"Obviously," Ryerson said. "Otherwise I wouldn't be here. The UHF ships have already arrived. The trap's been sprung."

"Good. That's good. Now let me out."

Ryerson did, and they set about freeing Moreno, along with all of the others that had aided in their first mutiny attempt. Their failed attempt.

This one will be different. Keyes will have no chance to play his rotten tricks.

CHAPTER 36

Win or Die

Keyes kept the *Providence* constantly in motion, refusing to give the six enemy warships a stationary target.

"Captain, the five corvettes have abandoned their trajectory toward the darkgate into Petrichor and are headed back to join the engagement."

Nodding at Werner, Keyes returned to scrutinizing the tactical display. "They know there's no longer any need to head us off. We can't extract ourselves from an engagement with two destroyers and four missile cruisers without suffering heavy damage. Right now, our choice looks a lot like win or die."

"Surrender is also an option, Captain," Laudano said. The XO had been quiet for most of the engagement, which was unusual, given his habit of constant sniping.

Keyes returned Laudano's gaze for a moment, fighting to keep his anger from showing on his face. "When surrender means humanity's extinction, it is *not* an option, Laudano."

He turned back to the tactical display and saw that the battle had assumed the configuration he'd been striving for. The supercarrier's superior engines had brought her once more to the periphery of the battle, denying the enemy the opportunity to surround her. The closest warship was the missile cruiser Fesky and the other pilots were having trouble with.

"Helm, bring us about, and Tactical, prepare to open fire on that cruiser with our main rail gun. Warn Fesky of our intentions, Coms."

"Yes, sir," all three officers said at once.

Within minutes, the shot was lined up, even as the other UHF ships struggled to catch up to the *Providence* and defend her target.

Too late. "Fire."

Occupied as she was with the swarm of Condors, there remained little the opposing missile cruiser could do about the stream of kinetic impactors. Her captain did attempt to flee toward the other UHF ships, angling the cruiser in a blatant attempt to put some Condors between her and the *Providence*. But Fesky was too sharp a commander for that, and the firing lane remained clear.

Well before the other ships drew near enough to back up the cruiser, it exploded.

Keyes clenched his fists in victory, but the celebration inside the CIC was limited to that. The tension remained too high to give birth to cheering, and they had too many enemy ships left to contend with. *But that was meaningful. The cruiser was becoming a huge pain.*

Lieutenant Laudano leapt to his feet, pulling out a pistol and rushing the Tactical station. Before anyone could react, his gun rested firmly on the back of Arsenyev's head.

"No one move, or I swear to God I'll unload this clip into her brain."

Keyes's innards felt cold. "What's this about, Laudano?" The rest of his CIC crew had gone rigid in their seats, scarcely breathing, from the looks of it.

"This is about the end of your little misadventure, Keyes. Contact the admiral and tell her you surrender. Then I want you to order your crew to prepare to be boarded, and following that you can step away from your console."

"Why didn't you point the gun at my head?"

"Because I know you'd be stupid enough to try something, even then. But you won't gamble with Arsenyev's life. Not your precious XO-in-training. Don't think I missed how you were grooming her to replace me." Laudano's com beeped, and he slapped it with one hand, never taking his eyes off of Keyes.

Laudano must have had his com on speaker mode, because a voice Keyes recognized as Private Ryerson's came through it: "We're here."

At that, Laudano seized Arsenyev by the arm and dragged her roughly from her station, forcing her to accompany him to Keyes's console, where he tapped the screen to open the CIC's hatch.

Ryerson, Bronson, and Moreno strolled in, surrounded by almost a squad's worth of marines, who pointed their guns at Keyes's CIC crew. "Hands up and toss your firearms on the floor, nice and easy," one of the marines barked.

"Has he surrendered to the admiral yet?" Ryerson asked.

Laudano shook his head, pulling Arsenyev away from Keyes. "Not yet."

Moreno marched over, his eyes gleaming with cold hatred. "Stand up."

Glaring at the mutineer, Keyes slowly complied, his shoulders back.

The traitor backhanded him, causing Keyes's head to snap sideways. Otherwise, he didn't move, though he felt a trickle of blood crawling down his chin.

Apparently dissatisfied, Moreno struck him again. Pain flared through Keyes's jaw and neck, but he still maintained his stance, calmly returning his gaze to lock onto Moreno's.

"Come on," Werner yelled. "Have some humanity."

Moreno ignored him, backhanding Keyes a third time, putting his full weight into it. Keyes staggered backward a foot.

"Cut it out," Bronson said, though he strode up to Keyes until he stood inches away. "I bet you don't feel like such a brilliant strategist now. All you ever had were tactics, Keyes. You can win battles, but you'll lose the war."

Keyes didn't bother pointing out that his actions had directly led to humanity winning the First Galactic War. There wasn't much point.

"Surrender to the admiral, Keyes, before she kills us all. Tell her you'll be recalling your Condors immediately. Come, now. The only reason you have to continue endangering your crew is pride."

Keyes sat down at his console, though it took an incredible effort of will to do so—to stop fighting. He ordered his Coms officer to patch him through to the admiral. And he did as Bronson said.

When it was done, Bronson told him to recall his Condors next. "And do *not* let on to them about what's happening here. If you give the slightest hint about it, I promise you we will end Arsenyev's life."

CHAPTER 37

Unravel

"Condors, return to base. We have surrendered to Admiral Jacobs. I repeat, return to base."

Keyes sounded dejected over the wide channel, as well he might. For his part, Husher felt numb. "Holy shit," he muttered, his hands leaving his fighter's controls. "I can't believe it. It's over."

He watched his tactical display as the other Condor pilots guided their birds back to their designated landing bays aboard the *Providence*.

Everything we've fought for...

Sighing heavily, he engaged his fighter's gyros until he was angled toward Flight Deck B. He was about to engage engines when Fesky's voice cut in over a two-way channel: "This isn't right."

"What do you mean?"

"This battle wasn't over."

Husher sniffed. "It looks pretty over to me, Madcap."

"I've known the captain for a long time. Fought with him, and then served under him. He would not have surrendered this battle. He would have found a way to pull through. I mean, we just took out that cruiser..."

"There are three more cruisers." And two destroyers, with several more ships on the way. But Fesky was right. He'd seen Keyes beat odds at least as harsh as these.

Husher sent Sergeant Caine a request to open a two-way channel, and she accepted. "Husher."

"Sergeant. Have you heard yet that Keyes is surrendering?"

"No, but someone just came to me from Engineering to tell me a group of marines took over two of their key control rooms."

Husher took a moment to fit that information into Keyes's order for the Condors to stand down. "So there's been a mutiny, and this time, it was successful." He stared at his HUD, which currently showed a view of space. "The captain gave us the stand-down order under duress."

"Wait. Keyes called the Condors back to base?"

"Yeah."

"Wow. This is real."

He nodded, though of course Caine couldn't see that. "Sergeant, our mission is now to get Senator Bernard off the ship and onto Zakros at all costs. If you can get her to a shuttle, I'll work on getting together some pilots to escort her to the planet."

"Escort her past past two destroyers and three missile cruisers?"

"I didn't say it would be easy." His mind was racing, and another idea struck him. "Get as many shuttles into the air as you can. Launch them all, if possible. That'll decrease the odds that Bernard's shuttle will get shot down. In the meantime, if you can manage it, try to evacuate other key personnel." Husher racked his brain, striving to think of who might prove important, for overthrowing Hurst, and for the war ahead. "Get Tort, the Gok. The Tumbran, Piper. Doctor Brusse—she's been working on some research the captain considers important. Other than that, help whoever you can to escape. And I want you and as many of your marines as possible to get out of there, too."

"Is there anything else you'd like with that? Maybe I could decipher the Ixan Prophecies while I'm at it."

Husher grinned, more glad to hear some of Caine's spunk returning than he was irritated at the jab. "You have your orders, Sergeant. Let's roll the dice."

"Yes, *sir.*" The response was clipped, and Husher expected her to sign off after it, which made him feel suddenly heavy in a way that had nothing to do with his Condor. But she spoke again, and when she did, his spirits lifted a little. "Hey, Husher, take care of yourself. Okay? Be careful."

"You too, Caine. We're gonna figure this thing out. We'll regroup, and then we'll figure out how we can win."

"Sure thing," she said, sounding about as convinced as he felt. With that, she was gone.

He switched over to a two-way with Fesky. "Madcap, there's been a mutiny. I've set things in motion for Sergeant Caine to get the senator off the ship. But we'll need an escort."

As she sometimes did when talking to him, the CAG sounded surprised. "All right, then, Spank. I'll see who I can round up."

"Only pilots you're sure we can trust."

"Obviously, human. I wasn't hatched yesterday."

CHAPTER 38

Wait and See

Markov double checked the clip he'd slammed inside his pistol moments ago, then he held it at the ready, between his legs, while he peeked around the corner just enough to keep one eye on the hatch into the CIC.

Many marines would have wanted an assault rifle or perhaps a shotgun for such a situation, but Markov loved his pistol. Too many soldiers fell under the spell of more powerful guns, and they sacrificed accuracy because of it, in his view.

Half of his squad waited in the cramped crew corridor behind him, with the other half waiting across the intersection. With any luck, when Bronson and his bastards left the CIC, they wouldn't check the cameras first. *I doubt they expect anyone's on to them this soon.* But everything depended on how cautious the mutineers were being.

Then again, Markov had orders to strike within ten minutes, whether anyone exited the CIC or not. If no one came out, he carried a breaching charge, and so did two other squad members. Markov didn't feel eager to use explosives inside the *Providence*, and he knew Keyes would make him pay for it if the captain ever got the chance, even if Markov somehow managed to take the ship back from the mutineers. But Caine said their mission was too important to place even the integrity of the ship above it.

The CIC hatch opened, and he breathed a sigh of relief. *Good old-fashioned combat.* He drew back from the corner, allowing time for enough of the enemy to emerge so that they couldn't easily disengage. Then he leaned out, lined up his shot, and popped off a round. His bullet found his target's neck, just above the body armor. Across the intersection, one of his marines fired a spray of ammunition from an assault rifle, hitting nothing.

Typical assault rifle user. "Let's move!" he shouted over a squad-wide channel, and then he performed a tactical roll, quickly finding his feet and squeezing off two more shots as he advanced toward the CIC. His marines moved up to join him, putting heavy pressure on the mutineers.

At last, the enemy managed to withdraw to safety, shutting the hatch. A hissing sound reached Markov's ears, and he turned around in time to see the corridor sealing off, blocking them from retreating through the ship.

His com beeped, and Markov took it out. An irrational spark of hope flared when he saw Captain Keyes's name on the screen.

But of course, it wasn't really him. The voice that spoke belonged to Bob Bronson.

"Corporal Markov. How unfortunate for you, to have highlighted your disloyalty in such a way. For the rest of the crew, there remains the chance of receiving pardons, but not for you.

I'll be using a trick I learned from Captain Keyes to quell your little uprising."

A whooshing noise began overhead. *He's pumping out the oxygen. And apparently we don't get a chance to surrender.*

"Everyone lie down on the deck," Markov told his squad. "It looks like we'll all be passing out, and there's no need for unnecessary injuries."

They did as he said, and Markov followed suit, hoping that Bronson intended to restore oxygen in time for them to continue living.

The world diminished until it was a pinprick at the end of a tunnel of blackness. Then, the darkness overtook him.

When he came to, he'd been stripped of his pistol and explosives and was being dragged through the ship's corridors.

Moreno marched nearby, and he sneered when he noticed Markov regaining consciousness. "That was the most pathetic rescue mission I've ever heard of, Markov. What did you think was going to happen?"

"Actually, our plan worked perfectly."

"What are you talking about?"

Markov grinned. "Wait and see."

CHAPTER 39

One Inch Closer

Airman Gaston climbed down from his Condor and headed toward the pilot locker room, his eyes on the floor. *I can't believe we surrendered.* A feeling of dread had settled in the pit of his stomach, showing no signs of dissipating anytime soon.

What would happen to him and the other Condor pilots now? The entire crew had to worry about the consequences of joining Keyes in his rebellion against the UHF, but Gaston and the rest of the Air Group had extra reason to be concerned. The *Providence* was the last carrier in operation. Would they keep her in the air? Gaston seriously doubted it. Keyes had been the only thing between the supercarrier and getting decommissioned.

When he entered the locker room, the only other Haymaker there so far was Sergeant Wicks. Gaston headed over to that corner, where most of his squadron had their lockers.

"Hey, Noodle," he said as he drew near, removing his helmet as he walked. "Noodle" was Wicks's somewhat unfortunate callsign.

"Hey, Voodoo. You seen Spank?"

Gaston shook his head. "I'm sure he'll be in here soon."

"He didn't even land."

Pausing with his hands on one of his flight suit's zippers, Gaston scrutinized Wicks's face. "Seriously?"

"Yeah. Madcap's still out there, too."

"Something's up, then." Releasing the zipper, Gaston pointed at Wicks's flight suit, which he'd half removed. "Put that back on. I'm gonna go do some snooping." He picked up his helmet and left the room.

He didn't have far to go. As soon as he exited the locker room, he spotted Sergeant Caine with five other *Providence* marines, escorting the senator as well as the corporal who'd come aboard with her. They were headed toward Hangar Bay B.

"Sergeant," he called, and she turned to face him, raising her gun a little.

"Whoa," he said, holding up his hands. "I just wanna know what's going on."

The sergeant only hesitated a moment. "There's been a mutiny. That's why Keyes surrendered. They have him, and if we don't get Senator Bernard to that planet then they'll have everything, and we can kiss any chance of saving humanity goodbye." She was studying his face closely, and Gaston realized she was gauging his reaction to the news. Trying to figure out whether he was a friend or foe.

I'll help you out with that. He had no idea why getting this lady to Zakros was so important, but he trusted Sergeant Caine. "I'll rally the Haymakers. We'll take on the enemy while you escape with the politician."

"You do realize 'the enemy' consists of two destroyers and three missile cruisers?"

"Yes, ma'am."

The sergeant lowered her gun and saluted. Gaston saluted back. There was nothing else to be said.

"I'd better get going, ma'am."

"God speed, Airman."

Gaston replaced his helmet and switched to a squadron-wide channel. "Haymakers, we're scrambling again. Don't ask questions, just know that this is important." Realizing that many of them had likely removed their helmets, he sent a message to their coms as well.

Within ten minutes, he was back in his Condor, and seven other Haymakers were too, prepping their birds for flight and guiding them toward the launch catapults. Gaston spotted three more Haymakers running across the flight deck.

"Voodoo, what's going on?" Perry, another Haymaker, asked him over a squadron-wide channel. Perry hadn't returned to his Condor yet.

"There's been a mutiny, Perry, and they have the captain. Sergeant Caine is trying to escape in a shuttle with the senator. Says it's important. I'm going out there to cover them. If any of you want to remain behind, I'll understand. Just leave your birds on the flight deck and go surrender with the rest of them. Me, I'm heading out for one more flight."

Before long, fifteen Haymakers waited in their Condors atop their catapults. The only one left was Husher, who was already out there.

Caine's voice came into his helmet, over a two-way channel. "We're ready, Gaston. We're launching multiple shuttles, to increase the odds of Bernard escaping."

"Just tell me when to launch, ma'am."

"Launch now."

He switched to a wide channel. "Haymakers, launch!"

They did, as one.

Gaston wasn't used to giving orders, but then, there was nothing usual about this situation, and no one questioned him. "Fluid-two formations, everybody. Sergeant Caine has authorized the launch of multiple shuttles, so I won't tell you which one the politician's in, because I don't know myself. If we favor one of them, the enemy will just target that one anyway. So we're going to have to protect them all."

Since Gaston normally paired up with Lieutenant Husher in fluid-two, he didn't have anyone to fly in formation with, so he went it alone. It took a minute for the enemy to catch on to what was happening, but before long, the first missile flew.

Gaston punched his acceleration up to eight Gs, screaming toward the Banshee. He shot it down, and started looking for the next.

"Voodoo." It was Lieutenant Husher, his voice coming over a two-way channel. "Voodoo, what in Sol are you doing?"

"We're making sure the politician escapes, Spank. The Haymakers got your back." Gaston's tactical display showed Husher flying near a shuttle that was moving away from the *Providence* at top speed.

"This is suicide. Those warships are going to swat you all down like flies."

"It's not suicide. It's about doing our part. If we can get humanity just one inch closer to surviving...well, we're willing to die for that inch, Spank."

Radio silence. Then: "Damn it, Voodoo. It's been good flying with you." If Gaston didn't know better, he would have said Husher sounded choked up.

"You too. Give em hell for me, all right?" He switched off the channel to focus on taking down the next missile headed toward a shuttle.

Already, his tactical display told him that only thirteen of the fifteen Haymakers who'd left the *Providence* survived. Then, thirteen became twelve. Eleven. Nine.

When the warships began focusing exclusively on the Condors running missile defense, and not on the ones escorting the shuttles, Gaston knew they were succeeding.

"Stay away from the missiles for as long as you possibly can, Haymakers," he said over the squadron-wide. "Fly like you've never flown before."

Gaston piled an Ocharium boost on top of his already considerable speed, causing him to accelerate faster than his body should have been able to tolerate while remaining conscious. *This is more Gs than I was ever able to handle in the centrifuge.*

He whipped his Condor around its short axis and fired into the cloud of fifteen Banshee missiles chasing him. They still gained on him, but very slowly, allowing him to pick them off.

A second barrage of missiles followed immediately after, and one of those got him.

CHAPTER 40

Scrap Metal

Admiral Jacobs strode into the CIC with her head high and shoulders back, the crispness of her posture incredible given her age. Even in his current situation, Keyes could still admire comportment like that.

An entire platoon of marines had accompanied her, half of which secured the area outside the CIC. The UHF was still treating his crew like an enemy, as well they might, considering the stunts Markov and Gaston had pulled.

Laudano had kept Keyes appraised of both those situations in real-time, remarking that it wouldn't bode well for him in court, that he'd brainwashed his crew so thoroughly they stood ready to throw away their lives for him.

"They're not doing it for me," Keyes had said. "They're doing it for humanity."

That his crew had managed to coordinate Senator Bernard's escape with a mutiny in progress made Keyes swell with pride, and it ignited a spark of hope inside him.

Jacobs carried herself with considerably more dignity than Bronson and his ilk, and it seemed odd to see her standing next to them. "You will be imprisoned in orbit over Hades," she told Keyes, her face devoid of warmth. "Indefinitely. No trial is necessary, since the Commonwealth has declared you a terrorist, and not entitled to due process."

"How convenient," Keyes said. Like many, he'd always considered it a little on the nose to name a prison planet "Hades," though it was in keeping with other planets that had taken their names from Ancient Greece. Located in a system accessible only from Caprice, the place was at once a prison for humanity's worst criminals and also the largest source of Ocharium ever discovered. For both reasons, its defenses were the most robust humanity had ever constructed, and widely considered impenetrable.

"In case you were wondering what would happen to your precious supercarrier," Bronson said, "I've been given the responsibility of overseeing its dismantling. For scrap metal, you understand."

Keyes's blood boiled hot, and he surged forward with a roar, breaking free of the marines restraining him. He raised his fist to strike Bronson, but the marines seized him again before he could land a blow.

"Always with the temper," Bronson said, shaking his head and grinning.

Keyes trembled with shame, but not over his failure to keep himself in check, or even his failure to hit his former XO.

In his heart of hearts, he'd known since this war began that winning it would almost certainly require him to sacrifice himself at some point, along with his ship.

But now they were separating him from the *Providence*. He was losing her, accomplishing nothing.

And humanity would burn in the offing.

CHAPTER 41

Vengeance

"Captain," Korbyn's sensors adjutant squawked, "attacking the Gok battle group you've designated will not yield the most optimal engagement available to us. There is a smaller Gok battle group just seven million miles farther out, which we should be able to eliminate while taking far less damage. Continuing to select suboptimal engagements is...well, it's suicidal."

Wingleader Korbyn clacked his beak. "Leave such assessments to the strategic adjutant."

"Sir, I sent my data to his console hours ago, and he should have made this recommendation himself. The fact that he hasn't indicates a serious lack—"

"Contact the sensors adjutant who has the next shift and tell her she's being called in early. You're relieved from duty and confined to quarters the moment she gets here." Korbyn said all of this without anger or indeed emotion of any kind. He felt like he'd been hollowed out and filled only with a drive to avenge the Fins. Nothing else remained.

The fact that the sensors adjutant felt differently made him a rarity among the Wingers. When his replacement arrived, the dissenting officer stood up, his feathers sticking up in multiple different directions. Then he marched stiffly from the bridge without another word.

"I wish to do the maximum amount of damage possible to the Gok forces," Korbyn told his bridge crew, "divorced from all other considerations. If we bypass the target battle group, it could escape us. Anyone who objects can consider themselves relieved from duty as well."

No one objected. He now had a bridge crew consisting of Wingers who felt exactly as he did. *Bytan would have condoned my actions, too. She'd be doing the same thing I am if she was still alive.* Nine other Roostships flew with Korbyn's, taking their orders directly from him without question.

He turned to his communications adjutant. "Patch me through to the fleetwide."

"It's done, Captain."

Korbyn clacked his beak—a habit that, not long ago, he'd fought to stamp out, both in his crew and in himself. "Fellow Wingers. The Gok will pay a heavy price for the genocide they have committed. One of my sensors adjutants, who I have just relieved from duty, called our line of action suicidal. I say: what of it? The Fins are gone, and all that remains to us is to avenge them. If we do not die in the process, how can we know that we've wreaked the maximum amount of vengeance possible?" *It's better if we die. For our failure to defend the Fins, we deserve it.*

He knew his words would sound insane from any rational perspective, and the fact that no one contested them was a testament to how foundational the Fins had been to the Wingers' identity as a species.

"Launch all Talons, and spare no ammunition to annihilate the Gok battle group I've designated. Only after every Gok ship has been obliterated will I get in touch with new orders." *Providing I'm still around to give them.*

At last, they reached the ugly Gok warships, who pounced eagerly on the Roostships, their cruisers spewing missiles, their carriers belching fighters.

Korbyn watched the tactical display blossom with hundreds of Talons launching simultaneously. To intercept Gok missiles, at least a couple of the Winger pilots simply flew their craft into the rockets rather than attempt to shoot them down.

For their part, the Gok warships didn't bother defending themselves from the Talons. They left that to their own fighters, even though they were woefully outnumbered.

Instead, the Gok ships pointed their weapons at the Roostships and fired away. It occurred to Korbyn that before the Fins had been slaughtered, he'd never witnessed an engagement where neither side had any interest in self-preservation. *So this is what that looks like.*

When the battle was over, only three Roostships remained of the original ten. Korbyn immediately got back on the fleetwide and ordered the other captains to make for the nearest Gok battle group, which was the one his former sensors adjutant had indicated.

The only difference was that now, that battle group outnumbered them.

CHAPTER 42

A Seed of Hope

Husher gently guided his Condor under an overhang on the surface of Pirithous, one of Zakros' two moons. Its other natural satellite, Sisyphus, was colonized, but Pirithous would never accommodate a colony barring a prolonged terraforming project, and since more suitable prospects were within easy reach, no such effort had been made.

Which served Husher's purposes just fine. He double checked his pressure suit's integrity while Fesky nestled her Condor beside his. Satisfied that his suit would protect him from Pirithous, which lacked an atmosphere, he switched on his helmet's lamp and exited the craft, stepping out onto the moon's sky-colored regolith.

He waited for Fesky to perform her checks and join him in the darkness, which was lit only by the stars and their suit lights. They'd landed on Pirithous' dark side, with the hopes that it would shield their fighters from detection. Finding an overhang big enough to store them had been a stroke of luck. *I think we're entitled to a little bit of that.*

"What are we doing here, Husher?" Fesky said, and he noticed that she spoke to him over a wide channel. If Bernard and the others wanted to hear their conversation, they could.

"You know what we're doing, Fesky. We're meeting with Keyes's old associate, Ralston."

"Yes, but what are we actually doing? I'm not clear on the point of this mission. Are we still pretending that we're rebuilding the UHF, as it was 'meant to be,' or whatever that was about? Because if we are, military personnel don't normally get mixed up with civilian matters."

"We're no strangers to bending protocol, Fesky. And when humanity's life as a species is on the line, I think it's called for." *At least, that's the thinking that led us to this point.*

"What are we doing?" Fesky asked again.

"We're planting a seed of hope." In truth, Husher was nearly out of hope. But it was the last thing that remained to him to say.

Apparently, it was enough. Fesky didn't speak again. Emerging from under the overhang, they quickly spotted the shuttle waiting for them nearby. Its airlock opened as they approached, and they stepped inside while it repressurized the compartment.

Inside, Senator Bernard, Corporal Simpson, and Piper occupied crash seats normally used by marines. There was also a squad's worth of marines distributed throughout the shuttle. Bernard smiled at Husher and Fesky, but other than that, the mood was somber. No one spoke.

The Tumbran looks funny in a crash seat designed for some-one twice his size. The thought raised Husher's spirits just enough to allow him to return Bernard's smile.

He poked his head inside the shuttle's cockpit to find that their pilot was Skids, which broadened his smile a little more. For a moment, Husher allowed himself to believe that maybe everything would turn out half-decent. "Skids, it's good to see you. I need to send an encrypted message to the other pilots who escaped the *Providence*."

"Sure thing." Skids didn't sound much happier than the others looked. "It's recording now, sir."

Husher gazed into the camera, trying to resurrect his smile from moments ago. "Well, people, it doesn't get much worse than this. We have found rock-bottom. The good news is, after this, everything should feel like winning the lottery. My advice is to spread yourselves throughout the Feverfew System and try your best to remain hidden. If you see any of our new UHF friends approaching, flee, as best you know how. I'll be in touch about our next steps as soon as I'm done here, and we'll figure out how we can leave this system then. I doubt that'll be as easy as it was aboard the *Providence*, with Captain Keyes in command, but we'll find a way. Husher out."

"That's the message, then, Lieutenant?"

For a moment, Husher considered recording it again. *I could have done more to lift morale. Not sure the dark humor's going to work very well.*

But he doubted they could afford for him to spend precious minutes getting his word choice exactly right. "Transmit it, and take us down to Zakros. We'll be going through the official channels. I don't think trying to hide will serve us very well, down there. Set a course for the spaceport nearest Ralston, and broadcast it to the local officials, so they know we're not hostile."

"Yes, sir."

An hour later, he was standing near the shuttle's airlock while Bernard and her companion, Simpson, made their way into the airlock, along with Fesky and Piper. The marines would remain aboard to watch the shuttle and to underscore the fact that they intended no harm.

Husher, Fesky, and Simpson left their firearms aboard the shuttle. Getting them through customs would have proven difficult, especially considering Husher and Fesky were technically fugitives.

Private Simmons saluted Husher before he joined the others in the airlock, and he saluted back, trying to put more energy into it than he felt.

Part of him didn't expect to make it past the spaceport. But Bernard's credentials as a senator went a long way, especially coupled with her overwhelming popularity—in stark contrast to President Hurst's plummeting approval rating, which had fallen almost into the single digits, at least according to what Husher overheard a security official telling Bernard.

Security personnel did perform thorough searches of Husher and Fesky in addition to insisting on installing tracking software on their coms, to be removed only when they left the planet. Other than that, they were free to enter the city where Ralston lived.

Bernard ordered them up some transportation through a ride-sharing service. During the drive, Husher offered a silent prayer that Keyes was right about Ralston being worth all of this.

Sadly, Husher already knew the answer to that. Nothing could be worth losing the *Providence.*

CHAPTER 43

Chief Ralston

The house creaked, and Calum Ralston started, head whipping around. *It was just the house settling.* He knew that, but it wouldn't stop him from nearly jumping out of his skin the next time it happened, and the next.

Turning around in his chair to face his kitchen table once more, he raised his coffee mug halfway to his lips before he remembered it had gone cold at least an hour ago. *Make some more,* he told himself, but of course he wouldn't.

It had been this way ever since the First Galactic War, when he'd returned from a mission in the Ixan home system and was found psychologically unfit for duty. He'd been honorably discharged with full veteran's benefits—benefits that had slowly eroded with each subsequent Commonwealth president. And he'd been left alone to rot.

Ralston often felt like he was rotting. Mentally, for certain. Every attempt he'd made to return to something that resembled a normal social life had ended with driving away whomever he tried to befriend, even though he lived in an area of town with many other people of Scottish descent. Hell, even the children that lived on his street avoided him, and whenever he looked in the mirror and saw his scowl, he understood why. He never meant to scowl, but his face always seemed to wear one.

They don't know what I've seen.

A knock on the front door made him leap from his chair, knocking it over. He righted it, cursing, and went to tell whoever it was to go away. To come another day. *After I'm dead, maybe.*

When he opened the door to a woman who looked identical to Senator Sandy Bernard, he shook his head, blinking, trying to clear away the mirage. *It's happened, then. I've lost the last shred of sanity I was clinging to.*

"Chief Calum Ralston?" the apparition said.

"Yes, ma'am." Ralston's gaze wandered beyond the hallucination and found more figments of his imagination. Behind the senator stood a Winger, a Tumbran, a human woman, and a man who looked like a young Warren Husher. *Strange that my sanity would abandon me in quite this manner.* It wasn't unusual to see Tumbra on human planets, though they never visited Ralston.

"May we come in?" Bernard's spectral doppelgänger asked.

He decided to run with it. "Sure."

Leading them to his smallish living room, he waited until the visions all took seats before speaking again. "Uh, can I get you tea?"

"If you don't mind my saying, Chief Ralston, our presence appears to have caused you considerable distress." Bernard had one leg crossed over the other, and she spoke calmly.

"I'm not convinced you're real," Ralston said.

"We're real," the Tumbran said. "Captain Leonard Keyes recommended we visit you."

"Keyes." Of course. He would be behind this. "His last great act, I suppose, as captain of the *Providence*. According to the news, they arrested him and took his ship to the Vermillion Shipyards to become scrap."

Young Warren Husher's fists tightened on his lap, and Ralston could tell he was barely holding back some venom.

Ralston squinted at him. "Are you a relative of Warren Husher?"

"I'm his son."

"Wonderful. The flesh-and-blood son of a traitor has come for a visit."

"Did you know my father?"

"I served under him, and I was one of the few who hated it. I didn't like the unorthodox way he went about everything. Or the constant wisecracks."

Husher the younger nodded. "The more you speak, the more respect I'm gaining for my father. I'll have to commend you to him."

Grunting, Ralston marched out of the room to make tea. He toyed briefly with the idea of not making the boy a cup, but decided not to be that petty.

He returned with the tray, and everyone took a mug. Husher started drinking from his right away. *Should have spat in that one.*

Ralston sipped from his coffee and grimaced. It was the same one from before, and just as cold. He replaced it on the tray. "I've always liked you, Senator."

Inclining her head, Bernard said, "Thank you."

"I recognize another soldier when I see one. I don't always agree with your policies, but it's not hard to tell you mean what you say. You actually believe in something, which pretty much makes you a unicorn among politicians, and you're prepared to fight for it."

"Allow me to get right to our purpose in visiting you," Bernard said. "As kind as your praise is, there isn't much time to waste on making nice."

Ralston nodded. As when he'd seen her on TV, he liked the way Bernard talked.

"Have you heard of the movement to pressure Hurst to resign?" Bernard said.

"Of course. It's all over the micronet. They're saying she lost her legitimacy when she ordered civilians massacred, and they're calling her insane for continuing to attack the Wingers when we'll clearly need them to answer this new threat from the Ixa, not to mention the Gok. Can't say I disagree with any of that. But the movement will never succeed."

"Maybe not with its current level of intensity, no. What if I told you that I intend to lend my support to the movement?"

Ralston pondered the idea, reaching absently for his cold coffee before letting his hand drop. "I'd call it noble, and I think it would mean a lot to the defenders—that's what the protesters are calling themselves, if you didn't know. But I doubt your support would be enough to force Hurst to quit."

"I've designed a set of algorithms that I hope will help," the Tumbran said. The alien hadn't touched its tea. *Maybe they don't drink tea.*

"Algorithms? What do algorithms have to with anything?"

"The humans have dubbed my invention the 'revolution gauge,' which is admittedly a bit pat, but—"

"I'm pretty sure you came up with that name," the Winger cut in, drawing a glare from the Tumbran.

"As I was saying," the diminutive creature said, "using both historical records and a holistic analysis of the contemporary news cycle, my tool will provide the public with an exact measure of its progress toward the stated goal, namely, toppling Hurst's government. Given a concrete visualization of its own momentum, my hope is that the public will..."

As the Tumbran spoke, Ralston gazed at Bernard, squinting. "Am I supposed to be understanding this little runt, then?"

Laughter burst from Husher at that, which he quickly stifled with the back of his hand. The Tumbran fell silent, stiffening in its seat.

Sandy Bernard cleared her throat. "It's not really crucial that you understand Piper's invention. We're here to ask your help in executing a plan formulated by Captain Keyes."

"This should be good."

"I hope so. The captain's plan involves bringing together UHF veterans who oppose the way Hurst is using the military to serve a corporate agenda, an agenda bound to bring a swift end to our species. If veterans join the protest en masse, it will put unprecedented pressure on the government. Can you imagine how it will appear to citizens when they see footage of police brutalizing veterans? That's if they even dare to use the same oppressive tactics they've been using on the defenders. I know the risk I'm asking you and your fellow veterans to take on is tremendous, but—"

"I'll do it."

Bernard blinked. "You will?"

He nodded. "I don't know how many veterans I'll actually be able to get together. I'm not very persuasive. But I'll try, and you'll have me, at the very least."

"Thank you, Chief Ralston. On behalf of the people of the Commonwealth, thank you."

The Winger spoke again, shifting its wings, which were clearly being poorly accommodated by Ralston's threadbare couch. "Do you have any news of how my people are faring?"

"Um..." Ralston shrugged. "The news isn't good. According to the TV, the Wingers have lost all battle sense. They're just throwing themselves at the Gok with everything they have, while the UHF decimates their colonies. I'm sorry, but it looks like the Wingers are done for."

The well-muscled Winger sitting in his living room rose to its full height. "That's it. I'm leaving."

Husher nodded, getting to his feet as well. "Me too. We've done all we can here. We have a war to fight."

Bernard joined them in standing. "I appreciate everything you've done, both of you." The senator shook the human's hand as well as the Winger's talons.

The Tumbran stood, too. "The senator has my algorithm, and so my contribution here is also at an end. I'll lend you my aid in passing through the darkgates, Lieutenant Husher, if you want it."

Husher raised his eyebrows. "You can do that?"

"Yes. The Tumbra have only ever done what they consider best to maintain the galactic balance of power. Once I convince my brethren that letting us pass serves that purpose, we shouldn't experience any problems."

"You can take the shuttle," Bernard said. "I'm where I need to be."

"I'll stay with Sandy," the other woman said, looking at Ralston. "I'm Corporal Simpson, by the way. Since you didn't ask."

"That's that, then." Husher also stared at Ralston. "We'll leave. I hope you're as valuable as Keyes seemed to think. We sacrificed more than you know to get here."

A biting retort leapt to Ralston's tongue, but he swallowed it. "I'll try my best to be," he said instead.

CHAPTER 44

Revolution Gauge

Once Husher and the others left, Ralston had led Bernard and Simpson to a small study on the same floor as the living room. There, a lapcom sat on a desk whose wood veneer had begun to peel.

They uploaded Piper's revolution gauge to the micronet, running into no technical problems, which Bernard gave thanks for. Without the Tumbran around to provide tech support, their plan might have sputtered out before it began.

Then she, Simpson, and Ralston stood around the cramped study and waited. For hours. She considered suggesting they move the lapcom to the living room, but she didn't want to impose on their host any more than they already had.

At last, the AI finished analyzing news sites, social media, and historical data it pulled from archives. Then it presented them with its calculation for how close they were to toppling Hurst's government:

Seven percent.

"Wow," Simpson said. "We have a lot of work to do."

"And fast." Bernard crossed her arms in front of her, rubbing her elbows. "I thought we could start our work here on Zakros, but this makes me think we should head straight for Mars." The red planet was considered humanity's adopted homeworld, after the total degradation of Earth. "I don't think we'll have quite the impact we need to, here."

The corporal nodded. "I think I can secure us discreet transport. I'll need micronet access, though."

"Ralston will need his lapcom to start contacting other veterans. Can you not get on the net with your com?"

"Nope. Military coms aren't designed to access the civilian micronet."

"Then use mine." Bernard handed Simpson her own personal com.

Ralston leaned back in the study's only chair. "Senator, before I get started, I have to ask you a question. If things don't go your way on Mars, do you envision these veterans taking up arms against Hurst? Is a military coup among the options you're considering? Because I'm not sure how I feel about that. Or that I'm up to it, physically."

"Absolutely not," Bernard said. "I will urge all protesters to remain peaceful, and I will make clear that any violent actors will be disowned by the movement. To turn violent would be to sink to the level of the government, and to give the media an excuse to vilify us. Not to mention that the police would gain an actual justification for cracking down as brutally as they have. They'd likely start brutalizing the defenders even more."

"That's what I needed to hear," Ralston said, turning to his lapcom without another word.

As the others worked, Bernard sat on the hard laminate with her back against the study wall and thought about what she planned to say to the defenders once she reached one of their camps.

It wasn't long before Ralston started muttering to himself. Bernard particularly enjoyed that, since she loved the man's Scottish accent, though she didn't want to risk embarrassing him by saying so.

"It's gonna cost money, especially if I manage to get more veterans than just me. Better start a fundraiser."

Bernard peered up at the screen. From the floor, she could only see the display's top-right quadrant, but that was enough for her to recognize the website of a popular crowdfunding service.

"What if I get a hundred veterans?" The Scot gave a derisive grunt, still apparently talking to himself. "Pie in the sky. Not possible." The clatter of his fingers on the keyboard followed, but stopped suddenly, with Ralston's head twitching upward. "What if I get *two*-hundred?"

Bernard felt a smile spreading across her face. "You'll get a thousand, Chief. Mark my words."

Ralston turned, apparently unperturbed about Bernard interrupting his conversation with himself. "Do you really think so?"

"I do."

"This could be huge, you know that? Like nothing we've ever seen before."

Inclining her head, Bernard said, "I think that's exactly what Captain Keyes envisioned."

CHAPTER 45

Juktas

Ek emerged from a long, low building on the tropical planet of Juktas. After the air-conditioned interior, the heat hit her like a wave, and the AI governing her suit kicked into overdrive to extract what moisture it could from the air, using it to keep her skin from drying out.

"Another warlord in the bag?" Warren Husher called to her from underneath a squat tree with rigid leaves that extended farther than seemed possible.

She crossed the distance between them, joining him under the tree's shade. "It would seem so," she said, relishing the sudden coolness.

"I've never met a woman so adept at convincing people to risk their short-term security for long-term gains. Most people are pretty resistant to that notion."

"Technically, the term 'woman' does not apply to me."

"You're right." Warren grinned. "If it did, I'd probably have a crush on you. Maybe I do anyway."

"You do."

Warren's gray eyebrows shot up, and his mouth hung open, in the middle of forming whatever he had been about to say. "I was only..." He sighed. "Ah, well. Don't tell my wife."

"I do not know your wife."

"Yeah. Neither do I." The nearby ocean sparkled under the Yclept System's blazing star, and Warren's eyes took on a wistful look as he stared at it. He returned his gaze to Ek. "Do you ever worry that you're making these radicals too powerful? Too united?"

"All signs point to their willingness to fight the UHF, and then the Ixa. For now, that has to be enough."

"I guess so. On that note, did they tell you I'm leaving?"

Now came Ek's turn to study Warren. *Is he truly with us?* Other than the strange fabrication aboard the Ixan shuttle, she had detected no reason to believe otherwise. But she did not have time to unravel the mystery of Warren Husher's mind. Everything barreled forward now, and events would soon come to a head. She needed to focus on mustering enough firepower for the coming fight. *And I need to continue distracting myself from the fact of my murdered people.*

"I'm taking the Ixan shuttle to Pinnacle," Warren said, clearly uncomfortable with Ek's silence. "Thresh says his orbital sensors detected Wingers taking some of the derelict UHF ships there. Those are human ships, and I plan to demand them back. They don't appear to be using them, anyhow."

"What purpose will your mission serve?"

"I'm getting the ships for the radicals to use. Why else do you think they're letting me go?" Warren shrugged. "I can't very well fly them all myself."

"You continue to call Thresh and the others radicals. I do not think they appreciate you regurgitating Commonwealth propaganda."

He shrugged. "How else will you know who I'm talking about?" The former captain ran a hand through his storm-cloud hair. "The real reason I'm doing this...I've been thinking a lot about what you said. About my possibly being this 'phoenix' person, from the Ixan Prophecies, and about humanity needing me. And I've decided, if they really do need me, I'd better figure out exactly how they need me, and quick. This seems like a good way to start."

"I see. Have you considered that the Wingers may simply arrest you, as they did before?"

"Yeah. But I have to risk it, Ek. I need to do something. I'm hoping these Wingers won't recognize me, but if they do, hopefully they'll also recognize that I'm working with the good guys. Oh, I almost forgot." Digging in his pocket, Warren pulled out a scrap of paper with a long string of characters written on it. He passed it to her. "You'll need this. It's a decryption key. The radicals are sending a Falcon just inside the Larkspur System, to relay any encrypted messages I send."

"Are you certain the encryption is secure?"

"Of course. It's the Köhler-Tremblay cryptosystem, the best public-key encryption scheme I know of." Warren cleared his throat. "Listen, are you picking up on anything, uh, weird about me? I've been wondering more and more about what exactly the Ixa did to me for two decades."

After a brief calculation, Ek decided she would tell him. "Aboard the Ixan shuttle, when I asked how you knew to refer to the Bastion Sector insurgents as radicals, you told me Wingers taught you the term. Your microexpressions gave every indication you were lying, and yet I also could tell you were not aware of your lie. Very odd, but that is what I perceived."

"That is odd," Warren said, and she could tell that while he had no memory of lying, he also took her words seriously.

He has seen too much of Fin perception to question it, by now. "Monitor yourself closely, Warren Husher. Your contributions are appreciated, but if the Ixa are able to exploit your position in some way, it could erase all the good you have done, or will do."

"Yeah," he said. "Okay. Thanks." But as he walked away, Ek noted his stiff gait, and the way his shoulders hunched.

Warren Husher was clearly even more concerned than before.

CHAPTER 46

Regroup

Husher picked his way over the uneven terrain carefully, knowing that a single misstep could send him and Doctor Brusse careening into space. The shuttles could pick them up if that happened, but it would be a waste of fuel. *Plus I'd never hear the end of it.*

The Condors that had escaped the *Providence* surrounded the asteroid where the shuttles currently sat. Many of them belonged to Fesky's main squadron, the Divebombers. She'd ordered the pilots to shut down all noncritical systems, to conserve fuel and to minimize the chances of getting detected.

The moment she and Husher had left Zakros, he'd instructed Skids to send out an encrypted message summoning all shuttles and fighters to this location. It had taken hours for everyone to assemble, but here they finally were, all accounted for.

They chose his and Fesky's shuttle to hold the meeting where they would decide their next move. Piper had his own Tumbran-sized pressure suit, but Husher didn't like the idea of transporting the diminutive alien across the asteroid, envisioning him flying off into space at the slightest mishap. And despite the initial tension between him and the Tumbran, Piper was proving incredibly useful. Husher wouldn't feel right excluding him from the meeting.

So Husher was currently escorting Doctor Brusse across the asteroid, as she had no experience with EVAs. The marines had all crossed without incident.

Other than a minor stumble, Husher and Brusse reached the shuttle safely. Once inside and past the airlock, they both removed their helmets.

"Thank you," Brusse said with a smile.

"Don't mention it."

The others were already seated in crash seats inside the troop compartment. Taking a seat in one himself, Husher decided not to waste any time. "Would anyone like to submit their idea for what we should do next?"

Looking around the shuttle, Husher saw that the faces he'd come to know well now rested in various states of dejection. Caine furrowed her brow slightly as his eyes fell on her. Fesky sat stiffly, feathers flared. Wahlburg stared into space, and Piper...well, actually, Piper looked bored.

"All right, then," Husher said. "Here's what I think. I say we take our little fleet and head back to the Bastion Sector, with Piper's help. If we can convince the Wingers on Pinnacle to give us back the UHF warships Keyes ordered hauled there, we'll be back on our feet. We can assess the situation and figure out how best to strike back at the Fleet. Any objections?"

"What about Captain Keyes?" Fesky said.

Wahlburg looked up at that, and Caine's eyes were locked on Husher's, too.

"I think...I think the captain would want us to continue fighting the UHF, not use up our resources trying to free him. He'll be taken to Hades, there's no doubt about that. The defenses there are impenetrable, provided decades of jailbreak attempts are any indication. If we're going to have a shot at beating the Ixa, we need to stop the UHF as soon as we can."

"But it's Captain Keyes," the Winger said.

"I know, Fesky. I respect Keyes more than I respect anyone. Honestly. I know this is hard, but I also know it's the right thing. We have to do the right thing." He glanced at Caine, who looked away the moment his eyes fell on her. *It is the right thing.*

"Technically, as a lieutenant colonel, I outrank you," Fesky said. "And if I give the order, then we're going to go try a rescue."

"You'd be sentencing us all to death. I think you know that."

Fesky clacked her beak. "I know how to fly a Condor. I know how to whip pilots into shape, get them flying in formation, and get them to actualize a strategy I've devised. But I know I still have a lot to learn about leadership. You've been a captain before, Husher. So you're in command. I'll defer to you."

"Thank you." He cleared his throat. "I think the next topic should be figuring out how the mutiny against Keyes came about, and exactly who participated in it. I have my guesses, but I won't point the finger without actual evidence."

Caine leaned forward. "One of my people saw Ryerson with Bronson and a squad of marines, in the corridor outside the CIC. She told me the hatch opened for them, and they strolled right in."

"They must have had someone on the inside, then." *Laudano.* Husher would have bet his life on it. "Wasn't Ryerson supposed to be confined to quarters?"

"He was gone," Doctor Brusse said, the first time she'd spoken since sitting. "I went to check his wound for infection and found his chambers empty."

"I thought it was his pain meds," Caine said.

"Pardon?"

"Werner messaged me to ask if I'd seen Ryerson. He told me Keyes said you'd gone to give him pain meds and found him missing."

"I went for both. To administer more pain medication and to check his wound."

"Let's move to another topic for a moment," Husher said, and he noticed a flicker of relief pass across Brusse's face. "How is Tort doing, Doctor?"

"I'll soon be out of the only sedative I've found to be effective on him, but for now the Gok is staying relatively calm, other than some restlessness."

"Any progress with curing the virophage?"

"None. Gok biology is like nothing I've ever encountered. My training has no intersection with the type of knowledge I need, here."

Husher nodded. "Which sedative are you using?"

A beat of silence passed before Brusse said, "Secobarbital." She was staring at Husher, totally unblinking.

"And exactly how much of that remains?"

"A few days' worth."

"How many days?"

"Four."

"Private Ryerson was clearly pretty xenophobic, considering he tried to kill Tort, even as the Gok was chained to a steel pallet. That must have been hard for you, to have that happen in your sick bay. On your watch."

The corner of Brusse's eye twitched. "Yes."

"And then you found Ryerson missing from his chambers. Also quite distressing for you, I'm sure."

Brusse didn't answer.

"You just unlocked the hatch to his chambers, opened it, and...poof. He was gone."

"He was gone when I opened the hatch, yes."

"Where do you keep the sedative you've been using on Tort?"

It took several moments for the doctor to answer Husher's question. "In my case," she said at last.

Husher took out his com and radioed the pilot of Brusse's shuttle. "Ozone, can you do me a favor?"

"Yeah, Spank. What's up?"

"I want you to open up Doctor Brusse's case and read the labels. Tell me how much secobarbital you find."

With that, Brusse leapt from her crash seat and ran toward the airlock. "Stop her," Husher said, without lowering the com from his ear.

Brusse managed to hit the airlock control, but before the inner hatch could open, Caine crossed the shuttle in a few strides and slammed the doctor against the bulkhead. Within seconds, she had Brusse in an armlock from which she had little hope of escape.

"Nothing called secobarbital in here, sir," Ozone said. "Plenty of starch syrup, though."

Husher blinked. "Starch syrup?" He looked at Brusse, who didn't look very comfortable at the moment. "What were you doing with starch syrup?"

"Gok don't get their energy from glucose," Piper said. "It's one of the things that makes their physiology so unusual. In fact, glucose actually clogs up the nested membranes they have in place of a circulatory system. Over time, a Gok will die from ingesting glucose."

A ringing started up in Husher's ears. He glared at Brusse. "Seems like you knew a lot more about Gok physiology than you were letting on."

"That thing is a monster," Brusse said, her voice ragged. "The UHF doesn't let them on their ships for a reason."

"And so you took part in a mutiny?"

The doctor didn't answer.

"Captain Keyes has so much respect for you. Do you know that?"

Still, she said nothing.

Husher shook his head, trying to stuff down his anger before it overwhelmed him. "I want her put in restraints until we have a brig to throw her in. Hey Ozone, I'd like you to dock with our shuttle. We don't need to deal with dragging a struggling mutineer across this dust speck of an asteroid. Today's been eventful enough for my taste."

"No problem, Spank. You know, I thought the doc was acting kind of weird. She kept asking to use the shuttle's transmitter."

"Tell me you didn't let her."

"Nah. Obviously we want to stay radio silent as much as we can."

"Yeah." He briefly considered telling Ozone to let him know the next time someone acted weird, but he discarded the idea. Everyone from the *Providence* was weird.

"Lieutenant," Piper said, and Husher looked at him.

"Yes?"

"I don't see why it's necessary to transport the doctor back to her original shuttle. Why not simply hold her on this one?"

"I want her to witness as we bring Tort back to health. Which brings me to my next order. You're going over to the shuttle, too. You'll start work on a cure for the virophage right away."

"What? Why me?"

Husher shrugged. "You're the closest thing we have to a doctor, now."

"Because I'm a Tumbran?"

"You did know the thing about the glucose."

"This is ridiculous."

"Just do it." Husher switched his com over to a wide channel. "All right, pilots. Take a good look at this pebble we're on, because we'll be leaving it forever within the hour. It's time to see a Winger about a spaceship."

CHAPTER 47

Compelled to Obey

Warren Husher woke with these words ringing in his ears: "*You will be compelled to obey.*"

Obey what? The phrase comprised the only clear memory from a string of muddled nightmares about his time as a prisoner of the Ixa. He didn't know whether the dreams were taken from the actual past or from his deepest fears. Nor did he know for certain whether anyone had ever actually spoken the words that still clogged his head.

I'm pretty sure they're real. I just don't know what they expect me to obey.

He unstrapped himself from the crash seat where he'd been asleep since parting ways with the Falcon who would relay his messages to Juktas. Then he made his way toward the Ixan shuttle's cockpit.

Am I really in charge of myself? Am I me?

Nothing made sense. He remained convinced that his release had involved a bargain of some kind. But why would the Ixa release him if he was just going to act against them? His mission to

Pinnacle involved recruiting more ships for the Ixa's enemies, and he had no intention of ever helping the Ixa. He never had.

Bringing up the shuttle's course, he saw that it had almost reached Pinnacle, on the periphery of the Larkspur System. Over nine hours ago, he'd transitioned back into this system and set the ship to follow a course here, with instructions to alert him if anything dangerous-looking came around. Nothing had, clearly—which was lucky, considering Gok still rampaged through the Bastion Sector.

The cockpit washed blue, indicating he had a transmission request. When he accepted, a disheveled officer from the Wingers' Interplanetary Defense Force appeared on-screen.

"What can I do for you?" Warren said.

"You can explain to me why you're piloting an Ixan craft, for starters." The bird clacked its beak. "I must say, I'm relieved to find you're not an actual Ixan."

It doesn't seem to recognize me. That's good. "So am I," he said. "I was a prisoner of the Ixa since the First Galactic War. I escaped in this shuttle." As far as he knew, this version of events was somewhat removed from the truth. But he doubted it would help his mission to start talking about half-remembered bargains.

"Escaped from the Ixa? They aren't supposed to have any prisoners of war."

"They told the UHF I'd died, which was a misrepresentation. Evidently."

"Yes. Well, congratulations on your escape."

"Thanks."

"What's your business on Pinnacle? And what's your name, for that matter?"

"I don't actually intend to land on Pinnacle. My business can be conducted in its entirety without ever landing on the planet."

"That's for the best. Pinnacle's our most important world, after the loss of Spire. And officials are a little touchy about alien visitors."

"Understandably."

"What did you say your name was?"

"Uh...Harry Wisher." Warren feared his real name would ring a bell for the Winger.

The Winger stared at him with its enormous, unblinking eyes. Finally, it clacked its beak. "Human names are strange. What is your business, then?"

"I'm here to commandeer the derelict UHF ships you have in orbit over Pinnacle."

"I see. Are you working for the UHF?"

"No. I plan to use the ships to fight them. I have enough people to crew the entire battle group, and I'll send them a message to come here once I have your go-ahead."

"And you expect us to simply hand them over?"

"I do. They're human ships, and anyway, you don't appear to be using them for anything. I'm sure even you will admit that your overall strategy kind of sucks, right now. If the ships are left there in orbit, they'll likely be destroyed before long, or actually seized by the UHF. At least, if you give them to me, I'll use them to take the fight to the Fleet, clearing the way for you

Wingers to continue your suicidal headlong charge into a wall of Gok."

The Winger paused for several moments, and Warren resisted the urge to start fidgeting. Finally, it said, "I will contact my superiors with your request."

"Thank you."

Warren put his feet up on the shuttle's wide console, careful not to place them in an area with too many controls governing critical systems. He fully expected to wait days while the Wingers deliberated, and the response would likely be a firm negative. That had been his expectation since leaving Juktas, but he'd still wanted to try. *Better than sitting around watching Ek make yet another warlord dance to her tune.*

So when the cockpit washed blue again twenty minutes later, Warren nearly fell out of his seat.

The same Winger appeared on the viewscreen. "They're all yours," it said.

"Wait, what?"

"You may have the ships, under the condition that we inspect the humans that come to crew them. We will know if your people are UHF. We maintain quite an extensive database of their personnel, and if your people are in it, we won't let you access the warships."

"That's very reasonable."

"Yes. Good luck in your fight, Harry Wisher."

The transmission terminated as suddenly as it had begun. Astounded at his success, he began encrypting a message with the good news. Once he finished, he transmitted it to the messenger ship waiting just outside the Larkspur-Yclept darkgate.

CHAPTER 48

Demerits

A tense silence prevailed inside the *Excalibur*'s CIC. Admiral Carrow knew his crew didn't relish their current task, of chasing down Captain Vaghn in the *Firedrake* and bringing her to justice for her insubordination.

Vaghn was one of those officers who was hated by Command but loved by those she'd served with. And she'd served with pretty much everyone during her climb through the ranks, given how often she'd been shuffled from ship to ship, with Command taking every excuse available to deny her each promotion for as long as possible.

Giving her the *Firedrake* had been intended as a warning to follow orders and keep her nose clean, but clearly that had backfired.

In truth, the necessity of arresting or killing Vaghn annoyed Carrow as well. He'd much rather continue the task of wiping out the Winger military and annexing their colonies, mainly because he hated to abandon a job once he'd begun it.

We'll get back to it soon. Vaghn couldn't run for long. He'd assigned a battle group to guard the entrance into Pirate's Path, and beyond that, Vaghn's options included fleeing deeper into the dead-end Bastion Sector or entering Commonwealth space.

"Admiral," his Coms officer said, "I've just intercepted an encrypted transmission."

Carrow scratched his stubbled cheek. He hated how lax his personal grooming had become since the start of this campaign. *I need to get on top of that.* "What are our chances of decrypting it within a meaningful timeframe?"

"They're excellent. The encryption scheme being used is twenty years old. I should have the cleartext within twenty minutes, if you'd like me to start work on it."

"I do. And make it fifteen minutes, Ensign."

"Yes, sir."

Carrow caught the ghost of a grimace that flitted across the Coms officer's face. He considered it a sign that his ability to command was as sharp as ever. *Always press them. Always demand better than their best.* It was a policy that had propelled him to the top of the UHF quicker than almost every other admiral in Fleet history.

"Sir..." the Coms officer said seventeen minutes later. Carrow made a mental note to apply a demerit to his permanent record for his failure to stay within the assigned timeframe.

"Yes? What is it?"

"The sender of this message claims to be Warren Husher."

Skin tingling, Carrow shook his head. "That isn't possible. Husher's dead. What does the message say?"

"It appears to be inviting radicals waiting on Juktas to come and commandeer a derelict UHF battle group in orbit over the Winger colony Pinnacle."

Carrow turned to his sensor operator. "Examine our sensor data of Pinnacle. The sender of this message can't be Warren Husher, but whoever it is, we can easily verify the claim."

A minute later, his sensor operator was nodding. "It's as the message says. There is a battle group of human ships over Pinnacle, and their profiles match warships from the UHF database. They appear to be basically undefended."

"Incredible." *They must be left over from the ships whose crews were vaporized by the malfunctioned wormholes.* Command had assumed that Keyes had destroyed what ships he didn't take, but apparently he'd had some of them flown to the Winger colony, as a reserve. "Nav, set a course for Pinnacle that prioritizes speed, and then relay it to the rest of the ships in our battle group. Allowing the enemy a battle group of our ships would be far worse than letting Vaghn escape, and anyway, she has nowhere to go. We can hunt her down after we destroy those ships."

His Coms officer furrowed his brow. "Destroy them, sir?"

"Of course. We can't spare the crew to operate them. But we certainly can't afford to let Wingers keep them, let alone radicals."

Carrow gave his Nav officer six minutes to calculate the new course. She did it in seven. *Another demerit.*

The *Excalibur* turned toward Pinnacle, and so did the two destroyers, four missile cruisers, five corvettes, and eight frigates that accompanied her.

CHAPTER 49

Hades

Tennyson Steele strolled into the observation room that looked in on the cell where they interrogated Leonard Keyes. He visited Hades whenever he could. Ocharium was the lifeblood of his company, and as the CFO for years and now CEO of Darkstream, he considered it his duty to ensure that lifeblood flowed strong.

But this was the first time he'd ever taken an interest in any of the prisoners kept aboard the orbital defense platforms. Most of those prisoners were forced to operate and maintain the platforms' systems. Most of them. But not Keyes. They kept him here for another purpose altogether.

Keyes looked more disheveled than harmed. The enhanced interrogation techniques used by guards here on Hades and by Commonwealth spy agencies were designed to leave emotional and psychological scars instead of physical ones. The idea was to leave room for plausible deniability for those overseeing the prison, in the event that a detainee had to be presented to the media.

Currently, the former captain's hands and feet were chained close to an eyebolt in the floor. This was called a stress position, meant to induce moderate discomfort. He was also naked.

"You haven't gotten anything out of him," Steele said. It wasn't a question.

"Not yet," one of the interrogators said.

"And you expect to? Treating him like that? You might as well give him a feather mattress." Steele felt his lip curl in an involuntary sneer.

"We're planning a steady ramp-up of our interrogation's intensity."

"There's no time for a steady ramp-up. We're fighting the Wingers *now*. We need to know their plans, their capabilities, how many ships and troops they have left. We're not historians."

The interrogator gazed up at Steele from where he sat, and his expression made Steele shake his head, which caused his jowls to shift from side to side. *I might as well be speaking a different language.*

"I want some time with him," he said, removing his recent purchase from his pocket. He smiled down at it, remembering the VR training sessions from the last few days. It was amazing, the tutorials you could find on the micronet. And having a concrete goal motivated one to learn quickly.

"Are those brass knuckles?"

"Actual brass knuckles are a rarity, these days. Most of the ones you'll find are knockoffs, made from cheaper metals, and an actual set of brass knuckles will set you back a small fortune.

Their illegality doesn't help matters. But to answer your question: yes. These are brass knuckles."

"You can't use those on him. We have orders from high up not to leave any visible marks. You don't want to screw with the people these orders came from."

"I have President Hurst's ear, you idiot. Open the door." Steele slid his fleshy fingers through the loops. *Quite a snug fit.*

The interrogator continued to look at him, his mouth open slightly. Steele pretended his own stare was a laser, boring through the man's head and melting the wall behind it. "Open the door and unchain his hands. Immediately."

Moving as Steele imagined a zombie would, the interrogator did as instructed.

"Get out," Steele said once the peon had finished unshackling Keyes's hands.

Finally, he was alone with the man he hated most.

"Do you know who I am?" Steele closed the door behind the interrogator, never taking his eyes off Keyes.

The disgraced captain still hadn't stood. He looked up, then replaced his head on the floor.

"Oh, yes. You know. We've never actually met, but you know who I am." Steele began circling the room, well out of Keyes's reach, given the short chain that bound his ankles to the concrete. "And I know you. All too well. You bear the distinction of having cost Darkstream more money than anyone else since its inception. Get up."

Keyes complied, dragging himself slowly to his feet and staring at Steele with his famous blank stare.

Heaving his bulk forward, Steele thrust his fist into the man's face, remembering to compensate for his extended reach. The brass met Keyes's face with a *crack* that sounded like a tooth splitting. The man tripped over the short chain and landed hard on his back.

How satisfying. Steele had no intention of actually trying to extract any information. In fact, the less information they obtained from Keyes, the longer the war with the Wingers would last. And the higher company profits would soar.

"Darkstream is humanity's only hope against the evils lurking inside the cave of space," Steele said, feeling not in the least winded. That was one of the things he'd learned from the training programs. You let the brass knuckles do the work. "Humanity's only hope. That makes you Satan for opposing us. Do you realize that, Keyes? Satan."

No answer.

"Get up."

Keyes rose to his feet and leveled the same bluff-faced stare at Steele. Scarlet leaked from his mouth, dribbling down his dark skin.

The brass knuckles crashed into Keyes's face once more, producing another *crack* and sending him back to the floor.

"I think that was your nose shattering," Steele remarked. "Very doubtful it'll ever heal properly. But I suppose you don't need to look pretty to be a traitor. Just like your old friend Warren Husher. Hmm?"

Keyes stayed silent, but Steele could see from the way his back heaved that he still lived. *What if he dies?* Steele would remind a panicked Hurst of her place, and there would be a cover-up. *Not an issue.*

"Corporations have always lifted humanity from the muck it seems to enjoy wallowing in. I know you have no children, for reasons clear to everyone, I'm sure. But I have a daughter. Her name is Lila. And when you oppose Darkstream, I see that as opposing her. My company is the dominant corporation right now, and without it, humanity would burn before the Ixa, who have the good sense not to hinder their corporations. Get up."

Incredibly, the traitor dragged himself to his feet, his eyes locking onto Steele's once again. Rivers of red flowed over his chin, falling in steady streams to the floor.

"You're probably surprised to hear me acknowledge the Ixan threat. Honestly, it doesn't worry me. The UHF is cutting its teeth on the Wingers after decades of inactivity. If the Ixa come, we will crush them."

Steele threw the brass knuckles into Keyes's forehead, knocking him down once again.

The door flew open, and a pair of guards rushed toward Steele, but not before he could pounce on Keyes and drive the metal knuckles into his face's soft flesh once more. One of the guards caught Steele's arm as he drew it back for another blow, and together they dragged his bulk off of the detainee.

"You have to leave the station," said one of the guards.

Looking back as they escorted him out, Steele noticed the unfocused way Keyes's eyes wandered the room.

A smile crawled across the CEO's face. "Not a problem. I've done what I came here to do."

CHAPTER 50

Within the Hour

Warren Husher woke from troubled dreams to find the cockpit flashing blue. He wondered how long it had been doing that. *I wish it made some sort of sound to go with the blue light.* He supposed the shuttle's Ixan designers hadn't anticipated the pilot sleeping at the console.

When he accepted the transmission, he found his son staring at him from the viewscreen. "Vincent."

"Vin."

"Right. What are you doing here?" *Wow. Couldn't you find something a little more fatherly to say?* After missing most of his son's childhood and all of his adolescence, he had absolutely no clue how to be a parent.

"I was about to ask you the same thing. I, uh..." Vin cleared his throat. "I thought you might have died on Spire."

"Well, I didn't. I mean, obviously. Ek sprung me from jail, and we escaped."

"Where's Ek now?"

"With the radicals."

"Radicals?"

"Yeah, you know. The ones the UHF's been bombing for two decades. They captured us near Thessaly, but Ek makes friends quick, and now she has them eating out of her palm, or fin, or whatever."

Vin nodded, looking a little overwhelmed. "Right. Well, I'm glad to hear she's alive."

"Thanks. Meanwhile, I've been busy securing these ships from the Wingers, for the radicals to fly in the fight against the UHF."

"You're giving warships to people you actually refer to as radicals?"

"Uh, yeah." Warren scratched behind his ear. "It seemed like a good idea at the time." He slapped the console, zooming in on a view of the Larkspur-Yclept darkgate. "Oh, look. The radicals are entering the system now."

"I doubt they're going to get here in time."

Squinting at the viewscreen, Warren said, "Get here in time? How do you mean?"

Vin blinked. "Are you telling me you haven't noticed the giant UHF battle group making a beeline for Pinnacle?"

Expanding the tactical display showed him the battle group in question. "Hmm. Wow. That is a big one."

"Yeah. Your, um, 'radical' friends should probably reverse course, if they don't want to get taken apart by the *Excalibur*. In the meantime, we have some ships to get up and running. Carrow will be here within a few hours."

"That's Carrow commanding those ships? I always thought that guy was an ass."

"You're not wrong. Listen, I doubt I have enough people to crew even one of these ships. Do you think the Wingers can help us out at all?"

"I'll ask. They seem to like me."

"You do that. I'm going to take my people into the missile cruiser, start bringing its systems online."

Vin disappeared from the viewscreen, and Warren flipped through the shuttle's logs, locating the transmission code for the Winger he'd spoken to before. *Got it.* Within a few minutes, the alien appeared on the viewscreen.

"Hey, old buddy," Warren said. "Do you happen to have any Wingers kicking around with experience operating warships?" He wondered briefly how well knowledge of Roostships translated into operating human-made warships. "You see, there's an experienced UHF admiral who seems pretty eager to get here, and he's got a whole whack of firepower, and I doubt that spells good news for either me or your—"

"Yes, human," the Winger said, sounding much more irritated than before. "The crews of three Roostships did manage to escape the destruction of Spire and flee to Pinnacle. But since your species insists on making its warships as complicated as possible, they require much larger crews, and we only have enough Wingers to operate a frigate and a corvette."

That's not good. "Okay. Once you fill up those two ships, will you have any crew left over?"

"We have the Talon pilots, who will join the battle in their fighters. And, yes, we have three-hundred extra crewmembers. But that isn't enough to operate another warship."

"That's perfect! Send them over to the missile cruiser. My son's already over there, working to get it up and running." Warren had no idea whether Vin had enough people with him to adequately make up the difference, but judging by Carrow's proximity, there wasn't time to pursue another line of action. This was it.

"Your son?" The Winger clacked its beak. "What is his name?"

"Vin Husher."

"I thought you said your name was Wisher."

Warren slammed the shuttle's console with his fist. "I can spend an hour bringing you up to speed on human family nomenclature, or we can get these ships operational in time to give the UHF a fight! Which option do you like better?"

"Very well, human! Very well. I'll send over the crewmembers now."

"That's more like it." Warren cut off the transmission and stared at the cockpit's ceiling. "Now what?" he asked it.

With such a short distance, it took him only a few minutes to set a course for the missile cruiser his son had chosen. *I wonder whether he'll let me inside.*

According to the tactical display, Admiral Carrow would be upon them within the hour.

CHAPTER 51

No Better than the Gok

Husher's head pulsed with pain as the tumult inside the *Contest*'s CIC mounted. His slapped-together crew traded frustrated shouts, and a shoving match broke out between a human and a Winger near the Tactical station.

Drawing a deep breath, he squared his shoulders and shouted. "*Hey!*" The clamor broke off immediately, and the tussling pair froze. He pointed at them first. "You should be ashamed of yourselves. If we weren't about to become the UHF's lunch, I'd send you both to the brig immediately. Rest assured, there will be consequences for your misconduct, if we manage to get out of this situation alive. To the rest of you, I expect better than this. I expect the crisp comportment befitting military personnel of any species."

The human who'd been wrestling a Winger stepped away from the alien and dusted himself off. It was one of the *Providence*'s Condor pilots. "Sir, these birds think they can come in here and take over."

"No one's taking over. I'm in command, and it's going to stay that way. But we who have come from the *Providence,* we're mostly marines and Condor pilots. We have no experience actually running a warship. These Wingers do, and so for the most part we will defer to that experience."

The Wingers were well-organized, with detailed knowledge of the crewmembers they'd brought aboard, and so Husher gave a team of them full authority to assign both Wingers and humans to posts according to their abilities. Soon he had a full CIC crew, comprised mostly of Wingers, with the rest of his crew being rapidly sorted out. He went on the shipwide to let it be known that anyone who didn't cooperate with his admin team would face harsh disciplinary measures.

All the while, he kept a close eye on the tactical display, where Admiral Carrow's battle group inched inexorably closer.

He palmed sweat from his brow. With his crew almost sorted out, all that remained was to choose the manner in which he would be defeated.

With just a missile cruiser, a corvette, and a frigate at his disposal, he doubted even a keen tactician like Captain Keyes could have won against a battle group as large as the one that approached. And Husher wasn't Captain Keyes. He didn't have anywhere near the man's battle experience, and he didn't have his talent.

He turned to his sensor operator, a brown-feathered Winger with snowy patches. "How long until the enemy battle group arrives?"

"Just under thirty minutes, Captain."

Now that the *Contest* was operational, Husher knew they needed to get clear of Carrow, in the hopes of joining up with a larger force and then taking on the admiral. But the missile cruiser didn't have engines like the *Providence*. It was just as slow as the approaching UHF ships, and likely slower than some of them. Carrow would not allow his quarry to escape easily. He'd order them harried until they hit a dead end or ran out of the fuel.

If Husher had more time, he would have called a meeting of his officers to develop a plan. But given the present urgency, he opted for thinking out loud.

"UHF ships built after the advent of dark tech were designed to be flown with minimal personnel," he said, suppressing a wince at what he was about to say. "That's providing nothing goes wrong with the ship's systems, and it rules out firing any weapons. But if some of us were willing to shuttle over to the empty ships and fly them on collision courses with Carrow's..."

Chief Taylor, one of the few humans in the CIC, spoke up from the Nav station. "Sir, you'd be ordering good people to their deaths. And it would make us no better than the Gok."

"I'm not *ordering* anyone to go on this mission," Husher said. "I'm asking for volunteers." He inhaled deeply, and took care not to let his breath come out as a sigh. "It's the only way I can see to preserve the assets we've just acquired."

"My species has already become no better than the Gok," said the Winger at the Tactical console. "After the Fins' extermination, we have lost our way. We are eager to throw ourselves between the enemy's teeth, even if it only causes them a toothache.

Many of our Talon pilots are also trained as navigation adjutants. I can easily find volunteers for the mission you propose, Captain."

Husher swallowed, hard. "Do it. Now. And don't bother clearing them with me. As soon as you have your volunteers, tell them to double-time it to the shuttle bay."

"Yes, sir."

Within fifteen minutes, four shuttles had departed the *Contest*, as well as three each from the frigate and the corvette. Ten shuttles carrying ten Wingers, all of them intent on using the ten remaining derelict ships to inflict as much damage as possible on Carrow's battle group.

"We're getting a transmission request from the *Excalibur*, sir," the Coms officer said.

Husher felt the hair on the back of his neck stir. *Just what I need.* "Put it on the screen."

Admiral Carrow's pinched countenance appeared, wearing its customary sneer. "Husher. How low you've fallen."

"Make it snappy, Carrow. I'm busy."

"Yes, I expect you are. I imagine a man becomes rather preoccupied in the moments before he is brought to justice."

"I wouldn't know. Actually, you're the first person I'd ask for insight on that."

"Irrational as ever. You're reminding me of the way you flushed your military career down the head, even after you were given your own command at such a young age." Carrow chuckled. "It's too bad you're not as lucky as Keyes. If you were, your crew would mutiny and hand you over to me. Unfortunately, this encounter will likely end with your death."

I'm done with this. Husher gestured at his Coms officer to terminate the transmission. As he did, two of the derelict destroyers began moving toward Carrow's flagship. Husher hadn't had enough crew to properly operate them, but if they could make it to the opposing battle group they'd do considerable damage.

"Tactical, I want six Banshees fired at each opposing ship, with the exception of the *Excalibur*. Take care not to hit the friendly ships moving toward their targets, and alert all Talon pilots that missiles will fly soon."

His idea involved keeping the rest of the enemy battle group busy, giving the Wingers in the derelict ships an opportunity to disable or even destroy the flagship. Husher wanted that outcome badly, but he doubted he'd get it. Either way, he'd given Carrow a lot to deal with.

Having already set his Nav officer to calculating a retreat vector, he now got on the fleetwide to order it executed. "Captains of the *Stevenson* and the *Active*, I've transmitted a course to your Nav officers, which I—"

He broke off as something on the tactical display caught his eye. The *Active*, the corvette, had broken formation and was heading toward the enemy under full power.

"*Active*, report! What are you doing?"

"It's as I said." The Tactical officer's voice was tinged with sadness. "The Wingers are blinded by vengeance. We have lost our way."

Husher felt something in his chest clench. *What am I doing, here? What's the point of any of this?*

"Captain?" his Nav officer said.

"Maintain course," he said, barely able to grunt the words out. On the tactical display, Carrow's battle group had already begun the process of obliterating the *Active*.

Husher stood, clawing at the collar of his uniform. His UHF uniform, which he had no right to wear. Not anymore.

I need to get out. Who do I give the command to? Who...

He didn't have it in him to remain long enough to figure it out. The knowledge that the war was lost, that humanity was truly doomed, bore down on him like a collapsing wall.

"Figure out who ranks highest," he rasped. "Whoever that is, they have the command."

Husher staggered out of the CIC.

CHAPTER 52

Fin Candor

"Captain, Juktas is under attack by Gok," Vaghn's sensor operator said the moment they transitioned into the Yclept System.

"Bring up a tactical display on the main screen," Vaghn said, unable to keep her fatigue out of her voice. *Is there no end to this parade of disasters?* She'd had no idea Gok had progressed this far into the Bastion Sector.

Then again, the crew of the *Firedrake* hadn't had much time for intelligence gathering. It had taken everything they had just to stay ahead of Admiral Carrow.

At least that danger had been lifted, for now anyway. Carrow had broken away from the chase for some reason, leaving Vaghn with little option but to flee into Yclept in the hopes of finding refuge.

She squinted at the vicious conflict over Juktas, between two Gok carriers and a swarm of Falcons. *That's probably all the refuge you're going to get,* she told herself.

"Set a course for Juktas and bring engines to full. Those Falcons are done for if they don't get some backup soon, and it looks like we're it."

Thankfully, Juktas and the Yclept-Larkspur darkgate were almost as close to each other as their orbits ever brought them, and it took less than two hours for the *Firedrake* to get close enough to engage.

"Let's target the carriers themselves first," Vaghn said. "The Falcons don't have a hope of taking them on, not with all those Gok fighters dogging them. I want to focus our primary laser on the closest one, and follow up with a healthy helping of Banshees, if necessary."

As she'd expected, the Gok warship didn't seem much interested in anything resembling an evasive maneuver. Its only response to the *Firedrake*'s laser was to point its main guns at her, one of which had been melted down by laser fire. The carrier managed one volley of kinetic impactors before Vaghn's Banshees arrived and turned it into space junk.

With the first carrier gone, and the remaining one distracted by the beating being administered by the *Firedrake*, the pressure on the Falcons lessened, allowing them to redouble their efforts against the enemy fighters. Nine Gok pilots lost their lives in the span of four minutes, and after that the Falcons had enough leeway to devote some of their number to helping Vaghn destroy the second enemy warship.

It would have been a rout, except for the Gok's refusal to retreat. Their willingness to fight to the death every time meant defeating them took a heavy toll on any force.

So it was with the Falcons and the *Firedrake*. The colony's defenders lost nearly a third of their remaining force, and Vaghn's corvette sustained heavy damage all along its port side. She ordered damage control teams to the affected areas and assigned a search party to look for the trio of crewmembers unaccounted for following the battle.

Other than that, she waited. Ever since the First Galactic War, the media had cast anyone piloting a Falcon as a radical. Whether that was accurate or not, Vaghn wanted her position at the negotiating table to be as strong as possible. That meant waiting for them to contact her.

"A transmission request is coming through from the planet's surface," her Coms officer said.

Vaghn gave a satisfied nod. "Accept and put it on-screen."

The tactical display disappeared from *Firedrake*'s viewscreen, replaced by a view of a massive conference table surrounded by a motley assortment of characters. But Vaghn's gaze was riveted by the figure sitting at the head of that table.

It was a Fin. A living Fin, with no water to be seen, a situation apparently enabled by the black, skintight bodysuit it wore.

And then it spoke. "Hello, Captain Vaghn."

"Uh...hi. How do you know...?" She cleared her throat.

"My associates have extensive intelligence on UHF warships and the officers that captain them. That is how I know your identity."

"I see."

"Making my acquaintance is normally an experience that inspires no end of curiosity. And while my species was known for encouraging intelligent inquiry, my associates and I consider time to be of the essence. The men and women you see around this table form a coalition of Bastion Sector warlords who have set aside their differences and disputes to unite and oppose the UHF. I am given to understand that you have also fallen into disfavor with your Fleet."

For a bunch of warlords, those around the table were certainly well-behaved. If she didn't know better, Vaghn would have said the Fin intimidated them. "And how do you know that?"

"I have surmised it. Anyone can plainly see that fighting Gok is far from current UHF policy. Since you have just aided us in defeating two Gok warships, it is exceedingly likely that you have gone rogue. In light of that fact, I would like to invite you to join our effort. You would be a great asset to it, given your evident battle prowess, your long military experience, and your knowledge of the UHF. A human leader would also prove much more palatable to my associates here, who have already begun to chafe under the weight of my influence."

A few of the men and women sitting near the Fin stirred in their seats, accompanied by a flurry of coughing and throat-clearing. Two of them exchanged glances, both blushing scarlet.

Obviously they still haven't grown accustomed to Fin candor.

"Despite their growing resentment, they still tend to yield to my logic. I will recommend to my associate Thresh, who you see to my right, that he make you his battle commander. I can assure you that once I take the time to impress upon him the significance of your pedigree and skill, along with the probable outcome of ignoring my advice, he will offer you the position.

And for that reason, I feel I can safely breach the usual protocol and simply offer it to you myself."

Vaghn felt pretty sure that no one was as surprised as she was to find her head bobbing up and down in acquiescence. "Yeah. Okay. Sure." She squeezed her eyes shut, and then returned to squinting at the viewscreen. "I guess fighting the UHF with you lot is better than getting hunted down by them on our own."

"I am inclined to agree," the Fin said.

CHAPTER 53

Automaton

Husher's com beeped, and he raised his head from the wardroom's table just enough to read the report displayed there, from his sensor operator.

Admiral Carrow's battle group has destroyed the warships piloted by Wingers. Only one succeeded in colliding with an enemy ship. The target was the Meade, *a destroyer, which took heavy damage but remains operational. The enemy ships are now attacking Pinnacle, and all other UHF warships in the Larkspur System appear to be heading toward that colony.*

Husher replaced his head on the table. If he had to guess, Carrow had ordered the UHF to regroup at Pinnacle for a final sweep of the Bastion Sector. Once the Wingers were put down, they'd no doubt choose to go after the Gok. *The more war the better, right?* They'd strayed so far from the Fleet's founding principle of only fighting in self-defense that preparing to fight the Ixa didn't even seem to factor into their calculus.

Ever since losing the *Firedrake*, Husher had yearned for another command. Now he finally had one, and he'd failed utterly.

Carrow had succeeded in showing him exactly how meaningless his efforts truly were.

It surprised him to find he felt more displaced now than he had when Command ordered him to leave the *Firedrake*, consigning him to the *Providence*. He'd come to consider the latter ship a true home. And it had been taken from him.

But what did it matter? *I'm bellyaching about having my feelings hurt while my entire species teeters on the brink of oblivion.*

Husher could not see the path forward for humanity. How could he possibly turn the tide against the UHF? He didn't have access to the micronet, and so he had no way of knowing whether Bernard's movement against Hurst was succeeding, but he had to assume it wasn't. The UHF was clearly still under the sway of Darkstream.

The wardroom door opened, and Husher experienced a burst of shame at his dejected posture. That made him sit up straight, and when he did, he saw that the visitor was his father.

"You're not supposed to be in here," Husher said. He hadn't meant it to sound friendly, but even he was surprised at the complete lack of warmth in his voice.

Warren Husher ignored him, choosing instead to take the seat directly opposite his son. His creased face hardened. "What the hell are you planning to do?"

"Excuse me?"

"I asked what your next move is. Because if it's sit in here and mope, then I guess our species really does deserve to die. Considering you're the best person it could find to lead the resistance."

Husher shook his head. "I don't lead the resistance."

"Who does, then?"

"I don't know."

Warren leaned closer. "I'll tell you who. It's whoever has the balls to stand up and get the job done. I'm going to ask again: what's your next move?"

"Continue fighting the UHF, I guess. Keep fighting them, and likely die in the process."

"Why in Sol would you want to do that?"

"Because the Wingers are in danger of extinction. And because stopping the UHF would give humanity the best chance of facing the Ixa."

"I asked why you want to do it. You. Vin Husher."

"I *don't* want to do it. But that doesn't matter. It's the right thing to do."

"Is it? Tell me, then—what do you actually *want* to do?"

Husher met his father's eyes for a long time. At last, he said, "I want to get the *Providence* back. And I want to bust Captain Keyes out of that hellhole."

Warren nodded. "Indeed."

"But being a good soldier isn't about what I want. It's about having principles that serve humanity and abiding by those principles."

His father let out a long sigh. "Principles are fine things, son. Fine things. But I think you're getting mixed up in your thinking. It sounds to me like a long time ago, you tried to program yourself to be a good person, and now you force yourself to live by that programming, without ever checking over the code. Like some sort of automaton."

"What are you talking about?"

"You're a human being, Vin. You're not a robot. Principles are great, but it's compassion, true compassion, that will lead humanity forward. And that doesn't have to mean abandoning your principles. It just means you don't sacrifice the people you care about to them." His father pointed at him. "In fact, the principle of banding together as people, of looking after each other, is a principle superior to every other."

Warren Husher stood from the table and headed for the wardroom's exit. He opened the hatch, and Husher listened for it to close again. But it didn't, just yet.

"I know you've programmed yourself to hate me, too," Warren said. "I understand it. You've had a rough life, and so has your mother. But I had no control over that. All I'm asking is that you have another glance at that code, too."

The hatch slammed shut, almost making Husher start. He hadn't expected it to be so loud.

He gave himself ten more minutes to sit at the wardroom table and stare at its gleaming metal surface. Then he rose slowly to his feet.

He entered the CIC three minutes later and forced himself to sit in the Captain's chair. His body didn't want to obey the orders he was giving it, but that was okay. Orders didn't need to be liked. So long as they were obeyed.

"Set a course for the Larkspur-Caprice darkgate," Husher said, and a sudden silence fell. The two other humans in the CIC looked at him wearing expressions of hope. Tightly restrained hope, but hope nonetheless.

"We're going to the Vermillion Shipyards," he said. "We're getting the *Providence* back."

CHAPTER 54

In the Way that She Cried

Ek left Juktas in an old combat shuttle, surrounded by a flock of Falcons, feeling confident that Thresh would follow her advice to continue recruiting warlords throughout the Bastion Sector. He had already put Captain Vaghn in charge of their forces, as Ek had recommended.

However, though her logic was undeniable, the warlords' compliance with it had grown more and more grudging. And that made it *most* logical for her to leave.

Without her, the warlords' path forward would cease to be the optimal one. They would make mistakes. A lot of mistakes.

But it *would* be a path forward, and for Ek to remain and continue trying to influence it would almost certainly result in them reversing course out of pride and stubbornness. That was the problem with even the best-intentioned leaders. They never knew when to leave well enough alone.

Ek did know. Besides, she had other work to do.

During the journey, she vomited twice into the shuttle's waste disposal unit, and the second time, she tripped on her return to the cockpit, stumbling into the bulkhead, head spinning. Though her suit kept her firmly anchored to the Majorana-laced deck, her body lacked Ocharium nanites, and it remained in constant freefall whenever she was in space. The harmful effects of that were finally catching up to her, it seemed.

The warning words of the Speakers for the Enclave echoed through her head, but she willed them away. *There is no time for that.* She forced herself back to her feet and marched into the cockpit.

The Bastion Sector insurgents had no access to carriers, or to support ships of any kind. For each mission, they had to carry with them whatever fuel and supplies they needed.

She knew the people with her were loyal, because she had asked them to embark on a mission that would take them past the point of no return. Past the point where they would have enough fuel to return to Juktas. She had asked, and they had agreed. So there was that.

The Fins had always refused to play the imperialist games that dominated galactic politics, and they had always counseled the Wingers against war, except when it was strictly necessary for their survival, as with the First Galactic War.

If the Fins could see what Ek was about to do, they would condemn her. They would probably disown her.

But the others were dead, and Ek was alive. If the Fins were anything, anymore, it was whatever she had become.

The Falcons took her to the center of the Larkspur System, as close to its sun as they could safely get. And when they arrived, Ek began her broadcast to every Winger in the system. To ensure every Winger heard her, she did not encrypt the message.

Nor did she record it. She knew what she wanted to say, and so there was no need for a redo. Ek spoke, and her words transmitted as soon as they were spoken.

"My beloved Wingers. You think the Fins are gone, and you rage against the void. You think the Fins are gone, but you are wrong. One of your sisters still lives, and her name is Ek."

She stared at the dark eye that recorded her image and words, flinging them out into space for those she loved to hear. For a long moment, she paused, and for her, at least, the silence was pregnant with meaning and emotion.

When Ek spoke again, she did something she rarely ever did. She spoke without thinking, instead letting feeling give birth to her speech. "Our species grew up together under the stars. The Fins lived because you allowed us to, and in return we used our talents to elevate you until you became one of the galaxy's most noble peoples. I see that war and terror has cast you low, and you see it, too. It is obvious to us both. But I believe you are missing one important point. Your nobility never left you. It remains inside, waiting for you to acknowledge it. I await that, too."

Ek spread her arms, calling to the Wingers with her eyes. With her soul. "If our shared childhood means anything to you, if our species' closeness ever meant anything at all, you will abandon this folly. And you will come to me. Join me at this system's heart. Join me, and together we will form the largest united force of Wingers the galaxy has ever known.

"Join me, and for the first time, a Fin will use her intellect and her perception to make war."

Ek cut off the transmission, and as soon as she did, she experienced another first. For the first time since the destruction of Spire, she felt something other than grief. She felt fear.

It took seven minutes for sensor data to reach her from the nearest Roostship. No message accompanied the data. The Wingers aboard the ship remained completely silent.

But their actions said more than enough. The Roostship broke from its pursuit of a Gok battle group and turned toward her.

The next Roostship also turned, the moment its Wingers heard her message. And the next Roostship. And the next.

A half hour later, her message had reached every Winger in the system. They were coming. All of them.

Ek's entire body trembled soundlessly, in the way that Fins cried. In the way that *she* cried.

CHAPTER 55

Calamity

Teth didn't like spending time among the other Ixa, who he mostly referred to as "useful fools," and so instead he took Ochrim cruising from system to system. True to his word about Ochrim not being made a prisoner, Teth gave his brother the option to go wherever he liked, including back to the humans. "Not that it would go very well for you, now," he'd said.

Ochrim remained. He shared Teth's disdain for their kind, and in return, their brethren treated the sons of Baxa with immense suspicion. Most Ixa now viewed Baxa as one might view a rabid wolf—a powerful ally, provided it can be controlled. But controlling it required incredible vigilance, and much of that caution transferred over to the Ixa's treatment of Teth and Ochrim.

And as his brother said, there was nowhere else for Ochrim to go.

"Soon enough, we'll have to return to my destroyer," Teth said. "Father wants every available warship assigned to cleaning up whatever remains of the aliens, once they've finished tearing each other apart."

Although Teth would never admit it, Ochrim could tell his brother yearned to return to Baxa, who, in his new form, expressed little interest in speaking with his sons. *It isn't as though he lacks the time.* No, Baxa was unique in his unlimited supply of that, with his ability to manufacture time from whole cloth, for whatever purpose he wished.

Ochrim did not consider Baxa his father anymore, not since his true designs had become clear, and certainly not in the tyrant's new form. For a short time, Ochrim had harbored the hope of changing Baxa, of working together to build a brighter future. One in which the Ixa still dominated out of necessity, but also one that didn't entail the extermination of every other species. The flame of that hope had sputtered out decades ago, and Ochrim had done everything he could to forget he had a father.

At least Teth's ship was comfortable. Baxa had custom-designed it for him, probably to keep his progeny out of the way. The ship sported a full suite of the new weaponry the Ixa had developed in secret since the First Galactic War, and it required no accompanying support ship. Teth had named it the *Watchman.* It also featured a spacious central area devoted to observation and reconnaissance, activities performed in total luxury.

Ochrim reclined on a couch made from a material invented by Baxa in one of his idle moments. Initially, sitting on it felt like lowering yourself into a puddle of water, which quickly tightened to support the sitter with maximum comfort. No cushions or other such implements were needed. In fact, they would almost certainly diminish the experience. It felt odd to think of a couch as a feat of engineering, but that was what it was.

"Today is a momentous day," Teth said from where he stood near the central display. "Historic."

The display appeared as a screen centered on you, no matter where you stood in the observation chamber. Currently, it showed a magnified view of the Auslaut System, which contained two major human colonies. The system was also a major connector on the path between human and Ixan space. Without its existence, the journey between them would be long and arduous.

"Do you remember the verse that corresponds to today's event?"

Ochrim studied his scale-covered fingers, spread out before him. Even they bore the white lines of age. Time had taken a much greater toll on him than it had on his brother, and he felt tired, so tired. Only scraps of sleep were available to him, these days.

"Unfortunately," he said.

"Recite it for me."

With a sigh, Ochrim did. "*Out of darkness comes calamity, the star-breaker. Look, ye doomed, to the path ahead. It is gone, and so goes your hope.*"

"Father considers it one of the most auspicious prophecies. Did you know that?"

"No." Ochrim made a point of not knowing such things.

"It's auspicious, but even so, today will motivate the enemy to make a study of the galaxy's network of dark energy. That will quickly lead to their ability to anticipate the supernovas. Father calls that a variable that must be closely monitored."

"A variable? There's room in the Prophecies for variables?"

"Of course not. All will unfold exactly as foretold, provided we continue to cultivate events carefully."

"And what does that entail?"

"We must achieve total victory within five years. But it won't be an issue. Father expects humanity's defeat inside one year."

Ochrim nodded, rubbing the rims of his facial depressions, the twin craters that housed his eyes. He knew the Ixa would prevail, and that it was the optimal outcome for the universe, however disastrous. But he could also see a way victory would take longer than a year. "Have the humans made any further contact with the Kaithe?"

"They have not. The Prophecies have succeeded in instilling sufficient suspicion of the children." Teth's gaze was suddenly riveted to the central display, and Ochrim followed it. "It's beginning."

They watched as the Auslaut System's sun ballooned outward. Unlike typical supernovas, those caused by disturbances in the dark energy network gave no advance warning. A handful of ships would likely escape the system via darkgate, racing ahead of the shockwave, but the vast majority of the population would perish over the next few hours.

CHAPTER 56

It Is Time

Bernard sat on her cabin's bed and used her com to thumb through page after page of information on the Auslaut System, complete with photos: some of important moments from its history, some of regular civilians going about their daily routines, enjoying the system's beautiful scenery, celebrating its holidays. On the micronet, it was as though Auslaut still existed, right down to social posts from its occupants mere hours ago.

She'd never visited Auslaut, except to pass through. *Always so preoccupied with work.* Now she was filled with a drive to visit all of the lands humanity had expanded into. But of course she would feel that way now, when it seemed very likely that those lands would soon vanish forever.

A knock on the hatch of her cabin. "Come in," Bernard called.

The hatch opened to reveal Corporal Simpson, who crossed the tiny cabin and lowered herself onto the bed, next to Bernard. "We just entered Caprice."

"Okay. Are the crew ready for me?"

"Yes."

Bernard drew in a long breath. "All right." Now that they had only two more darkgates to transition through, the risk of her uploading a message to the micronet was lessened. The cargo ship's captain feared that someone would identify his ship from the video, but she'd assured him she would show a green screen she'd brought for the purpose and nothing else.

It would have been better to wait until they'd transitioned through the final darkgate, into Sol. But the supernova had accelerated her schedule.

Before standing, Bernard asked, "What's the mood on the micronet?"

"Terrified. After Auslaut, a large part of the public is convinced the Prophecies are real and they're unfolding right now. And since the Prophecies predict the downfall of humanity..."

Bernard nodded.

"There's a lot of speculation," Simpson said. "People afraid of the worst. Which is fair enough, I guess, but the theories get pretty wild. Either way, with Auslaut gone, the Coreopsis System is totally cut off from us. The only way for them to reach us is through the Ixan home system." Simpson stared at the deck for a moment. "Anyway. The good news is that the revolution gauge jumped up to fourteen percent."

It wasn't enough. *Though it is doubled.* "Let's see whether we can't get it a little higher."

Bernard rose to her feet, and so did Simpson. Together, they left the cabin and walked to the cargo hold, where the video would be recorded. There, they found Chief Ralston and the seven veterans he'd managed to assemble before leaving Zakros, setting up a barricade of boxes and suitcases and blankets, meant to muffle the sound from Bernard's video and mask the fact that they were in a spacious cargo hold.

The captain and crew had treated their secret guests with great respect, which was remarkable in the face of their paranoia. *That's what greatness means. Acting in accordance with your principles, even while terrified.*

Several crew members had given up their cabins for their guests, and the captain had even offered his own to Bernard, though she'd declined that.

"All right," Ralston said. "That's as good as it's going to get."

Bernard sat on the stool that had been set up for her. Sweeping her bangs out of her eyes, she took another deep breath.

"We're rolling," said the veteran operating the camera.

Bernard leveled her eyes at it. "A few short weeks ago, we had an election in which you were given a choice that wasn't really a choice at all. It was a choice between bad and worse, and at the time it was difficult for the people of the Commonwealth to tell which one was worse. Well, we have more information today, and it looks like it was worse that won by the slimmest margin of votes in galactic history."

Bernard held up her hand, pointing at the air just above and to the right of the camera. "Sonya Hurst lost her legitimacy as president the day she ordered civilian protesters killed and then made a flimsy effort to cover it up. But even before that, we had plenty of clues as to what a disgrace she would be. She campaigned on a promise to reduce war, but instead, she did a complete one-eighty on the very day she was elected. Now, we're at war with two alien species, with a third one to be added soon. I want to be very clear: the Ixa are coming. Humanity is currently behaving exactly as the Ixa want us to, but for some reason our government is too blind to see it.

"On top of that, our government insists on continued use of a technology that has been found to cause stars to explode in catastrophes that have already killed billions of our people. Yes, their corporate-funded scientists say that dark tech isn't causing the supernovas, but the majority of scientists, who aren't funded by Darkstream, say that it is.

"Why is the government so blind? Why is it attacking our allies when we should be preparing for the largest fight in human history? Why were you given a choice between bad and worse in the presidential election? I'll tell you why. Our system is broken. Elections are broken, because of our corrupt campaign finance system, which undermines our democracy, and which allows corporations and billionaires to pour in huge sums of money to elect the candidates of their choice. And aligned with that system is a rigged economy, which is designed to funnel money out of your hands and into the hands of interplanetary corporations like Darkstream.

"It is time to take our government back. It is time to take our democracy back. We will demand the resignation of Sonya Hurst, who took power under a system tainted by corporate money, and we will hold a new election, funded only by you, the people. We will elect a candidate that the people actually want. And then we will dedicate ourselves to pulling back from the cliff we are currently barreling toward at breakneck speed. Thank you."

She nodded at the veteran holding the camera, who shut it off. Then she looked at Simpson, who was wearing a smile that stretched across her face.

"How was that, Trish?"

"That was good, Sandy. That was good."

CHAPTER 57

Ignition

Stress ruled Police Sergeant Doucet's life. Every morning, he woke up to find himself inside the temporary barracks they'd set up a short drive from the Martian Ocharium refinery, and every time he remembered where he was, he quietly cursed.

Today was no different, and as he pulled on his uniform, which he'd carefully ironed the night before, the curse echoed through his skull, bouncing off the walls of his cranium.

He ironed the uniform out of habit more than anything else, now, considering his winter gear went right over it and didn't come off until he turned in for the night. *I have no idea how the protesters are lasting.* True, they'd accumulated more clothing and equipment since their demonstration had begun, but their numbers kept growing, leaving them in constant short supply of everything. To increase that pressure, Doucet had ordered the road to the nearest town blocked off, citing safety and security reasons, and effectively forcing the demonstrators to travel three times as far for supplies and medical attention.

The protesters certainly had nowhere near the resources the police and security forces had. *We'll starve them out. We have to.*

On the drive to the refinery, he passed two news vans. The big news shows had finally started covering the protests. Doucet supposed that if they didn't, they'd lose viewers. Once something like this got big enough, you couldn't deny it, so he understood why the big shows had to cover it. *Doesn't mean I have to like it.*

When he reached the site, he found the protesters strung across the road, physically blocking access to the refinery. Just as they had been for the last two days.

That frustrated him to no end, and it was happening everywhere, with protesters disrupting Ocharium mining operations and also demonstrating outside every known Darkstream facility there was. *The stock market's going to take a dive.* Darkstream's stock was already taking a serious beating.

Doucet's superiors weren't taking it very well. He figured they were getting leaned on pretty heavily from above, and that meant even more weight on Doucet's shoulders. The chief of his police department called him twice a day now, demanding to know what he'd done recently to curtail the protests. But there was nothing he could do. There didn't seem to be any stopping them. Even blowing off that girl's arm had only galvanized them.

As he stepped out of his cruiser, his com beeped shrilly, like a smoke alarm. He took it out and saw that it was the chief. Gritting his teeth, he answered. "Doucet here."

"Doucet. There's been a change in policy."

"Policy, Chief?" A tiny hope began to take shape within him, a hope that he wasn't about to get chewed out for the tenth time this week.

"Public policy. Hurst and her party just rammed some new legislation through the Galactic Congress that removes the legal consequences of accidentally killing someone with a vehicle."

Doucet squeezed his eyes shut, thinking hard. Maybe the chief's words did make sense, and he was just too tired to piece together their relevance for the current situation. "So they legalized vehicular manslaughter?"

"Exactly."

"Uh...that's interesting, Chief. But what does it have to do with the protests?"

"I need you to listen very carefully. If someone were to *accidentally* kill a protester with a vehicle—a protester blocking a road to an Ocharium refinery, say—the driver of the vehicle would not face any consequences. The bill actually gives an example. It says here, if a driver were to 'accidentally depress the accelerator instead of the brake, that driver would be exempt from liability.' Am I getting any clearer, Doucet?"

Wiping his nose with the back of his hand, Doucet paused. "I think so," he said after several moments.

"Now, in this hypothetical situation, it would look very bad to the public if a police officer hypothetically did this. So I wouldn't want that. But if a factory worker were to do it, or another private citizen, that would be another story. And it would also do a lot of good, because the protesters would soon start to realize how unsafe it is to demonstrate in the middle of a road. In fact, I think we'd start seeing a lot less protesting overall. Don't you?"

"Yes, sir."

"Good. It's time for that protest to start fizzling, Doucet. I want results. Do you understand me?"

"Yes, sir."

"Excellent. Now get to work."

Doucet's boots felt like they were lined with lead as he approached the group of refinery workers waiting to see whether they would be able to get into work today. When he told them about Hurst's new law, none of them seemed very responsive. Doucet tried to talk in the same way the chief had, not actually asking anyone to do anything, but pointing things in the same general direction. All he got in return were set jaws and sullen stares.

In the end, they had to get a Darkstream Security employee to pose as a refinery worker and try to drive a truck through. When the protesters closed around his truck, linking hands, the employee pretended to panic, and the truck surged forward, right over a stocky man with streaks of gray shooting through his hair.

As the truck accelerated toward the safety of the refinery, Doucet watched as the downed man's left hand scrabbled weakly at the asphalt. He still appeared to be alive, but Doucet prayed for him to die.

Otherwise, he knew they'd have to do it again.

CHAPTER 58

A Fin at War

E k stepped onto the bridge of the Roostship from which she would command her growing fleet, her metal leg meeting the deck with a dull *clank*. Every Winger leapt from their seats and turned to her, saluting.

"Welcome, Flockhead Ek," Wingleader Ty, the captain, said. "I cede command of this Roostship to you."

That gave her a moment's pause. *Flockhead*. She supposed that was what she was, now.

"Thank you, Wingleader," she said. "But I ask that you remain by my side. While I feel reasonably confident in my ability to anticipate the enemy's strategy, my knowledge of this ship's capabilities pales beside yours."

"Yes, Honored One—I mean, Flockhead. If it suits you, I'll stay on as XO, and my current XO will enter the rotation of strategic adjutants."

"That will be fine." Ek settled into the Captain's chair and began studying the tactical display, which had been expanded to show the entire Larkspur System.

The UHF fleet had finished regrouping at Pinnacle, and as Ek had expected, they were rushing toward the center of the system. Reading their intentions did not require the perception of a Fin: they aimed to neutralize the growing Winger force before it became a meaningful threat.

But Ek did not stop at simply interpreting the enemy's objectives. Next, she considered what Carrow likely perceived about her own intentions.

Her message to the Wingers had been unencrypted, and so he would not only know that her reinforcements were on the way but also that, lacking the instantaneous communication enabled by dark tech, she was forced to linger at the center of the system to make sure those reinforcements reached her. She could not communicate a new destination to Wingers on their way from other Bastion Sector systems. And they would be on their way, once her message was relayed to them. So she needed to hold firm.

What else might Carrow anticipate? His current fleet, though comprised of dozens of battle groups totaling nearly five hundred ships, did not represent the UHF's full might. Over four hundred Fleet ships would be on their way from connecting systems, where they had been attacking Winger colonies. They would arrive soon, and almost certainly earlier than the Winger ships would.

With such an overwhelming force, Carrow likely felt confident, and understandably so. As a result, there were several factors he was probably failing to consider. Ek considered it reasonable to assume that the admiral saw only the battle before him: the relatively tiny Winger force at the system's center, growing steadily but not fast enough. Waiting to be flattened with a single hammer blow.

As Carrow's fleet screamed toward them and Ek's bridge crew began exhibiting signs of nervousness, likely due to her inaction, she stretched her strategic calculus to admit several other factors.

What of possible Gok involvement? That could not be counted on. Even if she could draw the Gok into the battle somehow, her Roostships stood just as great a chance of getting targeted by them as the UHF warships.

What of the Providence? Captain Keyes was captured, and the *Providence* waited in the Vermillion Shipyards to be dismantled. That news had reached her on Juktas.

And what of Captain Keyes's actions after the destruction of Spire but prior to his capture? Interesting. She quickly took stock of the individuals she knew to be aboard the *Providence* during that period, keeping that list in mind as she progressed with her thinking.

What of the Tumbra? It was absurd on the face of it. Even if they had wanted to contribute, Tumbra knew nothing of battle.

But they are well-versed in bookkeeping. They do not merely record the comings and goings of ships through darkgates, but also the ever-changing galactic balance of power. And what gets tracked gets managed.

She had learned much during her frequent visits to coffee stations, where every Tumbran she had met had demonstrated a willingness to tell her everything she cared to know. They had evidently cherished the opportunity to converse with a Fin, and they had sensed that she appreciated the value of discretion.

Wingleader Ty spoke, cutting into her thoughts. "Flockhead? I don't meant to question you, but the enemy ships will arrive in under two hours, and we haven't begun any preparations." He clacked his beak.

Ek could tell her presence had kindled a flame of hope inside the Wingers, but they dared not feed that flame too much fuel. From his body language, the wingleader clearly believed she had frozen at the sight of such an overwhelming enemy force.

"I require more time for thought," she said. "I would appreciate no further interruptions. If I must, I will seek seclusion to avoid them, but I would rather remain here, where I have immediate access to all relevant data and can dispense orders the moment I arrive at them."

"Yes, ma'am. Of course."

And what of the resistance against the current government of the human Commonwealth? Would it enjoy meaningful success, and if so, could that be leveraged in any way?

And again, the Tumbra... Surely they could see that galactic power was headed for a serious imbalance, in the form of the Ixa eradicating all other life, if events continued along their present course. Though not well-versed in military matters, the Tumbra had developed subtle ways of influencing power dynamics. Right now, human governance clearly needed a historic shift, and soon. She rated it as fairly probable that a Tumbran would find a way to help effect that shift, and sooner than anyone thought.

What else? There was Commander Vaghn and the warlords, who would likely come to Ek's aid, if their mettle was anywhere near as strong as she had judged. But she had no idea how long they would take to arrive.

And then there were non-military Wingers. Pirates. Reports abounded of their departure en masse from Pirate's Path, and if they had continued to spread, taking advantage of the unrest, there was little chance they would come to her aid. But if they had reversed course for any reason...

She reviewed all of the knowledge at her disposal in light of this new question. Captain Keyes's flight through the stars, the composition of his crew, the amount of resistance the pirates were likely to face from Tumbra who monitored the darkgates, widespread Winger resentment of the UHF...

Ek became conscious that the level of noise in the bridge had increased. Her crew shifted nervously in their seats, rustling their feathers, whispering to each other. A glance at the tactical display told her that the nearest enemy ships were a little over an hour away.

Finally, there were the Kaithe. *Are they likely to emerge from their long period of isolation?* Ek thought not. She was not certain a reason existed that would motivate them to do so. She also knew Captain Keyes did not trust the Kaithe, after they directed him to Ochrim, who had proceeded to betray humanity in the most heinous of ways.

"I have arrived at my first order."

A small amount of tension leaked out of Ty's otherwise stiff wings, and he turned his enormous black orbs toward her. "Yes? What is it, Flockhead Ek?"

"It is worthwhile for us to stall for time."

"Oh? Um, how do you propose we do that?"

"Fifteen minutes before Admiral Carrow reaches laser range, I would like the navigation adjutant to bring us about and then hard to port, in order to avoid any kinetic impactors the enemy has sent our way. Relay the same evasive maneuver to all other ships in our fleet. Following that, chart a swift course around the nearest side of the star, a course that encourages the enemy to keep to one side of it, without splitting its forces. And so it should also put considerable distance between us and the sun, to allay any fears the admiral has about us trying to loop back around it."

"Yes, ma'am."

Her crew executed the orders with an efficiency borne of long experience. Behind them, Admiral Carrow acted exactly as she expected. To him, her actions would look like a feint, like she wanted to portray to him that she was trying to escape, when he knew well that she had to remain at the star.

Of course, it would look like a poor feint. And her maneuver did not even leave open the opportunity to veer back around the star and buy time that way. Carrow would chalk it up to her lack of military experience.

His confidence proclaimed itself in the way his fleet gave chase in a thin convoy around the star, battle group after battle group, all following the most efficient intercept course possible.

Having accelerated all the way from Pinnacle, the enemy's momentum was much greater than that of the Roostships, and so they would quickly close the gap.

"We are receiving a transmission request from the flagship *Excalibur*," the communications adjutant said.

"Send a fleetwide order to spread out perpendicular to the enemy's trajectory, come fully about, and fire engines at full until our momentum has been arrested," Ek told the navigation adjutant.

"Yes, ma'am."

Admiral Carrow appeared on the screen. "A Fin admiral," he said. "Now I've seen it all. That was quite a message you sent to your bird friends, fish."

"Admiral Carrow, I have realized how low our chances are of winning this fight. I hereby surrender to you. I have already given the order to my fleet to spread out, come to a halt, and prepare to be boarded in as orderly a manner as possible."

She could hear a storm of beak-clacking and feather-rustling from all around the bridge. But as she had anticipated, the Wingers were too shocked to interject.

A smug smile crept across Carrow's face. "So you have an ounce of sense after all. Good move, Fin. I suppose I'll be meeting you in person shortly." He vanished from the bridge's main screen.

Ek cast her eyes around the bridge, meeting the aghast expressions worn by her crew. "Put me on the fleetwide."

The communications adjutant jerked in surprise, and then did as she was told. "It's done, Flockhead."

"The UHF has ruled the galaxy with an iron fist since the First Galactic War," Ek said to her fleet. "Now, it wages a fierce war against a former ally, a war it had every opportunity to cease, as the *Providence* did. Worst of all, the UHF stood by and did nothing as the Gok extinguished all life on Spire. The line of action I have chosen for us does not smack of honor. It will not make for a story to proudly tell your grandsires. But it *will* sow chaos among the enemy ranks, and it will maximize our chances of victory. You have granted me command of your ships. I demand that you continue to follow my orders. My people were all murdered, and I am full of cold fire."

"Our fleet has come to rest," the sensors adjutant said quietly. "The enemy nears, Flockhead."

"Launch all Talons with orders to attack. Fire lasers at the leading UHF ships. Fire kinetic impactors. Fire missiles."

Teach them the meaning of a Fin at war.

CHAPTER 59

The Cruiser and the Frigate

"Come in," Husher's father called the instant he knocked on the hatch. He opened it to find Warren sitting on a gleaming metal chair that looked sleek and modern and not very comfortable.

"What can I do for you?" Warren asked.

"I..." Husher cleared his throat. "I've come to ask you to be my XO. You have long military experience captaining warships, and I need all the help I can get."

Maybe because he was used to dealing with superiors who were older than him and mostly considered themselves infinitely wiser, Husher expected to detect at least a hint of gloating from his father over the request.

But Warren gave no sign of that. "I'd be honored."

With a curt nod, Husher said, "Very good. We'd better get to the CIC."

They'd transitioned into the Caprice System two hours ago, trailed by the Wingers in command of the *Stevenson*. That put them three hours out from the Vermillion Shipyards, where the UHF built most of its warships.

As they walked, his father wasted no time in breaking down his tactical analysis of the impending engagement. "I'm willing to bet the turrets on those shipyards are no joke. Have you given any thought to how you'll deal with them?"

"I have, but I've yet to come up with anything viable."

"Here's an idea. A trick I came up with during the First Galactic War. Prepare your Condors for launch from the shuttle bay they're in. Without their launch catapults, your pilots won't enter battle with the energy they're used to, but the shipyards' defenders won't expect to face Condors out of a missile cruiser. The element of surprise should compensate for the lower energy, if the Battle of Rik was any indication."

"That's perfect. We can launch shuttles filled with marines simultaneously, and to cover them we can order the Condors to target the platform's turrets with a heavy dose of Banshees, while we do the same from the *Contest*."

"Yep. Against a traditional orbital defense platform we might have had trouble, but a lot of the Vermillion Shipyards' mass is devoted to building warships, not to weapons. Which makes sense, I suppose."

Piper awaited them just outside the CIC, his thin-fingered hands clasped over his little pot belly, which poked out below the turtleneck-like garment that Tumbran monitors wore. The alien studiously ignored Warren, who, just hours ago, he'd encountered for the first time since the First Galactic War. Warren had immediately begun poking fun at him, asking whether he intended to smother the enemy in paperwork, and Piper had descended into a moody silence.

Apparently, he'd recovered from it. "Seeing the Wingers fly UHF ships solo gave me an idea for a program that would allow us to control their navigation systems remotely," he said, gazing solemnly up at Husher. "I've been working on the software since we left Pinnacle, and I believe I can finish it in time. Provided this mission is a success, perhaps we can use it to liberate some spaceworthy vessels from the shipyards. They may prove useful when we attempt to rescue Captain Keyes."

"That's brilliant, Piper," Husher said. "I take back everything I ever said about you."

The Tumbran bristled. "I do not."

Warren brayed laughter at that, and they continued into the CIC.

"Captain," his sensor operator said as they entered. "I was just about to get the communications adjutant to—"

"You mean the Coms officer." Husher didn't enjoy being a stickler, but the Wingers needed to remember they served under him now, and if he didn't remind them of that, it would anger the human members of the crew. *What a tedious balancing act this has become.*

"Yes. I was going to ask him to contact you. It seems you were correct that the apparent lack of warships defending the shipyards was a ruse. A destroyer has just lifted off from the Vermillion Shipyards and is approaching on an intercept course."

Husher's father gave a terse laugh as he settled into the XO's chair. "Cocky of them to leave the safety of the turrets."

"They want to avoid any damage to the shipyards and the warships under construction there," Husher said. "They think they can take out both the *Contest* and the *Stevenson* before we ever reach the platform, and they may be right. There's no question that a missile cruiser and a frigate will be outclassed by a destroyer. Possibly even with the addition of our Condors."

"There's a small chance we'd beat them with the Condors," Warren said. "But by deploying them early, we'd waste the opportunity to use them in order to bypass the shipyard turrets and reach the *Providence*."

"Yeah," Husher said, momentarily distracted by the way his father slouched in the XO's seat. *Is that how he used to sit in his Captain's chair, aboard the* Hornet*?* He'd heard about his father's reputation for doing things differently, which had fed into the narrative that he was a traitor. Now he was beginning to see the reputation was well-founded.

"Captain, the captain of the *Stevenson* has sent us a transmission request."

"Accept."

The white-feathered Winger in command of the frigate appeared on the main viewscreen. "Captain Husher, I am contacting you to offer to engage the destroyer alone, allowing you to speed past her toward the Vermillion Shipyards. We will harry and delay her for as long as we can."

Husher studied the alien's face carefully. "The Wingers aboard the *Active* were gripped by an urge to launch a suicidal attack against a superior enemy force. Have you been taken by a similar impulse?"

The Winger clacked its beak. "No, Captain. My proposal amounts to what you might call a sacrifice. Unlike many members of my species, I do not wish to die. But I understand that if I risk death now, it will be in service to all Wingers and to life in the galaxy as a whole."

"The very definition of sacrifice," Warren said.

"Yes," Husher said. "Thank you, then, Wingleader, on behalf of both our species."

The Winger nodded. "Our work begins." The viewscreen went dark.

CHAPTER 60

Oorah

The cargo ship had entered the Sol System and was now approaching Mars. As the planet grew large on the viewscreen in the crew's mess, the ship's captain entered and approached Bernard where she sat with Simpson and Ralston.

Once Husher and the others left, Ralston had led Bernard and Simpson to a small study on the same floor as the living room. There, a lapcom sat on a desk whose wood veneer had begun to peel.

They uploaded Piper's revolution gauge to the micronet, running into no technical problems, which Bernard gave thanks for. Without the Tumbran around to provide tech support, their plan might have sputtered out before it began.

Then she, Simpson, and Ralston stood around the cramped study and waited. For hours. She considered suggesting they move the lapcom to the living room, but she didn't want to impose on their host any more than they already had.

At last, the AI finished analyzing news sites, social media, and historical data it pulled from archives. Then it presented them with its calculation for how close they were to toppling Hurst's government:

Seven percent.

"Wow," Simpson said. "We have a lot of work to do."

"And fast." Bernard crossed her arms in front of her, rubbing her elbows. "I thought we could start our work here on Zakros, but this makes me think we should head straight for Mars." The red planet was considered humanity's adopted homeworld, after the total degradation of Earth. "I don't think we'll have quite the impact we need to, here."

The corporal nodded. "I think I can secure us discreet transport. I'll need micronet access, though."

"Ralston will need his lapcom to start contacting other veterans. Can you not get on the net with your com?"

"Nope. Military coms aren't designed to access the civilian micronet."

"Then use mine." Bernard handed Simpson her own personal com.

Ralston leaned back in the study's only chair. "Senator, before I get started, I have to ask you a question. If things don't go your way on Mars, do you envision these veterans taking up arms against Hurst? Is a military coup among the options you're considering? Because I'm not sure how I feel about that. Or that I'm up to it, physically."

"Absolutely not," Bernard said. "I will urge all protesters to remain peaceful, and I will make clear that any violent actors will be disowned by the movement. To turn violent would be to sink to the level of the government, and to give the media an excuse to vilify us. Not to mention that the police would gain an actual justification for cracking down as brutally as they have. They'd likely start brutalizing the defenders even more."

"That's what I needed to hear," Ralston said, turning to his lapcom without another word.

As the others worked, Bernard sat on the hard laminate with her back against the study wall and thought about what she planned to say to the defenders once she reached one of their camps.

It wasn't long before Ralston started muttering to himself. Bernard particularly enjoyed that, since she loved the man's Scottish accent, though she didn't want to risk embarrassing him by saying so.

"It's gonna cost money, especially if I manage to get more veterans than just me. Better start a fundraiser."

Bernard peered up at the screen. From the floor, she could only see the display's top-right quadrant, but that was enough for her to recognize the website of a popular crowdfunding service.

"What if I get a hundred veterans?" The Scot gave a derisive grunt, still apparently talking to himself. "Pie in the sky. Not possible." The clatter of his fingers on the keyboard followed, but stopped suddenly, with Ralston's head twitching upward. "What if I get *two*-hundred?"

Bernard felt a smile spreading across her face. "You'll get a thousand, Chief. Mark my words."

Ralston turned, apparently unperturbed about Bernard interrupting his conversation with himself. "Do you really think so?"

"I do."

"This could be huge, you know that? Like nothing we've ever seen before."

Inclining her head, Bernard said, "I think that's exactly what Captain Keyes envisioned."

CHAPTER 61

Fall Back

As the crowd chanted, Police Sergeant Doucet inched toward Corporal Bradley. "We need to move back."

Bradley looked at him, brow furrowed. "Sarge?"

"If we don't show these veterans some respect, the public backlash is going to be intense." Even Doucet could see that, and he was no PR expert.

Slowly, Bradley shook his head. "Don't you think we should check with the chief?"

"Yes. I do. But if he saw what we just did, I doubt he'll be saying any different."

Doucet realized his com was emitting its shrill beep, and he took it out, accepted the call, and put it to his ear.

It was the chief. "Doucet. You're at the site of unrest now, are you not?"

"Yes, sir, I am."

"We have to unblock the access roads immediately. If word gets out that we're denying veterans access to food and medicine, we'll be crucified. The way the Commonwealth treats veterans is already a sore point. This will ruin us. It could set the entire galaxy to rioting."

"I was just about to call you and say the same thing, Chief."

"Right. Just get to work. We're going to need to find another way to fight this." The chief sighed, and Doucet realized his boss felt just as tired as he did. "Hopefully Hurst comes up with something else. I thought the new law would do it. God. We can't even starve them out anymore. We need something else."

CHAPTER 62

Honor

Each Roostship would only be able to use its laser once, and so Ek ordered just half of them to do so in the initial barrage.

Some of the UHF ships had discharged their own primary lasers in their attack on Pinnacle, but many had not. As a result, their main capacitors were fully charged, and when they came under laser fire from the Wingers, they were ripped apart in titanic explosions.

Because of the enemy's tight formation, the resultant shrapnel punched through the hulls of several more ships, triggering yet more explosions.

Ek watched on the tactical display as the next battle groups in line slammed on their brakes, but too late. Their momentum carried them forward, and one of them collided with a corvette that had escaped the Wingers' assault, causing both to explode.

Most of the braking ships made it through the cloud of speeding shrapnel, and Ek knew they would be preparing to strike back.

"Fire the second laser salvo," she said over the fleetwide.

Lasers lanced forth from the half of her fleet with capacitors still charged, and more UHF ships exploded, increasing the amount of shrapnel. The rest of Carrow's fleet was reeling as each captain broke formation, taxing their engines to veer wildly in a desperate attempt to avoid the field of destruction ahead.

"How many ships?" Ek asked the sensors adjutant.

"Twenty-nine, Flockhead," the Winger said. "We neutralized twenty-nine enemy warships."

"Let us press the advantage." She studied the tactical display briefly and pointed at an area. "There. While their fleet is in disarray, let us strike there. The debris cloud we created will delay the others from backing them up."

"Yes, ma'am," the navigation adjutant said.

"Full power to engines, and fire a single volley of kinetic impactors from each ship just before we are in range of their lasers. As we near them, launch Talons to take advantage of their confusion."

Her crew worked with haste, and soon enough her fleet was on top of the wayward UHF ships. Talons spewed forth from every Roostship, joined by the Falcons that had first arrived with Ek. Together, they performed alpha strike after coordinated alpha strike. Eleven more enemy ships were obliterated.

No one inside the bridge celebrated in any way, and she suspected the situation was the same on every other Roostship. *They are as enraged and determined as I.*

On the tactical display, she watched as Carrow regained control of his captains, restoring order to their formations. "Take us back behind the debris field, keeping it between us and the enemy for as long as possible. I expect they will be much more cautious in their next approach."

"Ma'am, we're getting a transmission request," the communications adjutant said.

"Put it through."

Admiral Carrow appeared on the main viewscreen, his normally pale face flushed crimson. "Have you any honor at all?"

"Honor? I would ask *you*: can a creature who betrays his own species for money be said to have honor?"

"Of course not, but—"

"Then do not speak to me of honor. You have no authority on the subject."

Ek would not have considered it possible, but Carrow turned redder. "You can forget any more talk about surrender, fish. You just signed your own death warrant, along with every sky-rat under your command."

Carrow cut off the transmission, and the enemy began to inch around the growing debris field, approaching with much greater care this time. Instead of hugging the debris to come at Ek's fleet in a straight line again, Carrow arrayed his ships in an arc that kept its distance, snaking around the Roostship before tightening the noose.

I have bought all the time there was for sale. Now she could do nothing except expend her troops as efficiently as possible. Nothing but that, and hope.

The UHF began closing in, kinetic impactors screaming toward the Roostships, followed by a startlingly massive missile barrage.

"Take evasive action," she said. "Instruct all crew to brace for impact."

The impactors hit her command ship with a sound like prolonged thunder, and twin explosions rocked the bridge, one after another. Ek had strapped in at the beginning of the battle, and she had ordered her Wingers to do so as well, so everyone kept their seats.

"Instruct all Talons to initiate missile defense protocols immediately," she said. "Sensors adjutant, compile a damage report and relay it to me."

"The impactors rocked loose a poorly secured fuel cell, sending it crashing to the deck. The explosion detonated its neighbor. Alpha and beta decks are open to space in sections two, three, and four."

"Seal off the affected areas and deploy damage control teams."

"I have some good news, Flockhead. Captain Vaghn has just appeared out of the Larkspur-Yclept darkgate and is headed our way."

Ek suppressed a wince. *So close, and yet...* "It will take her hours to reach us. By then, I fear Carrow will be finished with us. How many Roostships are en route to join our fight?"

"Thirty-seven, four of them having recently entered the system, also from Yclept. Only one Roostship is due to reach us within the next hour, however. It's Wingleader Korbyn's. He's approaching the UHF from behind, though it doesn't seem likely he'll do any meaningful damage." The sensors adjutant tapped her console, and saw something that made her wings grow tense. "A sizable battle group has already broken away from the main body of Admiral Carrow's fleet to confront the wingleader."

A wave of nausea crashed over Ek, and she pitched forward against her chair's straps, suddenly losing all sense of balance, even from her seated position. It took an enormous effort of will to right herself. Her muscles would not cooperate.

"Honored One..." Wingleader Ty stared at her, his entire body proclaiming his agitation. "Are you well?"

"I am fine. Communications adjutant, send Wingleader Korbyn instructions to evade that battle group and attempt to find a safer route to join us."

"Yes, ma'am. Though I'm not certain he'll listen. The Wingers lost hope after Spire was destroyed, and Wingleader Korbyn has been particularly reckless. I doubt he'll hear reason."

Ek inhaled deeply from her respirator. *Do not waste your firepower like this, Korbyn. I need you.*

In truth, she needed thirty of him, at least. But one was better than none. Unfortunately, as Korbyn continued his approach despite her orders, the latter appeared more likely.

CHAPTER 63

Ready to Rock

Bronson's handlebar mustache twitched comically as he sneered at Husher from the *Contest*'s main viewscreen. "Why don't you stay and fight me instead of sending these sky-rats to do it for you?"

Husher yawned, mostly unsurprised to find Bronson in command of the destroyer sent to confront them. "Did you get in contact for a reason, traitor? Or is your repertoire limited to schoolyard taunts, now?"

"You oaf. Laudano and I are going to kill these Wingers, and after that we're coming to kill you."

"You're going to lose embarrassingly, Bronson. And you won't even look good doing it. Coms, cut the transmission."

"Yes, sir." Bronson vanished from the viewscreen.

"We'll reach the Vermillion Shipyards in twenty minutes, Captain," Husher's sensor operator said.

Husher nodded in acknowledgment, but the Winger wasn't done.

"There's something else, sir. The Tumbran is outside the CIC, requesting entry."

"Let him in."

The diminutive gray-skinned alien waddled inside once the hatch opened to admit him, his chin sack wobbling to and fro. Piper stopped in front of the Captain's chair and peered up with his dome-like eyes. To Husher, the Tumbran always looked somewhat long-suffering.

"What is it, Piper?"

"I've finished work on my algorithm for controlling UHF ships remotely."

"Some welcome news. How do we go about activating it? Can we install it remotely as well, from the *Contest*?"

"Unfortunately not," Piper said, raising his thin fingers to touch his face, something Husher had noticed the Tumbran did a lot, as though to make sure his head was still there. "UHF warships are designed to be impervious to hacking via any sort of signal. They can only be remotely accessed by Command, via the micronet. For us to compromise them, we must physically board each ship to upload my program."

As Husher digested what Piper had told him, he found himself wondering what Keyes would have done with the information. Devoting some of his forces to commandeering UHF ships would complicate the effort to recover the *Providence*. *But I can't just think about completing this mission. I also need to consider what I'll need in order to extricate Keyes from Hades.*

"This has to be a quick smash-and-grab, given that the destroyer will soon be back to ruin our day. That said, I don't think we can afford not to commandeer at least some ships. I'll assign some marines to the task, and that team will gain control of as many UHF warships as possible. Piper, I'll need you with that team, in case anything goes wrong with your algo, or we need your skills for anything else. Are you up to that?"

The alien tugged on his chin sack, which Husher had never seen a Tumbran do before. "As long as you don't ask me to try operating a firearm with these fingers." Piper held up his hands, spreading his spindly digits in front of his face.

Husher squinted. *Was that a joke? From a Tumbran?* "Uh...I won't."

"We'll be lucky to find spaceworthy vessels to commandeer," his father said from the XO's chair. "Seems to me they'll need to be pretty late in the construction process, for them to be viable targets for us to nab."

"You're right," Piper said. "Though I'm loathe to admit it. Life support systems are normally installed last, since until then the shipyard can simply use its supplies of atmosphere to pressurize whatever sections construction crews are currently working on. My algorithm doesn't require life support, so as long as we can find ships that have navigational systems but not life support, this should work."

"Fifteen minutes till arrival, sir," the sensor operator said.

Husher stood, turning to his father. "You have the ship. I'm going down there with Piper, to lead a team to secure the platform's control center. From there, Piper should be able to access information about how far along every ship is in the construction process, as well as the locations of viable targets. Caine will lead a team to retake the *Providence*, since she knows its layout a lot better than I do."

His father stared at him for a moment, mouth slightly open, as though he wanted to say something. Then he shut it again. "Yes, sir."

"Execute your plan to launch Condors from the shuttle bay, simultaneous to the shuttles' departure. Back up the Condors in neutralizing as many turrets as possible. Do it exactly as you described it to me." He turned to Piper. "Let's go."

To keep up with Husher's long strides on the way to the shuttle bay, the alien had to adopt a rapid waddle that was far from dignified. Piper didn't seem to care, though.

Husher decided that what many humans had interpreted as condescension from the Tumbra was actually just an extraordinary frankness. He also liked their total lack of concern for appearances. In fact, the more time Husher spent around Piper, the more the alien endeared himself to him.

As soon as Husher had donned his pressure suit's helmet, he tapped the transponder to patch him through to Fesky. "How are you doing, Madcap? Ready to rock?"

"Don't get too excited. This is going to be a tough mission, and you're not the one who has to go out there."

Husher chuckled, careful not to activate his transponder as he did. Now that she outranked him, Fesky was getting feistier by the day. "Actually, I'm taking a shuttle down to the shipyards. I'll be in every bit as much danger as you. And so will the crew aboard the *Contest*, for that matter. Don't let that Condor fool you into thinking you're the only piece of this operation that matters, Madcap. Everyone matters. And that's coming from a fellow pilot."

"Haven't seen you in a Condor much lately," Fesky snapped. Then she moderated her tone. "You're right, Husher. Sorry. I'm a little on edge lately."

"Understandably so. Just stay frosty out there, all right?"

"All right."

The *Contest* arrived at the military shipyards, and turret fire started hitting her right away. The sound of it didn't travel through the vacuum, of course; Husher knew because of the way the ship shuddered.

"Now," he said over a wide channel, and the shuttle bay door split open. Twenty Condors took wing. *Not even enough to make two squadrons.* But he trusted Fesky's ability.

The shuttles leapt for the exit seconds later, and carnage enveloped them right away, with the platform's turrets flashing as they fired, at the Condors, at the shuttles.

From the *Contest*, his father fired back, and on his shuttle's viewscreen, Husher saw a turret battery explode.

Their craft bucked, and Husher opened a two-way channel between him and the pilot. "That was a hit, wasn't it, Ozone? What kind of damage did it do?"

"Fairly negligible, sir. It—"

Another round hit them, birthing a tremendous sucking sound from the rear of the passenger cabin. Several of the marines clutched the straps holding them into their crash seats.

"That one took out our engines," Ozone said, and switched to a wide channel. "Brace for impact, everybody. We're coming in hot."

CHAPTER 64

Eviscerate

Wingleader Korbyn studied the tactical display for a moment, but he quickly gave up in frustration. There were too many icons approaching, with the cursed abbreviations the Interplanetary Defense Force assigned to the various classes of enemy ships. He never had been good at processing information visually, and the confusing display didn't help.

He clacked his beak. "Sensors adjutant, give me the composition of the approaching battle group."

His officers were accustomed to Korbyn's strengths and shortcomings. "The battle group coming to confront us consists of three destroyers, seven missile cruisers, nine corvettes, and five frigates, Captain."

"Essentially two battle groups mashed together, then." *Way too large to take on by ourselves.* He became aware that his feathers stood at attention with the tension of the decision he now had to make. That annoyed him. He hated how easily his body betrayed his emotions, but he'd never been able to curb the tendency. Few Wingers could, to be fair.

Bytan could. But Bytan was gone.

"All right," he said. "It's time. Communications, put me in touch with Blackwing."

Over the years, many had called Korbyn overconfident, but he knew he couldn't possibly be anywhere near as cocky as the former pirate. "Korbyn, I take it you need me?"

"That's *Wingleader* Korbyn to you."

"Not really. I haven't been part of the IDF for almost a decade. Why don't you tell me what you want?"

"You know what I want. Haven't you glanced at your tactical display lately?"

"I just wanted to hear you say you need me."

"If that's what it'll take for you to stop wasting the precious few moments we have before engaging to back up the last surviving Fin, then fine. I need you. Satisfied? Are you ready, you cursed pirate?"

"I've been ready since you were still pecking at your mother's flight feathers for second helpings."

Korbyn clacked his beak, but he refused to take the pirate's bait. They didn't have the time for a wingspan measuring contest. "Just stick to the plan, Blackwing. Korbyn out."

When Blackwing had first contacted Korbyn about abandoning his revenge against the Gok in order to help fight the UHF, he'd refused. Only the Fins mattered, and the Fins were gone, so Korbyn had intended to continue avenging them until he no longer could.

But for the same reason, when the message from Ek swept across the Larkspur System, Korbyn had gotten back in touch with Blackwing via an encrypted channel. His message had been brief: "I'm ready."

He turned to his strategic adjutant. "Fire our primary laser at the battle group's flagship. I want their attention riveted on us. Stand by to launch Talons, but refrain from doing so just yet."

"Yes, sir."

Korbyn ordered his sensors adjutant—the same one who'd questioned his tactics against the Gok, who Korbyn had since restored to duty—to put a magnified visual of the destroyer on the bridge's main viewscreen. It gave him a lot of satisfaction to watch the nose of the UHF ship warp and begin to melt.

The enemy battle group began to pick up speed, training their weapons on Korbyn's Roostship. "Prepare to take evasive action on my mark," he told his navigation adjutant. "Mark!"

Just as the Roostship adjusted its attitude upward relative to the ecliptic plane, sixty pirate stealth ships revealed their positions, directly behind the UHF battle group.

They revealed their positions by firing all weapons at the warships' sterns.

The UHF captains had no time to react, and over a third of their ships were destroyed or rendered inoperative almost instantly.

"Launch Talons!" Korbyn yelled as over half of the remaining ships in the enemy battle group began to come about in order to point their main guns at the pirates. "Send kinetic impactors at the ships still facing us, and follow up with missiles to keep their point defense turrets busy. I want this to be swift."

His wishes were carried out, and the battle ended almost as quickly as it had begun. Between them, Korbyn's Roostship and her Talons along with Blackwing's pirate fleet eviscerated the entire UHF battle group before the main body of Admiral Carrow's fleet had a chance to react at all.

No doubt Carrow had thought he was playing it safe by sending twenty-four warships to destroy one Roostship. The numbers favored him greatly in his battle against Ek, and so he'd felt he could afford to take zero risk in dealing with Korbyn.

Now he knows he was grossly overextending himself.

CHAPTER 65

Raid

"Is anyone injured?" Husher asked over a wide channel.

Radio silence. Marines shaking their heads was the only response.

"Piper?"

"I'm fine."

As their shuttle had careened toward the platform, Caine had managed to unstrap the Tumbran and strap him in with her, wrapping her arms tightly around his small frame. Husher didn't know how well Tumbran skeletons normally held up to crash landings, but they didn't look very hardy, and he suspected that if Caine hadn't acted so swiftly they'd have had an injured or dead alien on their hands. That would have been disastrous, given Piper's importance to their mission.

"Good thinking, Sergeant," he said over a wide channel, so everyone could hear his praise. "You may have just saved this mission."

She gave a curt nod. "And sticking around here and gabbing will endanger it again. Ozone, is the airlock still working?"

"Yeah, and you'd better use it. A lot of the atmosphere's leaked out already, but there's enough left to eject you pretty forcefully if we open both doors at once."

"Acknowledged," Husher said. "Open the interior door, and everyone in Caine's team get in. My two squads will go next. Ozone, you'd better come with us. I very much doubt we'll be taking this shuttle anywhere again. If we leave, we leave in the *Providence.*"

By the time he stood on the surface of the shipyards with Piper, Ozone, Wahlburg, and the rest of his team, Caine and her marines were nowhere to be seen. *Good.* He knew he could rely on her to liberate the supercarrier as quickly as possible. *And that means we're on her clock.* "Let's move, people."

As they made their way toward the shipyards' control center, the *Providence* loomed in the distance, dwarfing the ships under construction all around it. They encountered no resistance en route, which seemed strange until Husher realized the platform's defenders probably expected they were only here to recover Keyes's ship. The defenders didn't know about Piper's algorithm.

When they reached the airlock into the control center, they found it barred to them. Husher switched to the radio channel considered the standard for communicating in space when neither party had coordinated to choose another, more private channel.

"If there's any personnel in that control center, this is your one chance to open this airlock. We brought breaching charges with us, and we will use them to gain entry. Which is fine for us, but it won't work out very well for anyone inside."

He only had to wait a few seconds for the airlock to open. Motioning for his marines to crowd in, Husher did too, keeping a close eye on Piper. The Tumbran wasn't used to battle ops, and if someone didn't keep an eye on him, he could easily get into trouble. Or get the rest of them into trouble.

Inside the control center, they found shipyard personnel at their various consoles, frozen in place and staring at the marines as they fanned out through the area.

"Search them for sidearms, and corral them in the center of the room," Husher barked, turning to Piper. "Start checking the consoles to see whether any of the station personnel are still logged into the system. That could make our job a lot easier."

He assigned a marine to tail the Tumbran as the alien went from console to console. In the meantime, Husher took in their surroundings. The control center was divided into two levels, and the second level seemed inaccessible from where they stood. *No doubt that's a measure against exactly what's happening.* If intruders like him took control of the first level, the shipyards' defenders could simply use their special access to the second, firing down on the infiltrators from above.

Knowing one of these personnel had almost certainly sounded the alarm already, Husher turned to the nearest Winger under his command. "How easily can your pressure suits come off?"

"Very easily. We can have them off within seconds. They're designed that way, to take advantage of flight if needed."

"I figured." Husher already knew that Wingers injected themselves with fewer Ocharium nanites than humans did, allowing them to experience simulated gravity equivalent to the gravity on Spire, even while humans experienced one G. He switched to a wide channel. "All Winger marines, strip off your suits as quickly as you can and then use this chamber's air resistance to fly up to that second level. Once there, take up defensive positions, covering every entrance you can find. I'm expecting company up there soon—company that will want to get the drop on us. I'd like to surprise them by reversing that situation."

The Wingers complied, shedding their suits with impressive speed. They climbed on top of consoles, heedless of what commands they might be inadvertently entering, and they launched themselves into the air, their powerful torsos rippling as they propelled themselves to the upper level.

As a Winger pushed itself off of the console Piper was currently studying, the Tumbran turned to Husher, wearing what looked a lot like disgruntlement through the tiny faceplate. "The staff here were diligent. They're clearly following some sort of protocol designed to mitigate the damage from a raid, such as the one we've effected."

"What will we need to log in to the system?"

"Biometrics and a password. Note these sensors here." Piper brushed a rectangular black panel with the backs of his fingers. "They scan the user's retinas to determine whether he or she should be granted access to the system."

Husher contemplated the situation, his eyes wandering over the station personnel gathered in the center of the room.

From above came the *hiss* of an airlock opening, followed immediately by gunfire. *There's our company.* But how much? And how long would the element of surprise keep the single squad of Wingers up there alive?

Opening his mouth to address the woman who looked most likely to be the senior technician, Husher closed it again when Wahlburg stormed across the room without warning, seizing a man by his collar and dragging him over to the console where Piper stood.

Husher grimaced. "Wahlburg, cut it—"

The marine shoved his captive's face against the scanner by the back of the head.

Piper's gaze flitted rapidly between Husher and Wahlburg while the console emitted a pleasant beep. "Um...that's the biometric portion of the login taken care of..."

The sniper yanked his sidearm from its holster and pressed it against the back of the man's head while holding him in place by his neck. "You'll want to recite the password now, nice and slow, all right? We don't want our poor Tumbran here to have to re-type it. We *really* don't."

"Wahlburg, release him," Husher barked.

"Sir, I'm afraid you'll have to consider me insubordinate until our friend here recites the password we need. Feel free to court martial me afterward, or whatever protocol we've settled on for situations like these in this new military organization thingy we appear to have started up." The marine tapped his sidearm's barrel against his captive's skull. "Now, about that password. Yell it out real loud, so Piper can hear you over the gunfire."

Trembling, the man shouted each character, and Piper entered it in. It was at least twenty characters long, but finally they were done, and the Tumbran nodded. "I'm in."

Husher breathed a sigh of relief as Wahlburg released the technician, allowing him to return to his colleagues.

The sniper approached, his pistol's handle extended. "I'm sorry, sir," he said over a two-way. "I know that was out of line. But the last time we tried negotiating with personnel on an orbital platform, Davies got killed. I just—" Wahlburg's voice cracked, and his shoulders rose and fell as he took a moment, presumably to compose himself. "I lost it. I know I did. I'll surrender my firearms, if you want me off the mission."

Husher shook his head. "We need you on it. You can talk consequences with Captain Keyes, once we have the *Providence* back, with him in command. Understood?"

"Yes, sir."

A light over the airlock on their level turned blue, which Husher took to mean they were about to have some company, too. "Everyone find cover and prepare to answer an incursion from this level's airlock." Lowering his faceplate, he addressed the station personnel. "All of you, get behind my marines wherever there's space and lie down on the floor. If you try to cause trouble, it'll be a lot more dangerous for you than it will be for my people."

If he was thinking only of tactics, and not of ethics, he might have tried to leverage the prisoners against the platform security personnel about to enter. But if he behaved like that, then he'd only be proving there was nothing about humanity worth saving. *Which is why Wahlburg* will *have to face consequences for what he did.*

In the seconds he had before the airlock finished pressurizing and the inner door opened to admit the enemy, Husher radioed Caine. "Sergeant, we're holed up here in the control center, with station security pressuring us. I need the *Providence* up and running as soon as you can make it happen."

"That might not be as soon as you like, Lieutenant," Caine said. "I'm meeting heavy resistance, too."

But there was no time to answer. The inner door was opening, and Husher was raising his assault rifle to sight along the barrel at his first target.

CHAPTER 66

Sitting Duck

Fesky swung the outer shell of her Condor around its short axis, gunning her engines perpendicular to the firing solution one of the station's turrets currently had on her. Sensors informed her its kinetic impactors came within a meter of hitting her six.

But my six is always changing.

She changed it now, returning fire with a pair of Sidewinders before rotating all the way around to put some distance between her and the platform.

Her cockpit washed red, alerting her to a missile fired at her by another turret. But if she turned to deal with it, she would slow her progress, leaving herself exposed to a nearby battery that had just finished taking out one of her pilots.

"Fesky to *Contest*, a little help?"

A single Banshee left the missile cruiser, colliding with the missile heading her way. Both exploded in a flash that lasted for less than a second.

"Thanks. We need to take out as many of the shipyards' turrets as we can before Bronson gets back in his destroyer."

Glancing at the tactical display, she clacked her beak. *Wonderful. He's nearly here.*

"Acknowledged, Fesky," Warren Husher said into her ear. "Keep your Condors away from the *Contest*'s bow—we'll focus on neutralizing the turrets on that side." His words came as a relief, but she found it slightly odd that he was the one to actually contact her. *Shouldn't he be focusing a little more on tactics?*

Still, she shouldn't complain. So far, she'd lost a remarkably small number of pilots, and she was proud to see that fewer human pilots had gone down than Wingers. Not that she celebrated members of her species getting killed, but it did mean she'd trained her pilots to be at least as good as Wingers. It was important to acknowledge small victories, too.

Bronson had nearly arrived when she received another transmission, this time from Caine, of all people. "Fesky, there's no way I'm going to reach the *Providence* unless something gives. Can you help me out?"

"Oh, sure," Fesky snapped. "It's not like I'm busy with anything."

"Thanks," Caine said, and Fesky was sure she detected a note of amusement in the human's voice.

This species will be the death of me. "Condor pilots, continue to focus on the platform's turrets until the *Contest* requires your backup. I'm breaking away long enough to execute a strafing run."

Caine lit up her position on Fesky's heads-up, which seemed a little redundant, considering the *Providence* was sort of hard to miss, and the marines were trading fire within fifty meters of it.

Using visuals to carefully line up her shot so as not to do any damage to the supercarrier, Fesky began the run. Her kinetic impactors tore up the platform's surface in a staggered line, taking out three of the station's defenders before their formation started to fragment.

She hadn't even finished her first run when they scattered, and Caine's team pounced, taking full advantage of the confusion Fesky had caused. Another pass would not be needed.

"You're the best, Fesky," Caine said over a two-way.

Yeah, yeah. "Just watch your back inside the *Providence*, all right?"

"Why? You're not saying you'd miss me, are you?"

"Negative. I'm just worried about how much more aggravating Husher will get if you die."

That brought a chuckle from Caine. "All right then, Fesky. Good luck up there."

Turning back to the battle, scanning for a target, Fesky wasn't ready for what came next, and when it happened her talons nearly left the fighter's controls.

Bronson had arrived in his destroyer, and his first order of business was to blow the *Contest*'s main engines clean away, stripping her of the ability to maneuver in battle.

Not to mention our ability to escape this scrap heap. How could Warren have allowed this to happen?

Shaking off her dismay, she switched to a wide channel. "All Condors on missile defense for the *Contest*, now. Now! She's a sitting duck up there."

CHAPTER 67

You Knew I Was
Coming for You

Caine and her marines had no trouble entering the *Providence*, which didn't comfort her in the slightest. As far as she was concerned, it spelled only one thing: ambush.

So she reminded the others to proceed with extreme caution, checking around every corner before exposing themselves, and she kept the ship's layout in mind while selecting a route through her.

Caine also remembered Ek, and the way the Fin considered every factor in a situation, never missing an opportunity to leverage her knowledge against her adversaries. That was how Ek had helped uncover the conspiracy between Bronson and Moreno in the first place.

So who am I likely to face in here?

The war would not have left Command with much time to dwell on logistics, and since Bronson captained the destroyer battling the *Contest* overhead, it seemed likely that other conspirators would have been put in charge of preventing the *Providence* from being retaken. That meant Ryerson and Moreno.

Moreno she knew less well, but Ryerson had served under her for three years. And since Moreno was more accustomed to serving in a CIC, no doubt he'd let Ryerson lead the defense of the supercarrier.

Caine knew Ryerson. She knew how he thought—his strengths and his blind spots. *I can handle Ryerson.*

Simmons was on point, and when he checked around the next corner, gunfire roared. A bullet hit him, sending him careening backward.

Caine rushed to the private and yanked him away from the intersection, motioning the others to fall back. "You all right?"

"Yeah," he said, sounding hoarse. "Pretty sure." The pressure suit's torso was reinforced with a para-aramid fiber, designed to protect the wearer from gunshots, though an Ocharium-sped round would still leave a nasty bruise.

"Tough it out, marine," she said. "Everyone, retreat as quickly and orderly as you can. Follow me."

Her route may have seemed odd to the others, since it was far from a direct one to the CIC. But that was because it ensured they were never far from a cargo bay, hangar deck, or other open space.

Now they fell back to a starboard-side cargo bay, one that had two entrances. Ryerson wouldn't be able to resist an opportunity like that.

But because he'd chosen to ambush her here instead of waiting inside the CIC, he had no clue about her team's composition, and she'd reacted too quickly for him to glimpse it. As they poured into the cargo bay, Caine instructed her Winger marines to shrug out of their suits and fly up to conceal themselves in elevated positions, taking advantage of crates stacked high, a towering forklift, and crisscrossing rafters.

That done, Caine and the human marines dragged the Wingers' discarded pressure suits out of sight as they withdrew deep into the rear of the cargo bay.

And then they waited. "Do not fire except on my mark," she instructed the Wingers above, over the encrypted channel she'd set up before leaving the *Contest*.

It took several minutes for Ryerson to order his people into the cargo bay to investigate why Caine wasn't offering any resistance.

When she heard them enter, their footfalls picked up and amplified by her helmet, Caine opened a two-way channel with the Winger she judged to have the best vantage point. "Tell me what you're seeing," she whispered.

"There are fifteen of them," the Winger marine said, "threading through the cargo, searching."

"Notify me once they're almost on top of us."

"That would be now."

Caine slapped her helmet to switch back to the wide channel. "All Winger marines, fire!"

Assault rifles, shotguns, and sniper rifles spat fire from overhead. One of Ryerson's men dashed past the boxes concealing Caine's human soldiers, and she took him out with a well-placed pistol shot, sending him crashing to the deck face-first.

She shot him once more, to ensure he was dead, and then she motioned for her human marines to engage. When they emerged from their cover, only four of Ryerson's people remained standing, and Caine and the others dispatched them with ease.

"All marines converge on my position. We're hitting the others right now." She jogged toward the door, holstering her pistol and readying her assault rifle as she went.

They made for the leftmost entrance, with four of her marines remaining behind to defend it, on her orders. If they circled around and pinned Ryerson down near the other entrance to the cargo bay, he would have nowhere to run, since it was located down a corridor that didn't lead anywhere else.

When they reached the intersection again, Caine glimpsed a solitary figure disappearing around a corner up ahead. *Ryerson.* He'd be headed for the CIC, and if he reached it, he could cause more trouble for them.

Caine took off after him, and her conditioning allowed her to speak orders as she ran. "Take out the rest of the group that ambushed us. I'm going to head off Ryerson."

The private was nowhere to be seen when she reached the corner he'd vanished around, but she didn't slow down to search for him, instead taking the most efficient route to the CIC. His speed came as something of a surprise, given he was still recovering from his injury. *He must be using stims.*

Ryerson's knowledge of the *Providence*'s layout would probably be about as good as hers, given how long they'd served on it together. But she couldn't let that give her pause. Instead, she increased her pace, glancing down corridors that crossed her path and clutching her assault rifle close, ready to react if the bastard tried to get the drop on her.

In the end, it turned out Ryerson had taken a different route. They met at the intersection just outside the CIC, with him just ahead of her. Laying on even more speed, she jumped, tackling him to the deck.

Ryerson pushed her off, and Caine staggered to her feet, recovering quickly, with her assault rifle pointing at Ryerson's head. "It's over, Private. Toss your weapon."

"Going to shoot me again, Sergeant? Like you did on the Kaithe planet?" After throwing his pistol at her feet, he patted his sides from a kneeling position. "That's all I had."

"Pretty cocky, carrying so little. You knew I was coming for you."

Ryerson's eyes burned as he stared up at her. "I can't believe you're okay siding with aliens, Sergeant. You should have known all our problems started when we began letting them influence us."

"Humanity's problems started long before that."

Her former subordinate glanced past her, and Caine instantly realized what was happening. She dropped, turning as she fell, to hit the deck in prone position.

Sure enough, Moreno was coming around the corner behind her with a shotgun. She popped off a burst into his face, throwing him backward.

When she rolled onto her back, Ryerson stood over her, his pistol in hand. They both fired.

Ryerson fell back, two bullet holes marring his forehead. His shot had gotten her in the stomach, which hurt like hell. But her reinforced pressure suit had saved her.

She managed to regain her feet, her belly feeling like it was full of ruptured organs. Which was possible, but she suspected it would feel like that either way. Ocharium-enhanced bullets shot at point blank range...it wasn't what she would have called good for you.

"Husher," she said over a two-way. "I just took out Moreno and Ryerson. The *Providence* is ours. How are you doing?"

"There are fewer of us. But we fought through, and we got Piper's algorithm installed onto five ships. That's all we have time for. We'll head your way now."

CHAPTER 68

Battle Scars

Warren Husher watched on the tactical display as another missile made its way past the handful of Condors defending the *Contest*, past her overtaxed point defense turrets, and slammed into the hull. Another one followed, hitting near the same area and rocking the missile cruiser violently.

Bronson's destroyer was pelting them with everything it had, and if it hadn't already used its primary laser to destroy the *Stevenson*, it would surely have won already.

Most of the destroyer's missiles got taken down by Fesky's pilots or by the *Contest*'s point defense system, but too many were getting through, and kinetic impactors peppered her hull all the while—from the destroyer, and from the few remaining turrets on the orbital platform. Without engines, they simply had to sit there and take it.

Even if I had engines, I would not strand my son down there. "Get me a damage report on that latest," Warren said, though he was tired of speaking the words, and his chest tightened every time he did.

"Decks three through nine are leaking atmosphere into space between sections eleven and seventeen," his sensor operator said, clacking her beak. "Twenty-nine crew are unaccounted for."

Warren ran a hand over his face. Was this really the best he could do as a captain? He didn't seem to recall losing this hard during the First Galactic War. His CIC crew had started shooting him worried glances since he'd allowed their engines to get taken out. *They expected better from me.*

He felt like he was trying his best, but he also considered the possibility that the Ixa had removed the part of him that made him a great captain. Or maybe they'd added something to his brain that made him *think* he was giving an engagement his all when he was really holding back.

"Another missile's about to get through, Captain," his sensor operator said. "Maybe you should tell the crew to brace for another impact."

"Yes. You're right. Coms, put me on the—"

Too late. The missile struck, throwing Warren against the straps holding him in the Captain's chair. In the CIC, they had the luxury of strapping into their seats, but most of the crew's work required the ability to move around. *It's my job to warn them of impacts. And I didn't. Stupid, Warren. Stupid.* He really had lost it.

"Sir," the sensor operator said, and Warren winced, gripping his seat's armrests so hard his arms trembled.

"Yes?" he said, bracing for what had to be the finishing blow. "What is it?"

"Sir, it's the *Providence*. She's rising."

He opened his eyes, having squeezed them shut. "Give me a visual."

She did, and it was majestic...the most gorgeous thing Warren had ever seen. The old supercarrier didn't gleam with newness, like it had in Warren's day, during the First Galactic War. But somehow, as she labored toward the stars, her battle scars made her all the more beautiful.

That's what decades of hard service to humanity looks like. Who else can claim it?

"Sir, the destroyer has already turned its weapons on the *Providence*. She's swatting down whatever missiles it sends, and returning a healthy dose of her own."

"Put up a tactical display, for God's sake."

The main viewscreen changed to show a clear layout of the battle, and Warren felt a thrill shoot through him as the supercarrier's arrival warped the entire engagement.

Without the need to focus so intensely on missile defense, Fesky organized her fighters into alpha strike formation and began hitting the destroyer hard. More Condors streamed from the *Providence*'s flight decks to join them.

"Fire Banshees at that thing, Tactical," Warren barked. "And kinetic impactors, too. We don't have to worry about missile defense anymore."

"The destroyer is turning, sir," his sensor operator said. "It appears Bronson intends to flee."

"Let's make that as unpleasant an experience as possible. Tactical, direct our missiles at the destroyer's engines. I want to put them in our shoes."

"Yes, sir."

But Bronson's point defense turrets were robust, and he expertly met many of the *Contest*'s Banshees with missiles of his own. The Condors were doing damage, but those that had just emerged from the *Providence* had not yet reached the destroyer, and they weren't likely to, now.

A flock of missiles sprang from the supercarrier herself, helping Bronson on his way. Three of them made it through, causing brief explosions to blossom on the destroyer's hull, and causing Warren's heart to blossom, as well. *A welcome sight.*

"We're receiving a transmission request from the *Providence*, Captain."

"Put it on-screen."

His son appeared on the CIC's main viewscreen, and Warren's shoulders rose and fell in a sigh of relief. "Vin."

Vin gave a curt nod. "Captain. It looks like Bronson's destroyer is going to limp out of here after all."

"We should give chase. He doesn't deserve to continue operating freely."

"I'd love to, and we'd overtake him, in time. But we can't waste a second in getting to Hades. Not to mention, I'm uncertain how long your ship's going to continue being spaceworthy. I want you to get the crew to all available shuttles and escape pods, and I want you to use them to get over here as quickly as possible."

"All right. I guess that makes sense. How'd you have enough people to fly the *Providence*, by the way?"

"Most of them were imprisoned in their quarters. A testament to the UHF and the Commonwealth having their hands so full. Some have been sent to Hades, but they were keeping most of them here until they figured out what to do with them."

Warren nodded. *Figured out how guilty they considered them, more like.*

"I need you to hurry, Dad. Get over here. Husher out."

To his surprise, Warren's eyes stung. That was the first time in over twenty years that his son had called him "Dad."

His Winger sensor operator turned to him, her brown feathers surprisingly smoothed, denoting calm. "Sir, five UHF ships just lifted off from the Vermillion Shipyards and are forming up with the *Providence*."

He nodded. "Piper's algorithm at work." *Maybe we'll have a chance at Hades after all.*

CHAPTER 69

The Ultimate Whetstone

Korbyn's arrival had finally cracked the Wingers' veneer, and they had permitted themselves a few seconds' cheering when the stealth ships revealed themselves by decimating a sizable UHF battle group.

Ek did not join the celebrations. To do so would risk disrupting the flow state she had occupied since the battle's outset, which her deteriorating condition was already doing enough to jeopardize.

Instead of celebrating, she had continued to study the enemy's ever-shifting disposition, as well as that of her own fleet, and she derived many insights thereby.

Two hours had passed since Korbyn's gambit had paid off so lucratively. It had bought them the time they had needed so desperately, time enough for more Winger battle groups to arrive, taking the pressure off the main body of Ek's growing fleet.

Though the pirates were highly unlikely to regain the advantage of stealth during this engagement, their ships were nimble, darting in to harry the edge of Carrow's fleet and darting away again before getting picked off. The tactic was getting to the UHF captains, many of who had given chase out of frustration. When they did, the pirates turned on them, backed up by Korbyn and his Talons. They had destroyed several more ships that way.

As new Roostship battle groups arrived, Ek sent them encrypted orders to emulate the pirates' tactic. Her strategy remained the same as before: minimize losses, maximize targets neutralized, and hold out for another game-changing event, as Korbyn's arrival with the pirates had been.

She had been correct in her calculation that such events were probable, making it worth it to hold on as long as possible. Vaghn's approach, for instance, was a certainty, however Ek was rather uncertain she could keep enough of her fleet alive for the rogue captain's arrival to matter.

The *Firedrake*, Vaghn's ship, was a corvette, not a carrier. And so her speed was limited by the older Falcons accompanying her. It would take at least another five hours for her to get here.

By Ek's estimation of the numbers in play, more pirate stealth ships were unlikely to materialize.

And so, barring the rapid fruition of another possibility she had considered, she knew how long she needed to hold on for: five hours.

The tactical display was a mass of multi-colored icons, constantly shifting. She absorbed the battle in its entirety, holding it whole within her, dissecting it, leveraging her intellect and perception like never before.

Was it possible that war-making offered the ultimate whetstone for Fin intelligence?

She tapped her console and dragged a finger over it, highlighting a formation of UHF missile cruisers, which also highlighted it on every Roostship bridge's main display.

"The conservative fashion in which these cruisers are engaging indicates an intention to act as a temporary shield for the four destroyers loosely bunched behind them," she said over the fleetwide. "The latter's loose formation is a ruse, and once these two groups drift close enough to the nearby Roostship battle group, the cruisers will peel away, allowing the destroyers to hammer the Roostships with their main guns. We will leverage that tactic against them. The Roostships in question are to deploy their Talons into the debris field, as though intending to use it as a staging area for further harrying tactics. The moment the cruisers peel away, the Roostships are to take immediate evasive action, adjusting their attitude twenty degrees up from the ecliptic plane and engaging all engine power. The Talons will then emerge from the debris field en masse, engaging the destroyers from their aft starboard side. Simultaneously, their Roostships will level out and direct all available weapons at the destroyers. Following their destruction, the Roostships and Talons will work together to isolate and eliminate any missile cruisers that remain in the vicinity. Is that understood?"

"Understood, Flockhead," one of the Roostship captains in question said, and the others echoed him.

Ek highlighted another battle group. "These warships were constructed recently, and their design favors firepower over defensive capabilities. They have not incorporated a sufficient number of missile cruisers into their battle group to compensate for the weakness of their point defense systems. We cannot expect that situation to persist, and so it behooves us to devote the two nearest Roostship battle groups to its destruction." Highlighting the Roostships she meant, Ek continued. "Focus first on the missile cruisers, using the Talons' nimbleness to swoop in and neutralize them. After that, the rest of the enemy battle group should quickly fall to a concentrated barrage of Talon and Roostship missiles."

Not daring to stop, Ek moved on to the next scenario that required managing. And the next. Her voice grew hoarse, but still she talked on, watching as her orders were executed before her eyes. Whenever the overall situation evolved, she altered previous orders, and assigned follow-on orders to Roostships about to complete their current tasks. Every asset was in motion; nothing was wasted.

She had already pegged Carrow as a micromanager and not a delegator, and so he was in the same position as her, attempting to make the best use of multiple battle assets. But there were two key differences: his fleet was large and unwieldy, and also she was a Fin. Carrow was not.

Nevertheless, his long experience and his superior numbers were beginning to prevail. On top of that, reinforcements poured into the system for him as well, sometimes engaging the Roostships on their way to the center of the system.

A new Winger battle group managed to join the fray, emulating the tactics of those that had come before. This time, the UHF fleet bent inward, creating a hollow to bait the Roostships. It worked, and before Ek could warn the endangered Wingers, the human ships surged forward, enveloping them. They quickly fell.

I need to change tack.

Another thought followed on the heels of that one, a useless thought, but it followed nonetheless:

I need more time.

CHAPTER 70

People Can't Eat Money

Wandering through the camp, Bernard could feel the positive energy flowing through it. It felt hokey to think that, but it was true. This was a movement like nothing seen before, like nothing she'd have dared imagine possible. *I guess if you isolate people from hope for long enough, they get angry.* This *angry*.

"Senator Bernard!" called a mother whose head poked out of a tent. Behind her, Bernard could see two small children peering out at her, smiling.

"Good to see you," Bernard said.

"I just wanted to thank you. For all you've done. I voted for you, you know. I hate the way they rigged things against you. It won't be like that, next time."

"You're right. It won't. We won't let it." Her grin widening, Bernard continued on her way, readjusting her scarf against the biting wind. "Take care."

She picked her way through the camp, weaving through rows of tents until she reached the heart of it all, the logistics tent, where Flo was in the middle of a nervous breakdown.

The woman currently held a clump of hair in each hand as she revolved slowly in place, taking in the supplies stacked around her with widening eyes.

"Flo."

The logistics coordinator gave a start, then turned to face her. Her face relaxed one jot. "Senator. Hello."

"You seem concerned about something."

"I...I just—" Flo broke off, interrupted by a sob that seemed to surprise even her. After that, the dam broke, and tears fell freely down her face to drip on her puffy winter coat. "Four thousand veterans, Senator. Four thousand. That's how many Ralston just told me are on their way."

"Oh my." Bernard's reaction took a direction quite distinct from Flo's, though her sudden rush of adrenaline also made her want to cry. *It's happening. It's happening.* "I'm sure they must have the funds to match. With so many veterans coming, the corresponding public attention on it must be—"

"Tremendous, yes, yes. But people can't eat money. Someone needs to take the money to a store and buy food and supplies with it. And I'm the one who needs to make sure the money is invested wisely, so that we don't have supplies that simply go bad or get lost, that we pick reliable people to go on the supply runs, that we're able to access the nearest stores via the most fuel-efficient—"

"Wait. We can't be the only group to get veterans."

"No, you're right, and I pity the poor logistics people at the other camps as much as I pity myself. The veterans are showing up everywhere. Hundreds of thousands of them, descending on hapless logistics coordinators, demanding to be sheltered and fed and..."

Flo kept talking, but Bernard tuned her out, too excited by what this meant. Hurst couldn't deny such a unified front—not only the people demanded her resignation, but also the very veterans that had defended humanity for so long. *What an incredibly powerful message.*

She left Flo to her task, which the poor woman didn't make any easier on herself. They all needed people like Flo. They needed her now, and they'd need her going forward, more than ever. Bernard just wished she could stop moaning and find some peace.

Outside the tent, she ran into Corporal Simpson. "Trish," she said, and got excited all over again. "Have you heard the news? The veterans—so many—"

"Thousands," Simpson said, nodding, a smile sprouting across her face. "Keyes's plan is working, and Ralston executed it flawlessly. This is catching fire. And not only that. News just came in that the *Providence* was liberated, a mere seven hours ago. The revolution gauge jumped up to forty-nine percent, Sandy."

Bernard nodded, and now the tears did come. Not quite as loud or prolific as Flo's, but they came all the same.

The people have had enough. It's happening.

CHAPTER 71

Goliath

As Fesky finished briefing her pilots on the coming fight, she tried not to marvel at just how many of them the *Providence* had serving on her now.

For the first time in years, she had to set up the old telepresence system to properly brief all of her pilots, who now filled four ready rooms. There'd been no time to get it running during the UHF ambush in the Feverfew System, but that entire affair had been a debacle. *To be fair, I should have set it up before then.* She'd still been reeling from the loss of Spire, but she recognized that as a flimsy excuse.

"We now have the ability to put one hundred and ninety-four Condors in the air," she told her pilots, who stared back at her with the set jaws and narrowed eyes of experienced soldiers on the cusp of battle. "That's almost fifty percent of the supercarrier's total capacity. The *Providence* is returning to her former glory. Let's show Hades exactly what that means."

As her pilots filed out of the ready room to prepare for the coming battle, Fesky's com beeped, and when she took it out she saw it was Husher calling. The human had grown on her since they'd first met in the crew's mess, the night the war had begun. But she didn't know how she felt about him captaining the ship. For that matter, she sensed that *he* didn't know how to feel about it, either.

All the more reason to win this engagement handily and get Captain Keyes home.

"Madcap," he said, sounding calm enough. *Maybe he is ready.* "You ready to launch?"

"Affirmative."

"Good. You briefed them on the *Goliath*, right?"

"Obviously." A briefing on a mission to Hades would not have been much of one without exhaustively covering the dusty old destroyer charged with guarding the prison.

"Good. Because she clearly knows we're coming. She's parked right over one of the orbital platforms, giving us good reason to believe that's where they're keeping Keyes. The *Goliath*'s captain isn't making the same mistake Bronson did. He clearly has no intention of leaving the protection of the platform's arsenal."

"Smart." The Hades orbital defense platforms all wielded far greater firepower than the Vermillion Shipyards had. And the destroyer herself, while old, had been built just after the advent of dark tech, meaning it barely relied on that technology at all.

The *Goliath* was aptly named. A behemoth of a ship, she'd make a worthy opponent for the *Providence*, especially backed up by the platform's many guns.

"I know how well you've trained your pilots, Madcap, and this time you'll have the *Providence* fighting alongside you. But that doesn't mean this engagement is likely to be anything except the most trying of both our careers."

"You haven't been around for most of my career, fledgling."

"Fair point. Either way, I need you and your pilots on your A game."

"You'll get it."

"Excellent. Good luck, Madcap."

"Good luck, Spank. Try to keep this ship in as few pieces as possible, all right?"

He chuckled. "Husher out."

Twenty minutes later, she was inside her Condor, atop a launch catapult, with preflight alignment complete and all checks ran through twice. She switched to a wide channel. "Launch."

All squadrons jolted into space, leaving the *Providence* and swirling around her in formation. All one hundred and ninety-four Condor pilots, doing what they lived for: scanning the void for the enemy and thrilling for the kill.

The *Goliath* acted on them first, rising from Hades to spit salvo after salvo of solid-core kinetic impactors at the Condors. Her captain's aim was frightening. He fired not at the fighters, but at the space the fighters would soon occupy, and in doing so he ripped an entire half-squadron to shreds.

Fesky tapped her helmet, telling her transponder to transmit fleetwide. "All right, pilots, the *Goliath*'s not screwing around. For this entire engagement, I want you to incorporate guns-D maneuvers into your flying. If we continue to follow predictable flight paths, we're toast. We have a real fight on our hands."

CHAPTER 72

Technically an Admiral

Husher tapped his helmet to open a two-way channel. "Piper, you have everything you need up there?"

"Yes, though having to share this chamber with your cretinous father is far from ideal. It's difficult enough to operate five ships remotely without his eternal rudeness."

Husher failed to suppress a chuckle, and he doubted Piper would appreciate his mirth. But he felt grateful for the opportunity to laugh even in the tensest situations, and his interactions with the Tumbran often provided him with those opportunities. "That chamber is a CIC, Piper, and my father is your commanding officer."

"I'm not a part of your military."

"And yet, right now you're technically commanding five ships at the same time. Technically, you're an admiral."

Sitting in a crash seat across from Husher, Caine stared at him with wide eyes, which only made him want to laugh more.

"Why don't you tell me what you want me to do with these ships?" Piper said.

"Good idea. With my father's guidance, I want you to array them so that they shield the *Providence* from as many of the platform's turrets as possible, while providing our Condors with cover if they need it."

"What about the warship you're currently in?"

"I'm getting to that. Arrange this one like the other shield ships, except I want you to make sure she's the closest one to the platform, and don't stop moving her. Continue bringing her closer to the platform, and keep us updated on the level of damage she's taking from the turrets. Skids is going to fly us out of her shuttle bay at the last possible minute, which will hopefully be close enough to the platform's surface that we won't get shot down."

"All right, then."

"Good luck, Piper. Husher out."

Caine still looked aghast. "You're a crazy person. You know that, right?"

"What? I think it's a great plan."

"I'm not talking about the plan. I'm talking about that." Caine pointed to the rear of the shuttle's troop compartment, where Tort thrashed against his restraints atop the reinforced gurney Husher had ordered assembled during the trip to Hades from the Caprice System. He'd also told them to put Tort back in the armored pressure suit he'd been wearing when they'd met him. *And* he'd ordered Piper to stop administering sedatives to the Gok.

"He's fine," Husher said.

"It's not him I'm worried about. I'm worried about what will happen to my men and women once you free him. He can't control his rage, Husher. He told us that himself."

"You're right, he can't. But he can redirect it. And I expect to have some new targets for him to focus it on fairly soon."

"It's irresponsible."

"Wrong, Caine. It would be irresponsible for me to neglect to use a single asset at my disposal in the effort to rescue Captain Keyes. Anyway, we brought a tranq gun, which Piper filled with enough sedative to take down a Gok of his weight. If he gets out of hand, we can make him sleep again at any time."

"You make it all sound so easy."

For the sake of morale, Husher had to appear this confident. But in truth, the Gok did worry him, and he wasn't the only one fueling his anxiety. Husher also couldn't stop thinking about the conversation he'd had with his father before departing the *Providence*.

"I don't know if I can do this, Vin," he'd said.

"You have to. Who else do I have with command experience? You're it, Dad."

"*You're* it. You should sit in the Captain's chair, not me."

Husher had shaken his head. "I have to go down there. I'm still not confident Caine's one hundred percent, after her lapse, and anyway, I can't send her down alone with Tort. I'm taking full responsibility for setting him free, and that means being there if things go wrong. I need to command that platoon."

"Vin, I think I've lost my edge. Letting the *Contest*'s engine get taken out, plus I'm slow to react, and—"

"Dad, from what Captain Keyes has said about you, I doubt there's anyone he'd trust more to fly the *Providence* while he's away. You're going to do this."

That brought a slow nod from his father, though it looked like it was being dragged out of him. "Yeah. Okay." The corners of Warren's lips turned upward. "The chance to command a supercarrier is kind of mind-blowing. They were the top-of-the-line badass ships, in my day. It's a shame she's the only one left."

Caine spoke again, yanking Husher out of his thoughts. "What if Captain Keyes isn't being held on the platform we're headed toward?" Her voice was much softer, now.

Drawing in a long breath, Husher said, "It's the one the *Goliath* is guarding. We have to assume that Keyes is a high-value enough detainee that they wouldn't risk a ruse like parking the destroyer over the wrong platform."

"If it is a ruse, we're screwed."

"I know that. But we just have to—"

"Roll the dice?"

Husher smiled, and Caine did too, for the first time in a while. "Yeah," he said, his heart suddenly racing.

Piper's voice cut into his helmet. "You're nearing the platform." They hadn't had time to sync up the shuttle's sensors with the ship they were riding in, and so Skids was relying on Piper to let them know the optimal time to leave the shuttle bay. And Piper was relying on Werner, who also had his eye on the engagement with the *Goliath.*

Is there any part of this mission that isn't extremely risky? "How near is nearing, Piper? And what does our ride look like from the outside?"

"It's taken a lot of damage. Hull breaches in several places. Honestly, I'm surprised it's held together this long."

"That would have been helpful to know a little earlier than this, Piper!"

Skids's voice interrupted their conversation, then. "We're getting a lot of billowing smoke inside the bay, sir. It's affecting visibility. I mean, I can fly out of here by feel, but it's not ideal."

"Get us out of here!" Husher barked. "Now!"

"Roger that."

The shuttle lurched forward, and the troop compartment's display switched to provide them with a stomach-churning view of a smoke-choked shuttle bay, which they hurtled through.

Husher couldn't see anything relevant through the billowing pillar that filled most of the screen, but hopefully Skids had access to a better view from the cockpit. *I could kill him for even taking the time to put a visual feed on our display.* Though it did fit Skids's sick sense of humor.

They screamed out of the shuttle bay at a height that looked a mere three or four meters above the platform's surface. A brilliant flash of light filled the display from behind, followed by pieces of the ship they'd just vacated speeding past them. Some of the shrapnel hit their shuttle, causing it to rock worryingly.

But Skids leveled them out, executing a surprisingly soft landing near what appeared to be an airlock leading into the prison.

"See?" the shuttle pilot said into Husher's ear. "That wasn't so bad, was it?"

The shuttle vibrated again, and the viewscreen switched automatically to show suited-up figures shooting at them from near the prison entrance.

"Let us out of here, Skids. If you want something to fly back to the *Providence* in, you'll open that airlock right now." He switched to a platoon-wide channel. "All right, everyone. Stay focused, and remember what we're here for. There's not one of us Captain Keyes hasn't looked after at some point, so now we're going to return the favor."

"Oorah," the marines shouted as one.

"Oh," Husher said. "And someone grab that Gok."

CHAPTER 73

Unfit

Warren stared dumbly at the computer before him, its function escaping him for the moment. He raised a finger to tap at it, then hesitated. *No. I might...* What? What might pawing at the computer do? The idea that it had an important purpose skittered around his brain as he tried to pin it down.

"Captain?"

He didn't know who that woman was addressing, but the answer could provide Warren with some valuable clues about his current situation. So he waited, listening for the response.

"*Captain!*"

Wait. Is she talking to me?

He looked up to find a room full of faces, staring at him wearing distraught expressions. "Are you...?"

Shaking his head, context slowly seeped back into his brain. He *was* the captain. Captain of...the *Providence*! It all came rushing back. His son had left him in charge of the only super-carrier left in the galaxy. He'd trusted him.

"Yes," he said. "Um..." *Think, Warren.* He was in the middle of a battle. Against...he glanced up at the large viewscreen, toward which every console was angled. *Against a really large destroyer.*

"What's our capacitor charge?" he said. They seemed like very fine words to say. Just the right ones, in fact. What a relief to have found them.

"Enough to fire tertiaries," the woman who'd spoken earlier answered slowly.

"Excellent. Fire tertiary lasers at the destroyer. Disrupt their aim, confuse their sensors."

"Sir, that's only likely to happen if we pair it with evasive movement, and even then it's not considered a very effective tactic. What it's much more likely to accomplish is disrupting communications between our own Condors."

Warren ground his teeth. He'd discovered the perfect words for the situation, and now this woman dared to defy him. "I gave an order."

The woman stood from her station. "And I'm belaying it. With the absence of a ship's doctor, and as one of the ranking officers in the CIC, I am declaring you mentally unfit to command this vessel. You are relieved from duty, Warren Husher. Retire to your quarters at once."

Even Warren could sense the tension as everyone watched to see how he would react. He became suddenly aware of the weight of the service pistol hanging in its holster from his belt. His eyes wandered to the woman's hands, which were perched on her own belt. *She's ready to draw if I do. But I was always quick...*

He shook his head to clear it. *What am I thinking?* He stood. "Yes," he blurted, afraid he would do something rash unless he committed himself to a course of action. "I am unfit. You're right. I'll leave."

The woman—*Arsenyev, isn't it?*—slowly nodded, and waited until he walked to the CIC's hatch.

He paused there. "Good luck," he said, smiling a little.

That brought a curt nod from Arsenyev, who still watched him, her body rigid with readiness.

Warren left the CIC.

CHAPTER 74

High-Value Target

For some reason, the *Goliath*'s point defense weapon system had become less occupied, allowing her turrets to devote increased attention to the Condors swarming all around her.

Fesky's HUD lit up with scarlet as two turrets painted her with a firing solution. Given her current trajectory, the only option left was to dive closer to the destroyer.

She took the opportunity to bury a row of kinetic impactors in her hull, but pulling away and avoiding the follow-up turret fire required the best guns-D flying of her life. Despite her intense focus, she couldn't help registering it as four other Condors went down on her tactical display, one of them a member of the Divebombers.

When she finally succeeded in maneuvering to a safe distance, it did not elate her. It made her mad.

Slapping her transponder, she squawked, "*Providence*, what happened to our suppressive fire? Those turrets just took down four of my pilots, all because it suddenly had no Banshees to deal with."

Arsenyev's voice filled her helmet. "Apologies, Fesky. I have taken temporary command of the *Providence*. Warren Husher has been found unfit."

At that, Fesky felt some of the weight she'd been carrying leave her. She didn't relish seeing a great captain cast low, but Warren had been acting erratically since taking command of the *Contest* during the Vermillion Shipyards engagement. Also, Fesky had a lot of faith in Arsenyev.

"All right, then. In that case, let's take down that beast. Our shield ships are taking a severe beating, and I doubt they'll hold together much longer. I've already lost too many Condors, and most of the pilots had no time to eject. We have limited supplies of both."

"I couldn't agree more," Arsenyev said.

Before Fesky could speak again, her cockpit washed red. The *Goliath* had sent a stream of missiles at her Condor, no doubt having identified her as a high-value target after the fancy flying she'd used to escape getting taken out moments before.

Fesky gunned the engine, laying the Ocharium boost on thick. That gained her some distance, allowing her to spin her fighter around its short axis and start picking off some of the guided bombs.

The *Providence* saw her plight and chipped in, sending Banshees to intercept some of the pursuing projectiles. Unfortunately, the *Goliath*'s captain was too smart to bunch the missiles together, meaning Arsenyev had to spend one Banshee for each one neutralized. They didn't have an unlimited supply of Banshees, either.

Whipping her Condor around once more, Fesky gunned the engines, making for the nearest shield ship, a corvette. Because of the time she'd taken to fire back at them, the remaining missiles were closing on her.

The Condor zipped toward the corvette's nose, and just before she drew flush with it, she rotated again, directing her engines parallel with the hull. *This will hurt.* Fesky punched it, soaking up every drop of acceleration her engines would give her and hugging the corvette's hull. Intense g-forces bore down on her, and merely remaining conscious required a high-intensity workout.

But the maneuver worked. Most of the missiles collided with the bow of the corvette, disintegrating it. A couple of them veered around it, continuing to give chase, but Fesky brought her Condor around and easily finished them off.

She took a deep breath, feeling utterly exhausted after the effort escaping the missiles had required. But this wasn't over. Looping around the corvette, she rejoined the battle, beginning by shooting down a pair of missiles chasing another of her pilots.

"Thanks, Madcap." It was Airman Bradley, who just a few short weeks ago had counted among her most vicious critics.

"Any time."

Her tactical display showed more and more Condors falling to the *Goliath*'s expert marksmanship. And the *Providence* wasn't spared from the barrage. The enemy ship's captain made such efficient use of his arsenal that he had enough to spare for defense as well as offense against both the Condors and their supercarrier.

I don't even want to consider what will happen once those shield ships go.

But she needed to consider it. Because when the enemy succeeded in destroying them, the *Providence* and her Condors would become completely exposed to every turret on the orbital defense platform.

And that would be a reality soon.

CHAPTER 75

No Going Back

Inside Hades' squat corridors, Husher couldn't leverage his Winger marines' ability to fly. Even so, they complemented the humans well. With their shorter statures, the other marines could easily fire over the Wingers' heads.

After overcoming the defenders guarding the airlock, the section they found themselves in appeared to have an administration function. That said, it had no shortage of prison guards and security personnel, pressing back hard against the marine incursion, refusing to give an inch. They'd had ample advance notice of the marines' arrival, and they'd prepared accordingly.

Even the prison's offices had steel-reinforced hatches as doors, and so Husher set his marines to making good use of them, opening them into the hallway and using them as cover.

It quickly became an old-fashioned slugfest. Neither side seemed eager to use grenades or other explosives. The guards had likely been ordered not to by their bosses, so as not to cause undue damage to the prison, and for Husher's part, he didn't want to risk depressurizing the entire section. He and his marines would be fine in that event, but if Keyes was here, he almost certainly wasn't wearing a pressure suit.

Husher popped out from behind the door he used for cover, fired off a single round, and then had to withdraw again.

"There's too many of them," Caine said from the other side of the corridor, behind a door of her own. "If this takes any longer, they'll no doubt get even more backup. We need to break them now. I hate to say it, but I think it's time to release the Gok."

"Music to my ears. Cover me?"

Caine nodded, pivoting around the hatch and sending suppressive fire at the enemy. For his part, Husher crouched and ran several hatches back, where Wahlburg stood watch over the gurney they'd dragged inside the prison with them. Husher nodded at the sniper, who held the tranq gun at the ready. Wahlburg was the only one Husher trusted with a shot that important, if it needed to be taken.

As far as Husher knew, the prison guards weren't aware of Tort's presence. Switching to a two-way channel, he addressed the Gok, who was straining tirelessly against the nanofabric straps holding him in place. "Tort. How are you feeling?"

"Am ready!" Tort bellowed into Husher's helmet, making him wince and turn down the volume.

He felt bad for returning the alien to this agitated state, but they clearly needed him right now. Besides, the Gok had asked Keyes to help find a cure for the virophage, and Keyes couldn't do that while imprisoned.

"My marines are all taking cover behind hatches. You'll see them as you pass. You must not harm them. I need you to focus all of your rage on the guards attacking us. We won't leave you to confront them alone—we'll be moving up along with you. If you harm a single man or woman under my command, Wahlburg will take you down, and I guarantee you'll get no help from us in curing the virophage that infects you. Is that clear?"

"Clear!" The Gok thrust upward with his fists, causing the straps to creak. He did it again. "*Clear!*"

God help us all. "Release him," he told Wahlburg.

The sniper nodded, reaching across the hulking alien to unfasten the restraints, first those holding down his legs, and then his torso.

"Your energy weapon is tied underneath the gurney," Husher told the Gok, just before Tort surged upward.

Instead of reaching underneath the gurney to free his gun, Tort picked up the entire thing with one hand and slammed it against the ceiling. That done, he ran toward the enemy with the steel-reinforced contraption held over his head, raining sparks down into the corridor.

Exchanging a brief glance with Wahlburg, whose eyes were large behind his faceplate, Husher switched to a wide channel. "Everybody, move! Back up Tort!"

The marines rushed from cover and fired around the Gok at any targets that exposed themselves.

One of the prison guards emerged from behind a hatch to fire at the charging Gok, but the bullets bounced harmlessly off of his titanium-plated armor. Tort flung the gurney at the hatch protecting the guard, and it slammed shut, knocking the guard off his feet. A second later, Tort reached the hatch on the opposite side of the hallway. He booted it closed, and the crunch of bone came through Husher's helmet audio, accompanied by a spurt of scarlet as the guard was crushed between the hatch and its frame.

Catching up to the gurney, Tort picked it up and ripped his directed-energy weapon from the thick ropes holding it in place. He threw the gurney down the hallway, catching a guard who had been popping out for another shot full in the face.

Tort reached the next set of hatches, kicked one shut, and grabbed the guard behind the opposite hatch by the front of his suit, slamming his skull against the ceiling and then dropping him like a used rag. The guard crumpled to the floor.

More emerged from cover to fire on Tort, and only then did the Gok return fire, sending bolts of light flying down the corridor. Flesh melted and popped where the energy beam touched it, and clothing caught fire.

The remaining guards turned and fled down the corridor, and Husher saw them run into another group on their way to provide backup, causing a great deal of confusion as those fleeing Tort tried to communicate the approaching danger.

Tort didn't wait for them to figure it out. He advanced down the corridor, firing bolt after bolt into the throng of guards. After a few seconds of carnage, they managed to organize themselves enough to return fire, but Husher had fought Gok soldiers over Spire, and he knew the precision required to penetrate their armor. At their remove, and with that level of panic, the guards weren't coming close. Soon enough, the entire group broke once again, turning to flee en masse.

As Husher trotted after Tort, Caine kept pace, and she caught his gaze through their faceplates, her eyebrows raised. "All right, then," she said.

He nodded. "All right, then."

As Tort rampaged through the station, backed up by the marine's supporting fire, they began passing cell blocks, each with an interactive information panel next to the entrance hatch. No security clearance was required to access the lists of prisoners. Evidently, the designers hadn't expected intruders to ever get this far.

Finally, they came to a hatch with only one prisoner listed: Leonard Keyes.

Husher opened a two-way with the Gok, who had ranged ahead, seeking more kills. "Hey, Tort. We found the captain. You can...uh, could you...?" He glanced at Wahlburg, who had recovered the gurney from where Tort had thrown it. He'd dragged it along with them while keeping the tranq gun near at hand.

I don't want to put Tort to sleep prematurely. "Tort, we need you to wait here while we extract Captain Keyes."

The Gok turned abruptly, running back toward him at full speed. Husher wanted to take a step backward, but instinct told him not to. He clutched his assault rifle.

Tort stopped a few meters away, where the corpse of a guard lay strewn on the metal floor. The Gok bent over it, first pounding it with his fists, and then slamming it against the wall viciously, quickly turning the body into a pulpy mess. "Hurry," Tort grunted. "Just...hurry."

Husher swallowed. "Yeah. Okay." He motioned to the others, and they opened the hatch.

The long, narrow room was bordered by tables full of computer equipment and what Husher recognized as torture implements. Those who stooped to such practices had another name for it, but Husher called it what it was. Torture.

The room also featured an observation window that looked into a cell, and inside that cell was Captain Keyes, slumped sideways against a wall.

Running to the door that separated the observation room from the cell, Husher found it locked. He stepped back and fired at the lock. After a few seconds, he tried again. This time, it opened. He rushed to Keyes's side.

No reaction from the captain. Husher put a hand on his shoulder, turning the man toward him.

He gasped. Keyes was almost unrecognizable. One of his eyes was swollen shut, and his face was covered in blistered abrasions, which had split in several places. The one eye that was visible seemed to stare into space at nothing.

Husher shook him gently. "Captain?"

At last, the eye focused on him. "Husher."

"We're getting you out of here. Can you walk?"

Keyes pushed himself up, leaning heavily on the wall. When Husher offered his arm, he leaned on that.

"Let's go," Husher said, and they made their way out of the cell, as quickly as the captain could manage.

In the hallway, Keyes glanced at the Gok, who was still savaging the corpse. But the captain made no remark.

Husher nodded at Wahlburg, and the sniper leveled the tranq gun at the alien, firing a diamond-tipped dart that punched through the fabric at the seam where Tort's helmet met his suit.

"Let's go," Husher said over a wide channel. "Work together to lift the Gok onto the gurney as fast as you can. We need to get back to the shuttle." They'd brought an extra pressure suit with them, for Keyes, but Husher decided to wait until they reached the airlock to get him into it.

He didn't feel as good as he'd expected to, freeing the captain. It felt like victory, but not quite as pure a victory as he'd hoped.

The captain seemed changed by his captivity. Husher had no idea what shape that change might take, going forward, but he felt certain that whatever it was, there would be no going back.

CHAPTER 76

Old Steel

Arsenyev instructed Piper to send the two shield ships in the best condition to meet the shuttle coming up from the platform. That way, the shuttle could fly between them, protected from turret fire for as long as the ships flanking it held together.

Since she'd taken command of the *Providence*, the battle had been slowly turning in their favor. Warren Husher's lapses had left a lot of tactical options unexplored, which she now pursued with a vengeance.

He'd simply been lobbing missiles at the destroyer in the hopes that it would allow the Condors to use alpha strikes in order to take out critical components. But Arsenyev chose her targets with care, alternately going after the destroyer's engines and the point defense turrets themselves.

That had the dual effect of diverting even more of the enemy captain's attention to the incoming missiles, given the criticality of their targets, while crippling the destroyer further whenever a Banshee did land. And as Arsenyev fired Banshees at one type of target, she directed kinetic impactors at the other.

Fesky quickly adapted to the tactics change from her captain, as any good CAG should. But Fesky wasn't just good. She was almost certainly the best, and she masterfully exploited the increased pressure applied by the *Providence*, organizing her pilots to take down yet more turrets.

When the destroyer's point defense system was sufficiently weakened, Fesky set her Air Group to executing rotating alpha strikes, with various squadrons targeting parts of the destroyer at random. Combined with Arsenyev's more methodical approach, the unpredictable nature of the air strikes served to wreak havoc on the enemy's disposition, which manifested in an increasing number of slip-ups. *We're doing it.*

But with two fewer shield ships, the *Providence* was taking heavy fire from the defense platform's turrets, and so it came as a relief when the captain of the *Goliath* sent a message signaling that he wished to yield.

"Get him on the main viewscreen, Coms," Arsenyev said.

"Yes, ma'am."

The man who appeared on the screen looked about as old and dusty as the destroyer he captained. His white beard badly needed a trim, and his wiry hair stuck up in a way that put Arsenyev in mind of a stressed-out Winger.

"I yield," he said. "Well fought."

"And you. I will accept your request, provided you can get Hades' turrets to stop firing at us immediately. You have thirty seconds."

The captain of the *Goliath* inclined his head and ended transmission. Within the timeframe Arsenyev had allotted, the orders had apparently been sent and accepted, since all pressure from the orbital defense platform ceased. That drew a sigh of relief from her. She switched to a fleetwide channel. "All Condors, return to base."

As soon as she received word that the shuttle containing Husher, Caine, and Captain Keyes was on board, Arsenyev ordered her Nav officer to set a course out of the system. To her surprise, just minutes later, the party from the shuttle entered the CIC.

She stifled a gasp when her eyes fell on the captain, and her heart rate felt like it tripled. *Oh no...*

Husher escorted Keyes to the Captain's chair, where Arsenyev still sat, gaping at him. She turned to the young officer supporting the captain. "Lieutenant, Captain Keyes is clearly in no condition—"

"Trust me, Ensign, I wanted to take him to sick bay. He insisted on coming here. Called it a direct order."

Though it must have caused him incredible pain to talk, Keyes moved his cracked lips, rasping, "If I may, Arsenyev."

Slowly, she nodded and rose to her feet, moving out of the captain's way.

Keyes settled into the chair, struggling to lift his arms to the armrests, as though they were metal weights. Once he'd arranged himself to his liking, he stared at the Captain's console for a long time, breath coming in ragged heaves. It occurred to Arsenyev that the captain was about to cry.

But he did not cry. He spoke again, with the deliberate manner of a man afraid of breaking something. Perhaps himself.

"This is where I belong. The next time I'm parted from this chair, it will be by my death."

A long silence followed, during which Keyes's eyes remained on the deck while he seemed to compose himself. *He keeps having to do that.* How long could the captain keep this up without first taking a long rest in sick bay?

But when Keyes raised his eyes again, some of their old steel had returned. They fell on Husher. "You captained my ship for a time. Did you not?"

"Yes."

"And yet you do not hold the rank of captain."

Husher paused before answering. "No."

"You held it once. The old UHF demoted you. This is the new UHF, and as an officer of it, I am promoting you again, from first lieutenant to captain."

"Yes, sir. Thank you, sir."

Keyes nodded, the same way he did everything now, slowly, deliberately. His eyes fell on Arsenyev. "Fesky has already been in touch to tell me what happened during this engagement. You held things together here when they were falling apart. I am promoting you to lieutenant, and I'm making you XO of this ship."

Warmth radiated through Arsenyev's chest, though her joy was tempered by her concern for the captain. "Thank you, sir. Thank you."

"The war continues, and we will hold brief promotion ceremonies for you both, but only provided the war effort leaves us with extra time. Somehow, I doubt it will. Bring me Warren Husher."

It took several minutes for a marine to escort the old war hero from his chambers. When he finally arrived, to stand before the Captain's chair with shoulders slumped, it occurred to Arsenyev that Warren Husher and the captain bore a resemblance now that they hadn't before. Both had been through terrible ordeals, and both labored under the weight of them.

Keyes's swollen face again began the painful process of speech. "Fesky tells me you faltered when the need was greatest, old friend."

Warren didn't seem able to take his eyes off of the deck. "It's true."

"What happened?"

"I don't know. Maybe, my time with the Ixa...they changed me, Leonard. Did something to my brain."

A nod from the captain. "Hmm. You did no irreparable damage. I hope, in time, you can free yourself from the Ixan taint. Until such time, you must hold no command. Indeed, you must hold no rank of any kind."

"I understand. I think...I think I can fight it off. In time."

But to Arsenyev, Warren didn't truly look convinced.

CHAPTER 77

Suicide Run

"A nother Roostship has fallen, Flockhead," the sensors adjutant said quietly.

But Ek already knew. She had noticed the icon vanish from the tactical display, even though the display was still populated by thousands of icons. Acknowledging the adjutant's report with the barest nod, she returned to giving the Winger fleet orders based on her comprehensive analysis of the state of play. Occasionally her vision swam, and at those times, only the seat's straps kept her in it. Even then, she did her best to ignore her body's trials, instead riveting her attention to her strategizing.

Talon pilots would fight to the death to protect their Roostships, and unfortunately, that was exactly what this battle required of them. With every hour that passed, they fell by the dozens, while the enemy's losses slowed. Carrow destroyed more and more Roostships, and the pirates' numbers were cut almost in half, with Korbyn's warship on its last wings.

More Roostships arrived in an irregular stream, but with Ek's main fleet dwindling, and UHF reinforcements arriving all the time, it was not enough to turn the tide. Vaghn's fleet was still over two hours away, and Ek now knew for certain that even the rogue captain's arrival would prove meaningless.

In spite of Ek's best efforts, she had lost too many ships too quickly. Defeat was inevitable.

The end to which I have led the Wingers is no more noble than the one they had chosen for themselves.

To get this far, enraging Carrow with her false surrender had been necessary, but now it prevented her from sparing any of her Wingers' lives.

Which meant this battle was nothing more than a glorified suicide run.

CHAPTER 78

Wartime Powers

It had taken Hurst a lot of effort to arrange this.

She'd fired official after official who refused to cooperate. It didn't cost her any sleep to do that. They were short-sighted idiots, who couldn't understand her plans for the galaxy.

Finally, she'd found a former planetary governor with the legal expertise and the willingness to help her draw up legislation that would give her sweeping wartime powers. They included the ability to pass laws without having to involve the Galactic Congress. And since she never intended for war to end during her lifetime, she would always possess these powers.

One of her first laws would suspend elections during war. For the security of the Commonwealth, of course.

Once the bill was finished, she handed it to top officials of her party, who had quickly learned not to oppose her. Since her party held a majority in both the Galactic Congress and Senate, and since the opposition party was nothing more than a collection of spineless suckholes, the bill passed with ease.

She already had her first law prepared. It was not the law suspending elections, though that would come soon. No, it was something to put a final end to the trouble being caused by all these economic terrorists.

Hurst signed the new law surrounded by top members of her cabinet, all of it recorded and broadcast by a multitude of cameras operated by fawning news organizations. She'd bent them all to her will during recent weeks. That had been easy enough, too.

Turning briefly to her pet reporter Horace Finkel, Hurst winked at him. He blinked, chin twitching, before he quickly replaced the uncertain expression with a pasted-on smile.

The new law was signed on camera because Hurst no longer cared about placating the public. Sure, the economy might take a hit, but the corporations need not worry, because she planned to give them completely free rein. There would follow an economic boom, because companies would never need to take anything but profit into consideration ever again.

As soon as the new law was signed, Hurst began handing down orders that were now perfectly legal. She had no intention of letting the public digest the implications of her new powers— they would witness the effects of them at the same time news of the law was being disseminated.

Even before the last camera left her office, Hurst had a small chuckle to herself about the protesters' main demand, that she resign. Resign? She didn't think so. The opposite, actually.

Everyone would soon get used to life under her.

CHAPTER 79

Life on the Line

Police Sergeant Doucet held his com to his ear, but he could barely feel it there. It was as though his entire body had gone numb.

"Chief, are...are you sure about this?"

The chief sighed. "I don't like it either, Doucet. And I don't mind telling you that I expect this to keep me up at night, for many months. But orders are orders, aren't they?"

"Yes, sir."

"Say it, Doucet."

"Orders are orders, sir."

"Good man. Now..." The chief cleared his throat. "Now go do your job. If you want to keep it, you'll do it." The call ended.

Stomach heavy, Doucet trudged toward the front of the police line, holding out his hand as he passed Corporal Bradley. "Give me the bullhorn," he said, his voice toneless and dull in his own ears. Bradley relinquished it.

"Form ranks," Doucet said into the bullhorn, and his police fell in, as orderly and efficient as always. He dropped the bullhorn to his side as he continued to the front, so that he could at least look the protesters in the eyes as he gave the next order. He owed them that much.

Noise levels had fallen to unusual lows, leaving only the sounds of the Martian winter, which were few. Gradually, more and more people were turning to focus on Doucet—demonstrators, reporters. The police remained in their ranks, staring forward.

Slowly, he raised the bullhorn to his lips once again, and he paused, eyes scanning the people assembled before him on the road. The veterans had arrayed themselves in front, all in full uniform, a reminder of the sacrifices they'd made for the Commonwealth. Of the risks they'd taken, and of the risks they continued to take.

Just say it. The next order he had to give consisted only of two words.

Open fire.

The protesters, who called themselves defenders, were eyeing him, wearing uncertain expressions. They didn't know what was about to happen. And soon, they wouldn't know anything. There would be nothing left for them to know.

Doucet opened his mouth, first taking a deep breath, feeling as though he was going to vomit. *Say it, Doucet. Say it.*

His hand fell to his side, and the bullhorn clattered to the pavement. Taking a step forward, he hesitated, and scooped up the bullhorn again. Then he crossed the open space between the police line and the protesters.

Bewildered expressions dawned on the faces of the protesters, and even on those of the veterans, who'd no doubt witnessed far more than the average person. Far more than they'd ever wanted to, probably.

Doucet stopped just in front of the veterans and turned around. Then he raised the bullhorn once more.

"I've been given the order to open fire on the protesters. Apparently, President Hurst decided the only way to bring the public in line with her thinking is to start killing them until those that survive are too afraid to continue objecting. I can't carry water for this president any longer. In my time as a police officer, I've put my life on the line too many times for the public. Now it's time for me to do that again. If your conscience allows you to follow Hurst's order, then I guess you'd better start firing. But I will be one of the people you kill."

In the silence that followed, Doucet unbuckled his gun belt and tossed it to land on the road a few feet away.

The police officers stared across the divide from their ranks, the same officers that he'd led in the effort to quell the protests over the past weeks. Many of them wore the blank expressions instilled by their training, but others wore their emotions plainly, with anger, fear, and confusion all warring on their faces.

Then, without warning, one of the newest officers unbuckled his gun belt and dropped it to the ground. He walked across the stretch of empty pavement to stand alongside Doucet, thumbs tucked into his pockets.

Another officer removed her gun belt too, letting it fall to the pavement before walking over.

The floodgates broke, then, and the police started crossing over to the protesters in twos and threes, fives and sixes. Soon, only the media stood on the side the police once had. They all looked dumbfounded, but they continued to do the one thing they knew how to. They recorded the event, and they broadcast it.

The veteran with the Scottish accent spoke from behind Doucet, quietly: "Oorah."

Doucet nodded, and he put his fist in the air, a little uncertainly at first. "Oorah," he said.

And then, just like that, the entire crowd was chanting it, the police officers included: "Oorah! Oorah! Oorah!"

CHAPTER 80

Immediate Self-Interest

E ven with certain death approaching, Ek did not stop analyzing the flow of the battle and giving the most effective orders she could based on her analysis. Retreat was not an option, and that did not come from any misguided notion of valor. If her fleet tried to disengage, Carrow would pounce, decimating them before they came anywhere near the closest darkgate.

Reason made her course of action clear: make the UHF pay as dear a price as possible for their victory, reducing their ability to continue doing damage to the galaxy. They would still possess considerable power to do that after killing her, but if she could lessen it even one iota, she would.

Vaghn still approached, and so did every Winger in the system, with more entering through the system's darkgates in a continual stream. Ek had sent them messages instructing them to turn around, but they came anyway. That saddened Ek. She had wanted a future filled with meaning for the Wingers. Now, they would merely break themselves against the might of the UHF instead of the Gok.

On the tactical display, something anomalous caught her eye. She looked at the sensors adjutant. "Are our sensors working properly?"

The Winger returned her gaze with a bemused one of her own. "As best as I can tell, Flockhead."

"Run diagnostics on them."

She waited while the adjutant bent over her console, rapidly tapping the touch controls and dragging elements around. In the meantime, more anomalies cropped up on the tactical display. *There has to be something malfunctioning.*

But when the Winger had the results of the diagnostics scan, they showed that everything was in perfect working order.

"That cannot be," Ek said. "According to the tactical display, the UHF ships are attacking each other."

"It's what I'm seeing too, Honored One," the sensors adjutant said.

"Flockhead, we're getting a transmission request," the communications adjutant said. "From the *Renown*. A UHF destroyer."

"Accept."

A lanky, raven-haired woman appeared on the main view screen. "Ek, isn't it?" she said.

"It is."

"All right, then. We don't have much time for chitchat, so let me get straight to what I have to convey. The Hurst administration has lost all legitimacy. She gave herself dictatorial powers

and then ordered the slaughter of civilians. Most police and security personnel refused to carry out the order, and the public
are in total revolt. Many of our captains agree with the public
that the government is now illegitimate and therefore should no
longer direct UHF strategy. We submitted our concerns to Carrow, urging him to withdraw from this engagement, but he
would not hear of it. And so we're revolting, too."

Ek could not remember the last time she experienced surprise, but even though this was one of the outcomes she had
considered possible, she now felt it all the same. "I see."

"Most of the captains here support us. It's best if we end this
as quickly as possible, so that there's something left of the UHF
once we're finished. To accomplish that, we need your help. If
you'll accept a data transfer, I can send you the list of ships on
our side, in the file format Roostships use. It'll paint your new
allies green."

"Yes. I will accept it."

"Thank you, Ek. Now if you'll excuse me, I have an admiral to
fight. Luck to us both."

"Good luck."

With her tactical display lit up with green, Ek saw new opportunities where before there had been only death. She also
had a new group's tactics to anticipate—her allies, over whom
she could exercise no control.

And so she turned her attention to perceiving their intentions, as well as to how she could direct her own forces in order
to amplify her allies' efforts against Carrow's.

"Here," she said over the fleetwide, highlighting a grouping of green icons. "These ships are about to be overwhelmed. The three Roostships nearest them will order their Talons to intercept as many missiles targeting those allies as possible, while directing a steady barrage of kinetic impactors at the ships firing them." Ek highlighted another friendly group. "This battle group intends a strike that, if successful, will split the enemy's forces down the middle, eventually allowing us to smash the half closest to us before neutralizing the other." Another highlight. "These five Roostships will assist, ensuring the strike *is* successful. And here—"

"Flockhead Ek, the *Excalibur* is moving to confront us."

Ek looked at the icon that represented her own ship, and at the large red icon approaching it. "So it is," she said, and with a glance at the tactical display, she saw that there were no nearby Roostships able to help. If she called any to her aid, she would only risk their destruction as well as her own. Even many of her own ship's Talons were deployed elsewhere, some assisting other Roostship Air Groups, others backing up allied UHF warships.

Quickly reviewing her options, Ek saw that for her and the Wingers serving on her ship, the situation had not been altered by most of the UHF captains changing sides. Carrow still was not likely to accept her surrender, or any other peaceful resolution. As well, the firepower at Ek's disposal paled before that of the *Excalibur*'s. There was still no way she could win.

And so I must open my heart to defeat. "Send Admiral Carrow a transmission request."

"It's done, Flockhead."

The admiral stared at her with eyebrows raised when he appeared on-screen. "I hope you know the only reason I accepted your request was to rub it in your fishy face before I kill you."

"I will die," Ek said, her dorsal fin rigid with tension. "But I will choose the manner of my death."

"What are you—"

"Navigation adjutant, bring the Roostship full ahead, straight toward the oncoming destroyer, maximum acceleration. Strategic adjutant, fire our entire payload of missiles at the admiral's engines, in quick succession, and use as many kinetic impactors as we have time to before the collision."

"*Collision?*" Carrow said, his face whitening. "Have you lost your mind?"

The gap between the speeding ships narrowed. "On the contrary, I have decided to make my death count. If I am to die, then taking you with me seems like a valuable service to the galaxy. I invite you to attempt to destroy my Roostship before we reach you, but I do not think you have time to do so. Even if you manage it, it is probable that our missiles will damage your engines while our kinetic rounds perforate your hull. The others will catch you as you attempt to limp out of the system, and then they will mete out whatever justice they see fit. Your day is just as done as mine is, Admiral. Goodbye."

"Missiles ready, Flockhead," the strategic adjutant said.

Ek opened her mouth to give the go ahead when Admiral Carrow interjected: "Wait. Wait!"

"Yes, Admiral?"

"I surrender, damn you. Alter your course and belay your order to fire all your missiles."

"Very well. I will adjust my attitude upward, and I suggest that you adjust yours downward."

They did so, and the Roostship passed over the destroyer, so close that many of the Winger officers winced as they monitored the visual displays on their consoles.

"Navigation adjutant, set a course to rejoin our allies while conserving as much of our speed as possible," Ek said. "I do not trust the admiral to keep his word, now that it no longer serves his immediate self-interest."

With the battle won by all appearances, she finally allowed herself to relax, and the moment she let her guard down the space sickness attacked. Darkness edged in from her peripheral vision, creeping inexorably toward the center, and she felt her body slump against the chair's straps.

"Honored One?" Wingleader Ty said, and it was the last thing Ek heard.

CHAPTER 81

Service Pistol

Warren felt unusually positive as he scraped away his stubble with a razor. Washing his face afterward, he studied himself, pleased. He'd aged a lot since the First Galactic War, but that didn't matter. As long as he stayed cleanly shaven and sharply dressed, he looked the part of a UHF officer.

His goal was to get back to a place of certainty about his own mind, so that he could contribute to the war against the Ixa. And that started with looking the part. Maybe, if he made enough progress, they would even give him his own command.

But his positivity had other sources, too. Sonya Hurst had resigned as president of the Commonwealth after the biggest popular uprising in human history, and her trial had already begun.

New elections were also underway, with each candidate already having delivered their stump speeches. The most successful candidates were those promising never to take corporate money and to reform the electoral system the moment they got into office, removing corporations' ability to control the government.

Sandy Bernard had decided not to run, but after an enormous public outcry heard all across the Commonwealth, she'd changed her mind, and was now the leading candidate by a wide margin.

Best of all, as far as Warren could see, was the widespread support for finally doing the right thing. For finding a way off of dark tech, and for working with the Wingers instead of slaughtering them. Together, along with the Tumbra and even the Bastion Sector's former insurgents, they would find a way to defeat the Gok and the Ixa. *We have to.*

Admiral Carrow would be tried by a court-martial, but Bob Bronson was nowhere to be found. He'd probably joined Tennyson Steele and many other Darkstream employees in fleeing the Commonwealth.

Rumors said that Darkstream had long held a trump card in its back pocket; a contingency plan, in case their doings within the halls of power ever turned sour.

According to the rumors, the company had concealed an enormous colony ship somewhere deep down Pirate's Path. Whatever the case, most of the company's personnel had vanished, and many people worried that they would continue to use dark tech, further destabilizing the fabric of the universe.

Warren thought it likely they wouldn't, since there was no longer as much money to be made from it. Darkstream had lost control of the galactic government they'd once corrupted and sucked dry of funds. They'd lost the public that had unwittingly fueled their profits.

He gave a sigh born of contentment and optimism. Today would begin with venturing out into the Martian winter, to visit a neurologist. Later, he would visit Ek in the infirmary where she was being examined and ministered to by the best available doctors, but first he needed to start the process of figuring out what the Ixa had done to his brain.

As he reached for his glove, his hand faltered, and then it dropped to his side. Today, he would...

Today...

His mind emptied of thought and memory, becoming a total blank, filled only with sensory input. The handle of the bedside table's drawer felt cool against his fingers, but when he took out the service pistol he'd been given during his time aboard the *Contest*, it felt positively cold.

Mechanically, he checked the chamber to ensure the gun was fully loaded, then he turned off the safety. He yanked out his carefully ironed shirt and tucked the pistol inside his belt, hanging the shirt down over it, concealing it.

In the hallway, he encountered Fesky, who clacked her beak. "Hello..." she said, trailing off, apparently uncertain how to address him now. She turned as he passed by her wordlessly, watching him. "All right, then."

A left turn, then another. Without knocking, he pushed open the door to a conference room. Gathered around the table were Vin, Keyes, Simpson, Piper, Bernard, and a few planetary officials.

"Hello, Warren," Keyes said.

Warren didn't answer. Instead, he walked around the table, as though planning to take the empty seat beside Sandy Bernard. He didn't, though. Instead, he stopped behind Bernard, lifted his shirt, removed the gun, and planted the barrel against the brown hair covering the back of her skull.

As everyone else at the table surged to their feet, Warren unloaded the pistol into Bernard's head, which fell forward, hitting the conference table with a *thud*. Scarlet spattered the mahogany.

Memory came rushing back instantly, and he began to process the horror of what he had just done. Without thinking, he nestled the barrel under his chin.

But Vin had reached him by then, and he knocked the gun aside, causing the bullet to implant in the ceiling.

Then his son was wrenching the gun from him, tossing it onto the floor, and walking him several feet to slam him face-first against the wall. The others reached them, and they treated Warren just as roughly, helping Vin to wrestle him to the floor while Keyes shouted into his com for someone to bring restraints.

Warren wept silently into the patterned carpet.

CHAPTER 82

Dark Tech

Aheera walked with the others in her band across the lush fields of Home, enjoying the way the towering grass tickled her legs and arms and head-tail. The sun's rays found their way through the grassy sea, warming her just enough. On beautiful days—and most days on Home were beautiful, even the scheduled rain days—the temperature lingered at exactly the right level for a Kaithian. When the day started to cool at last, it served as a signal that the time had arrived to retire for the night.

That time had not yet come. Now was the time to walk through the grass with her band and attempt to chart a course for the Kaithe. *Perhaps for the universe.*

"The humans have done well," Culkin said. "They've progressed faster than we ever did, and with fewer atrocities. Ironic, isn't it? Perhaps we were correct to grant Leonard Keyes help when he came to us with traitors in his midst."

"That is not the prevailing sentiment." Aheera brushed the grass lovingly with her tail. "And we made no provisions to safeguard dissenters from the consequences of our actions."

Culkin opened his mouth wider than was necessary to speak, which signified an objection. "Because time did not permit."

"True, but that doesn't change our situation. We acted swiftly, without seeking Consensus. And now we have a smaller mandate to act."

"Forget mandates." Now Culkin had stopped walking, and he gripped a grass stalk, as though poised to rip it from the ground in anger.

Aheera felt her mouth twist in distaste as she spoke. "Forget mandates, Culkin? Forget the norms that have kept our society stable for millennia?"

"None of that matters," said Pulpa, light-blue hands planted on her hips. "Whether we can achieve Consensus, whether we have a mandate, or even care—it doesn't matter. The Ixa have succeeded in turning the humans against the Kaithe. We no longer have their trust, if we ever did."

Culkin released the grass stalk, but none of his anger. Aheera felt the heat of it ripple through her mind. "We *owe* the humans—"

"We owe them nothing," Aheera said, taking a step closer to her bandmate. "The humans are young. They've barely achieved sentience, and now you speak of dedicating ourselves to *their* aims?"

"They're struggling against the Ixa, Aheera. The *Ixa!*"

"And what do we risk becoming, if we take up the practice of offensive war once again? What did we become the last time our species waged offensive war? No better than the Ixa."

"That's what I'm trying to tell you. This would not be an offensive war. The Ixa are burgeoning, and if we stand by while they defeat the humans, we will have no recourse to adequately defend ourselves. Attacking the Ixa *is* our only defense."

"The Consensus does not see it that way. They aren't convinced by arguments for defense that contain the word 'attack.'"

"Look," Pulpa said, pointing at the display they'd set to hover ahead of their band, which expanded the view from a micro-wormhole.

They all fell silent, then. Warren Husher was standing with a gun against Sandy Bernard's head. He shot her repeatedly, and she slumped forward.

Aheera's circulatory system proclaimed her fear, causing the skin all over her body to pulse slightly. She turned to Culkin. "What do you say now about their progress as a species?" she asked, her voice trembling.

"I say it has been jeopardized, and also that the slim chance they had of defeating the Ixa just grew much slimmer. We must act, Aheera. We must."

She knew Culkin was right, and that she needed to overcome her dislike for him so that she could acknowledge that fact.

But the relations between the members of their band was a distraction. There were far more important matters. Aheera approached the display, caressing the side, which switched off the micro-wormhole, enabled by dark tech.

"We shouldn't leave that on."

The Advance

C aptain Scavo preferred silence in the CIC of the *Parker*. During their routine patrols of the Coreopsis System's outskirts, the crew generally had no real need for talk, and Scavo came down hard on any chitchat that arose. While his officers were on duty, he permitted them only the words necessary to run the ship. What words they spilled during downtime was their own business.

The silence allowed him to pick over the carcasses of his decades-old memories in peace, and it ensured that when the time for talk did come, the sudden noise would punctuate the gravity of the situation.

Scavo was from Abydos, one of the Coreopsis System's three major colonies, and though he never visited his home planet anymore, he rarely left the system itself. Even on the few occasions his body had departed Coreopsis, he hadn't truly left.

No, he was always in this system, and he was always fighting the battle during which the UHF had lost it to the Ixa, over twenty years ago. After their victory, the reptiles had extermi-

nated anyone who spoke up against them, and Scavo's elderly
parents had been among those.

Everyone here was on edge since the supernova had seen to
the Auslaut System, which meant Scavo now had company. He
remained just as edgy as he always was.

The destruction of Auslaut had isolated Coreopsis from the
rest of humanity. On the heels of that had come the widespread
realization, seeping through the micronet like a poison, that the
Ixan Prophecies held real water.

For the inhabitants of Coreopsis, the only remaining path
back to the rest of humanity led through the Ixan home system,
and no one had quite gotten around to checking out how safe it
was.

Sure, reports continued flowing in from the monitors in
charge of watching the Ixa, reassuring their fellow humans that
everything was fine and dandy, and that the Ixa were behaving
just as they should. But people on the micronet had started
picking up on how glassy-eyed the monitors had become, how
overly earnest they seemed, especially when you compared the
footage to their reports from a few years ago.

And so Coreopsis was alone, defended only by the handful of
warships that hadn't been called to fight in the UHF's misguided war. Scavo didn't relish the knowledge that he would soon
die to the Ixa. It didn't rally his spirits like some storied hero.
He hated the fact, because all he wanted from life was to live to
see the Ixa killed. To be the one to murder them all, if that
wasn't too much to ask.

No, Scavo would die screaming and raging against the reptiles, unable to accept what they had done to him, and unable to accept that in the end, their reward was to kill him.

That was the sort of death he knew awaited him. But at least you could set your watch by it.

"Sir," his sensor operator said, and Scavo glared at the man, as a reminder that he'd better have a good reason for talking.

"What?"

"We have multiple contacts emerging from the nearest darkgate."

"The Ixa?"

"Yes, sir."

So the time had come. "They won't just come out of one darkgate. Radio the other captains and tell them to make for Croton. Against so many ships, we need to consolidate our defense, and the orbital platforms over Croton are the best in the system. We'll make our stand there."

"What about the other two colonies?" his Tactical officer asked.

Scavo glanced at her. "Forget about them. This system is about to be overrun, and today isn't about some screwball attempt to save it. Today is about kicking the Ixa in the nuts as hard as we can." He pointed at his Nav officer. "Set us a course for Croton, and tax the shit out of the engines. We won't be needing them again."

Several minutes passed, and sensor data arrived from the next-closest darkgate. "Sir, you were right. Ixa are now coming out of Coreopsis-Inkberry."

"And soon they'll be entering from Morchella."

"They—sir, there's no sign of it stopping. There are still ships coming through from both gates."

By the time the *Parker* reached Croton, Ixan warships were streaming from all three darkgates. Most of them made for Pinara and Abydos, quickly obliterating the defenses there, which Scavo had been petitioning the UHF to beef up for years. He watched, stony-faced, as hundreds of nukes carpeted his home world.

A handful of the Ixa's warships came to test Croton's defenses, darting in and out, attempting to draw out the human ships. Scavo kept the other captains tightly reined in, mostly by bawling at them over the fleetwide.

When the enemy finally finished entering Coreopsis, they had several thousand ships in-system. Far more than anyone would have expected them to have, and certainly far more than were needed for this attack.

Why? It took only a moment's consideration for Scavo to answer that question. The citizens on the surface of Croton would upload images of the carnage to the micronet, just as those on Pinara and Abydos had no doubt recorded the horror of their final moments.

This wasn't about ensuring defeat of Coreopsis' paltry defenses. This was about sending a message, a prophecy, and one that anyone could decipher: *We're coming.*

This was about intimidating humanity. And no matter how much he resented feeling that way, as the black Ixan tide finished swallowing the other two colonies and began hurtling toward Croton, Scavo did.

Scavo felt intimidated.

Draw your last breath, ye doomed
And, victor: judge not your prey harshly
Lesser forms quail when pressured
And terror drives them to unreason

Lovingly slash their throats
Tenderly shatter their hopes
Lavish generous ruin upon their homes

Peace will follow total war
Justice will come with a reckoning

-The Ixan Prophecies

Acknowledgments

Thank you to Sam Bauer, Inga Bögershausen, and Jeff Rudolph for offering insightful editorial input and helping to make this book as strong as it could be.

Thank you to Tom Edwards for creating such stunning cover art.

Thank you to my family - your support means everything.

Thank you to Cecily, my heart.

Thank you to the people who read my stories, write reviews, and help spread the word. I couldn't do this without you.

About the Author

Scott Bartlett was born 1987 in St. John's, Newfoundland, and he has been writing since he was fifteen. He has received various awards for his fiction, including the H. R. (Bill) Percy Prize, the Lawrence Jackson Writers' Award, and the Percy Janes First Novel Award.

In 2013, Scott placed 2nd in Grain Magazine's Canada-wide short story competition and in 2015 he was shortlisted for the Cuffer Prize. His novel *Taking Stock* was also a semi-finalist in the 2014 Best Kindle Book Awards.

Scott mostly writes science fiction nowadays, though he's dabbled in other genres.

Visit scottplots.com to learn about Scott's other books.

CPSIA information can be obtained
at www.ICGtesting.com
Printed in the USA
LVHW111254100622
720988LV00008B/66